THINGS KEEP GETTING DARKER...

I'm Lia Hebert. A year ago, I made angels fall to stop the Archangel, Raphael from closing the gates of Heaven. Raphael is still after me, but to make matters worse, now the Archangel, Michael, is coming for me too. And he doesn't want to use my ability. He wants to kill me because of it.

But I'm discovering more about my badass powers and about the man who calls himself the Redeemer. I'm so close to understanding my destiny and what I must do. I'm shuffling through the lies to get to the truth.

And it will change my whole world.

Books By L. M. Peralta

THE ARCADIAN STEEL SERIES
The Wings of Heaven and Hell
The Seven Archangels of Heaven
The Seven Princes of Hell

THE ELEMENTALS TRILOGY
The Elementals
The Council
The Creator

United Trace

the seven archangels of heaven

The Arcadian Steel Sequence
Book Two

L. M. Peralta

Summary: A year ago, the angels came to Hell in search of Lia, the girl who can make angels fall. Lia discovers Michael, the Arch-angel, wants to kill her to stop Raphael.

ISBN: 978-1-946470-00-3

prologue

THE reedy branches reached to the ashen sky. A slash of light hung among the clouds where the angels descended, their wings white and thickly feathered. The shining armor and Arcadian weapons they wielded gleamed in the light above them.

Never again would Adriel feel that eternal warmth or the tickle of feathers against his back. He was in a world of never-ending gloom from which he could never leave.

He trekked across the lands beyond the Angel District. Headstones were embedded in a vast plain of barren soil. In the distance the earth met the gray sky.

Adriel didn't dare think what was beyond that, the Circles perhaps. He thought of the cruel punishments Lucifer enacted on accursed souls, and for once, he felt pity. As an angel, he never held sympathy for the damned. They were damned for a reason, but now that he was damned too, these thoughts came readily to his mind.

Adriel avoided the grave markers that patterned the ground like gory stepping stones. Dust stung Adriel's nose, and sweat stained his brow.

He walked with a heavy stone upon his shoulder. The physical weight of it caused him little struggle, but its symbolism carried much weight.

He was fallen.

His stone would rest among the others. His name etched upon it. The marker was not like a headstone found on Earth, in remembrance of a loved one. It was not to honor what he was. It served as a symbol of his shame, of his fall from grace.

Adriel sank the stone into the ground, packed beside three others. Although he did not struggle, he did notice the weight of it. That had never happened before.

His hands were reddened from gripping the gritty surface of the stone. That had never happened before either.

He sighed as he beheld the sky.

A place of unimaginable bliss and serenity loomed far above him, and its gates were locked to him forever.

He didn't blame Lia, but he wondered if, given the chance, he could have retrieved his weapon and flew out of the Pit. But the Pit would have swallowed him up like a black hole. The farther he descended, the stronger the pull down would have been until he was lost in an endless fall. The pressure would have torn the feathers from his wings and the skin from his body. He would live through all that pain for an eternity.

What was worse, the pain or this hopelessness?

The air around him changed. Soft footfalls padded across the dry, cracked earth.

Adriel turned his head.

Nasriel approached him. He wore a black suit and a black shirt like a mourner at a funeral.

Appropriate, Adriel thought.

Nasriel stood over him as Adriel's fingertips bit into the flat headstone.

"I'm sorry," Nasriel said.

The wind pushed the hair around Adriel's face. A few strands stretched away from him as if they struggled to leave his ill-fated head. His hair was dark gray when the locks used to be black as midnight. It matched Nasriel's more closely now.

"Where's your headstone?" Adriel scanned the vast distance.

"Why? So you could put yours next to mine?" Nasriel asked.

The grittiness of the stone beneath his hands left impressions in his no longer impervious skin.

Nasriel shook his head. "I don't remember."

Adriel closed his eyes. "It feels so . . . lonely. I used to be able to sense the others, our brethren, but now, there's nothing. I just feel this terrible disgust for what I've become."

"That will change with time," Nasriel said.

"Will it?"

"A lot of time."

Adriel stood. Tension crept through his shoulders. Was his back bowed?

Nasriel glanced over Adriel's shoulder. "I can help you saw off the bones if you like."

Adriel had not yet looked in a mirror, and he did not want to. From the corner of his eye, he could see the blackened bones that had once been covered with soft, white feathers. He knew his golden-brown eyes had darkened to black, and his hair had become ashen. That transformation happened to all fallen angels, but he didn't want to see it.

"They can get in the way sometimes," Nasriel said, "and it's not like they're of any use anymore."

Nasriel needed no special shirts to accommodate his wings. They were gone. *How long had it been since he severed his wings from his body?* Knowing Nasriel, he probably chose to do it as soon as he plummeted to Hell. Nasriel never let emotions get in the way his aims. He always followed through no matter who got hurt in the process.

"No," Adriel said. "I want to keep them to remember what I was."

Nasriel grimaced. "You might as well rid yourself of them. It's not like angels have ever *risen* back into God's good graces."

"They remind me of my shame," Adriel said.

Nasriel raised his eyebrows. "This didn't happen to you because you went against your god. It happened because a girl burned you. That's the problem with you, with the others. Why would you want to follow a god who would slough you off so easily?"

"God didn't do this to me."

"No? The creator of all things can't find a way to bring your Grace back?" Nasriel laughed.

Adriel clenched his jaw, and the muscles in his body tensed. He knew what he felt, but the feeling was never so intense before.

Adriel's hand wrapped around Nasriel's neck. He didn't squeeze, but he held Nasriel in his grasp. He was proud of his control, especially in the face of such burning rage. The pride and wrath were unfamiliar, yet so satisfying.

Nasriel pulled Adriel's fingers from his neck and thrust his arm away. "You guarded his throne for millennia. We both did. Not once did he grace us with his presence or show his damned face. What do you owe him?"

"My life."

"I hope you're thinking about that when you enter the Angel District." Nasriel spit on the ground. He turned and walked away with his hands in his pockets, not bothering to avoid the headstones, but planting his feet down on them like they were pavers.

He became a black dot in the distance, a speck, a bug, a fly like the rest of them. Adriel was no better.

"It's time."

Adriel turned toward the voice.

A man stood a hand taller than Adriel. He wore a black suit and red tie. His hair was slicked back, and his golden wristwatch gleamed in the light.

"Beelzebub." Adriel's nose crinkled as he said the demon's name.

"You can call me Bob," he said.

"I'll call you by your true name," Adriel said.

"Suit yourself. You won't be seeing much more of me anyway."

"That will be a blessing."

"Trust me. Where you are going there are no blessings." Beelzebub strolled past Adriel and led the way to the lands beyond.

Adriel stared after him.

Beelzebub turned his head. "It's not a short walk." Beelzebub grinned, and when he did, there was no joy in it. His grin threatened like the smile of a crazed killer.

"You've been demoted to ferryman?" Adriel asked.

"I volunteered, my fallen friend."

"Why?"

"Isn't that interesting," Beelzebub said. "You've come with a newfound curiosity."

Adriel hadn't considered it. He had never asked many questions before. Now, he wanted to know the answers for reasons other than utility. He was, as Beelzebub had said, curious.

"Do you still want to know?"

Adriel was quiet. He was ashamed that he did *want* to know. It was a part of what he had become.

"Of course, you do," Beelzebub said. "I heard you were Seraphim. We don't get many of those down here. Since you're done polishing God's throne, you're not a Seraph anymore."

Adriel frowned. He was an exotic animal in a cage. Something to be spectated. "I left my post a long time ago," Adriel said.

Bob walked on, and Adriel followed.

"Against Michael's orders, I assume," Beelzebub said. "I never did understand that. How Michael, an Archangel of lower rank, can order around the highest choir of angels."

Adriel grimaced. He didn't like the familiar way Beelzebub spoke about his brethren.

"I know you won't tell me about it," Beelzebub said. "You're not the first angel who's fallen. They're all loyal to a fault when it comes to matters of Heaven or angels. Well, that is apart from the original Fallen. Most of their souls have been demonized. I've heard the guilt goes then. I could put in a good word for you."

Adriel cringed. He had never seen it, but he had heard of angels turning into demons. If anything was worse than becoming a fallen angel, it was becoming a demon. He couldn't imagine any fallen angel choosing that horror.

A cluster of buildings came into view beyond the horizon. A tall, iron gate surrounded the buildings.

Beelzebub stopped. "There it is," he said. "The Angel District. Welcome home." He approached the gates where two giants stood. They were identical except one had a swollen eyelid. The corner of the eye creased so he looked like he was winking.

They carried broadswords at their sides.

"Morning, Bob," the unblemished giant said. "Looks like you have a new one for us." He glanced over at Adriel.

"That I do," Beelzebub said.

"We'll take good care of 'im." Shut Eyed grabbed Adriel's shoulder.

The giant's hand was cold and moist.

Adriel shrugged him off.

"Testy one," Unblemished said.

Shut Eyed reached for the sword at his side and clubbed Adriel's head with the flat of the blade.

Adriel sank to the ground, putting his hands on the sides of his head. Ringing accosted his ears as he put his head to the ground, trying to make it stop. It wasn't the pain that bothered him, although it was there. If he stood right away, he knew he would stumble. He was on the ground the moment the blade hit him. He didn't want to let these demons see him stagger as well.

After a moment of spinning, Adriel stood up, careful not to show any expression of pain on his face. Pain was more acute now. He wouldn't forget that again. Next time, he wouldn't show it. He would set his feet and bear it.

"That's alright," Beelzebub said. "I wanted to take him in myself. We have ourselves a Seraph, boys."

"*This* is a Seraph?" Unblemished asked.

Shut Eyed laughed. "He don't look any different."

"I'm not Seraphim," Adriel said. "I'm a fallen angel."

"That's what I like about you lot," Unblemished said. "You got humility." He and Shut Eyed pulled either side of the gates and opened them to Beelzebub and Adriel.

"Good luck, ex-Seraph," Unblemished said as he and his twin brother sealed the gates behind them.

Beyond the gate, a gravel path curled into the cluster of buildings. Trees, naked of leaves, surrounded the path. Their branches leaned toward the trail as if they wanted to capture those who treaded it.

The music of the city grew louder. A series of beats sounded without vocals. Adriel's muscles tensed. Despair rose beneath the song. The screams and cries coming from the city echoed the feeling the music gave Adriel.

"What will happen to me in there?" Adriel asked.

"Others will hold a mirror to your shame," Beelzebub said. "And it won't matter because you'll feel it anyway, right?"

"Then, what's the point?"

"Those who feel shame are the weakest here. They hesitate and prefer to live in self-pity," Beelzebub said. "If you were human, your shame would damn you to the Circles. But fallen angels feel pain differently from humans. Their greatest pain is the shame. And no one has more shame than a fallen angel. That is why this place exists. Do you know the best way to make a man feel better about himself? Show him a man who's far worse off."

Beelzebub patted Adriel on the back. "You'll be an example to others. But don't look so glum, my boy. You've hit bottom. You need fear nothing more now. There isn't any further to fall."

Adriel recoiled at Beelzebub's touch and his words, but he was right. Adriel didn't have any further to fall. It didn't matter how he had fallen. He was down here. The Devil had him now.

Beelzebub strolled onto the street, and Adriel followed. Bright neon lights assaulted his eyes, and stabs of loud music came from all sides. Adriel's vision blurred.

"Whoa." Beelzebub gripped Adriel's arm to keep him upright. "I know. The lights are brighter to you now. It will take some getting used to. Your eyes aren't what they were when you used to look into the light of God, but they're still better than a demon's and certainly better than a human's. Come on."

Adriel blinked a few times, and his eyes adjusted to the light. The lights were pink, yellow, green, orange, and blue. Demons crowded the streets. They chatted, drank, and laughed. Their skins were crimson, obsidian, and burnt with eyes of black and red. Horns curled from a few heads, and teeth were like the points of daggers.

"Pick them up," a deep voice roared.

Desperate hands scrambled to grab the glittering coins from the ground. Fallen angels sank to the earth on their hands and knees, not in prayer, but to lift money from the dirt. Their necks were collared, and chains led from the collars to the hands of horned demons, barking at them while the crowd hooted and laughed.

"Eat it!"

A demon shoveled a thick, brown gruel into the mouth of a fallen angel in chains. The angel's stomach bloated like she was pregnant.

"Hit him!"

Demons forced another angel to lash the backs of his brethren with an Arcadian whip. Whelps and lines of black blood were drawn across the backs of angels who knelt on the ground.

Adriel's heart clenched, and a sting erupted behind his eyes. Both were sensations he wasn't accustomed to.

"What is this place?" Adriel grabbed the collar of Beelzebub's shirt.

A grin split Beelzebub's face.

Adriel fisted the fabric of his shirt. "Why are you smiling, you devil?"

"They let these things happen to them," Beelzebub said, "and you will too, because you hate yourself."

The fallen angels were collared, but they didn't fight. The collar seemed a mere symbol to their shame. Adriel, too, wanted to hurt himself. The thought of pain, the feeling of punishment, would for that moment cloud his mind and help him to forget he was doomed.

Adriel lowered his eyes and released Beelzebub. He did hate himself. Regardless of the circumstances, he had failed in his duty. He should have stayed at his post as defender of the Throne, but he left to find a friend and stayed to protect a girl who lost her guardian angel. None of which were his assignments yet he failed in those as well.

Beelzebub smoothed down his shirt. "Now, let's get a collar on you."

He twisted around the corner, and they strode down the street. Adriel's ears numbed to the music, the shouts, and the jeers. He didn't want to look at what happened to his fellow fallen angels.

"Here we are." Beelzebub opened a door in the alley. Graffiti marked the door with the word *dog-catcher*.

Inside, a fat man squatted at a workbench with a soldering tool. Hours of sweat drenched the front of his yellowed shirt. He held an iron collar that had not yet been welded shut. He glanced up at Beelzebub and Adriel as they walked in. He had a glass over one eye to help him see his work.

"It's done," he said. "Now, let's get it around his neck."

The room was dark, a relief to Adriel's eyes. But a bright light glowed above the table where the man worked. The brightness stung as Adriel bent his head, pressed his cheek onto the table, and allowed the man to reach his neck. The light caused him pain, but he *could* look into it. Beelzebub was wrong. Adriel could see the light of Heaven, only not without sacrifice.

part one
the fallen

One

I sat on the end of my bed. The rumpled blanket was cool to the touch. My feet dangled in the cold. My hands gripped the mattress. I closed my eyes and breathed in through my nose.

I wore a thick sweater and hadn't changed out of my pajama bottoms. What was the point?

Nash hadn't returned. I wasn't sure where he had gone.

But with the trainings, the hunt for angel weapons, and the attacks on over a dozen angels, I didn't have time to process my feelings for him. I had feelings, but they were jumbled puzzle pieces on the floor.

I hated the way he treated Adriel, but there was something about Nash, something undeniable.

Sim's food and water dish rested near the door. The food in it grew mold.

My feet padded across the cold floor. I picked up the dish and brought it to the bathroom. I tossed the food in the small trash can and rinsed the bowls in the sink.

Sim was never here. My skin crawled at the thought of the creature that was here—a Jinn, imitating my cat. The Jinn spied on me and reported to Raphael my whereabouts and what I was up to. That's how the angels knew when to come. That's how they knew to retrieve their angel weapons.

The real Sim, what became of her?

I grabbed a towel and dried the bowl.

It was my fault the angels attacked Sheol. Adriel losing the Twinblade and worse, his Grace, was my fault too. Worst of all, Raphael knew where I was, and he knew what I was after. I had no way to stop him. Dad and Mom were in Heaven, but because of me, they wouldn't be for long.

I dropped the towel and hummed the food tray against the wall. The plastic chipped and fell to the floor.

I screamed and beat the wall until the sting bit my hands. I gripped the edges of the sink.

"Lia?"

I walked to the door and slid it open.

Nash stood in the hallway. "Are you alright?"

"Sure." I struggled to keep the tremor out of my voice. "What's up? Why are you dressed like that?"

Nash wore a black suit like he was going to a funeral. "I was visiting a friend."

A dead friend? But all Nash's friends were dead and not dead at the same time. They were immortal. Everyone was. I will be or am too because when I die, I'll go to Heaven if Lucifer keeps her end of the deal. Big *if.*

"We have to go," Nash said. "Tom found a fallen angel. We need to bring her to Sheol."

Fallen angels and demons were standard Sheol Parole Officer fare. Nash oversaw enforcement. I wasn't complaining.

Hunting fallen angels and demons meant spending some time on Earth where the air wasn't so stale. I couldn't stand the stagnant air of Sheol and the way the weather never changed. I missed listening to rain drum against the windows while I strummed on my guitar.

"Okay. I'll get dressed." I slid the door closed and pulled on a pair of black pants and a shirt. I wrapped my belt around my waist and slid my sword into its sheath.

My hand stopped on the hilt of my sword. My skin prickled. *What if this was a trap?* Raphael might be trying to lure me back to Earth so he could send my friends to the Pit.

I rushed out of my room and met Tom as he came down the stairs from the third floor. "What if Raphael planned this?" I asked. "What if he made that angel fall to trap us? He can't come to Sheol, so he making us come to him."

Tom narrowed his eyes. "You sure don't bury the lead, do you?" Tom sighed. "The fact that you thought of it means Raphael won't do that. He wouldn't try something that even you could figure out. Besides, Raphael can't *make* an angel fall. Angels must go against an order they believe is from God."

I shook my head. "Then, why hasn't Raphael fallen?"

"Clearly, he believes he isn't going against God," Tom said.

I narrowed my eyes. "But he is. God made Heaven for humans, and he is directly opposed to that."

"It gets complicated when the message isn't coming from God Himself."

"Then from who?"

"You have a fallen angel to hunt," Tom said. "We can talk more about Heavenly politics when you return. But an angel can't decide to go against God to become fallen if he believed that very sacrifice to be in the name of God. Therefore, Raphael couldn't get one of his followers to do it unless they believed that what Raphael pursued was an act opposed to God, and, if they believed that, they wouldn't be one of his followers."

Choice and belief matter a lot in both Heaven and Hell. That fascinated me. You could end up in Hell because you believe you belong in eternal damnation, and angels could fall on the mere belief that their actions are against God.

Tom turned away from me and continued down the hallway.
"You aren't coming with us?" I asked.

"Can't," he said. "I have some scouting to do."

I considered what Tom said. I saw Raphael around every corner. I had to stop doing that or it would paralyze me.

Chandra leaned against a column at the landing of the stairs with her arms folded. Her hair was tied back, and her brass knuckles were secured to her belt. When she saw me, she grimaced, unhinged herself from the column, and walked away.

She didn't like me before, but after what happened to Alex, she'd never forgive me.

Adrianna, Kiran, and Nash chatted on the sofa in the living room. I stopped behind the wall and watched their reflections in the mirror opposite the room.

"It was that damn cat," Kiran said.

"It always tried to bite me." Adrianna looked at her nails. They were painted red and made her emerald green eyes pop. "I should have known something was wrong with it. Animals love me." She smiled.

"What are we going to do now?" Kiran's curved sword rested in its black sheath invisible against his pants except for the silver hilt.

"I haven't figure that out yet." Nash bent forward and rested his forearms on his legs. "But we can't go after the other angels, not yet. We need another strategy."

"I'm ready." I stepped through the archway and into the room.

Kiran and Adrianna gave each other an awkward glance.

"Good." Nash stood. "Let's go. Wait. Where's Chandra?"

"Here." Chandra walked into the living room. *Did she see me eavesdropping on their conversation?*

I looked at her. She didn't look at me. She avoided my existence. I was glad she ignored me. The only alternative relationship we could have had was one a lion has with an antelope.

Nash held out his hand and opened a portal. The edges of the portal glowed like a hole burned through the space and showed what lie beneath.

Chandra climbed through followed by Adrianna and Kiran. They disappeared onto the other side.

I clenched my locket, which protected the photographs of my parents. The only ones I had left. Letting my feelings out never helped me so what was the point of all that effort? Sometimes, I couldn't help it.

Despite what you might believe, bottled emotions aren't the dangers. The fear is that if you bottle up your emotions, they come out in a rush to meet you and not in the best of ways. But perhaps the true danger wasn't the emotions themselves and the consequences of the rush, but the very practice of keeping them quiet. If you keep them silent long enough maybe you become numb.

Numb was the opposite of what I felt with Nash.

"Go ahead," Nash said.

"What?" I asked.

"The portal."

"Right." I approached the glowing circle. I turned to Nash. "I'm sorry."

"For what?"

"For everything that happened. I'll never leave again, not until this is done. And I'm sorry about Sim too. I ruined everything."

"It threw things off course," Nash said, "but you didn't know about the cat. How could you? I'll figure out what needs to be done. In the meantime, stop blaming yourself. Self-pity doesn't look good on you." He nodded to the circle.

He was right. I couldn't let the thousand little thoughts in my head stop me from doing what I needed to do. I can't change the past, so let's start working on the future.

I stepped through the portal, ready to take a breath of clear, moving air. I breathed in a deep lungful. Dust tickled the back of my throat. I bent over, feeling like I might cough up my insides.

The air smelled of mold. The walls were gray blended with vomit green. Cracks ran through the plaster. Dim light struggled to get through the dirty paned glass window above the second landing.

I stood on the stairs. Black iron bars supported the stair rail. Cobwebs showed their wispy patterns between the bars. Light invaded the stairway through a small window on the front door. Someone had nailed boards to the doorframe.

The stairs groaned. I didn't want the distressed wood to give under my weight, so I rushed up to the landing before the next flight of stairs.

Chandra, Adrianna, and Kiran looked down at me from the second floor. Adrianna gestured for me to join them. Their weapons were drawn.

Nash's warmth suffused my back. He stood close behind me. I didn't hear him on the stairs. The portal must have sent him straight to the landing.

Strange. Portals changed location on Earth so quickly, but at least it kept us from running into each other.

We met the others upstairs.

The hallway walls ended in dirty baseboards. Cracked picture frames failed to protect the photographs inside, covered in thick layers of dust. The doors were ajar to two of the three rooms on the second floor.

A roach darted in front of me and scurried into a crack in the baseboard. *Don't worry. We aren't taking you to Hell.*

Chandra pointed to the room at the end of the hall. The door was closed. We crept toward the room with our weapons drawn. Chandra turned the knob and swung the door open.

I held my breath. Fallen angels get a burst of adrenaline right after they fall. The angel who attacked me in my bedroom didn't need his Grace to crush me like a monkey does a coconut.

The room was empty except for a curtain that floated in the breeze, which came in through the broken paned glass window. Holes blemished the torn, gray curtain.

"It's the only room we haven't checked," Chandra said.

"She must be downstairs." Kiran looked to Nash.

He nodded.

If I was a fallen angel, and I heard movement upstairs, impossible not to hear in this creaky, old house, I'd have made a run for it. We would have heard boards being torn from the front door if that was the case.

To my right was a closet with dingy, white folding doors. As I approached the closet, I squinted.

Low breathing came from behind the slats.

"Lia, what are you doing?" Adrianna asked.

"Shh! Listen." I stepped closer.

Dad always said I had excellent hearing despite all the Metal concerts I'd been to.

I imagined black eyes as they peered at me from the closet shutters. Imagining what waited for me wasn't hard to do. So many things jumped out at me from the dark. But I never got used to them. My skin crawled, and goose bumps erupted across my flesh.

I clenched the hilt of my sword.

My hand shook as I reached for the doorknob. Before my hand touched the knob, the door burst open. I jumped back.

The fallen angel emerged from the closet. She wore a dirty, shapeless dress. Her skin was pale and eyes as dark as the Pit.

Her dark gray hair was in stiff tangles. Her bony, featherless wings rose in the air above her head. Black cuts patterned her exposed skin.

She screamed and rushed us. Dark blood dripped from her mouth.

Adrianna grabbed her wrist and pinned her arm back, right between the bones of her wings. "You need to come with us."

The angel screamed like a wild animal and tried to pull away from Adrianna, but Adrianna's hold was firm.

The angel gritted her teeth. She forced herself forward and pulled until the loud crack of a bone breaking filled the room. She slipped from Adrianna's grasp and scooped a piece of broken glass from beneath the window.

The angel held up the piece of glass. The shard cut into her palm, and fresh blood dotted the floor. Her other arm rested limp and mangled at her side.

Kiran whipped his blade, and the sword flashed in front of the angel. The sword cut into the arm that held the glass. The shard and her hand fell.

The bloody stump was still raised to us in a grim salute.

The floor creaked and groaned and splintered. The floorboards gave.

My back hit a flat, hard surface. Plaster and dust fell on top of me. Despite the pain, I rolled over so nothing heavy could hit me in the face. I choked the dust out of my lungs and forced myself up. I sat on top of a dining room table.

Adrianna lay under a pile of floorboards and sheetrock. I moved the stuff off her as she came to.

Debris shifted across the room. Black bones angled out from beneath cracked floorboards and ceiling dust. Like a rabbit caught in a garden, the angel's eyes quivered.

She ran. I climbed over the debris and raced after her. I fell and grabbed her ankle. She struggled and plummeted. I grabbed my dagger from its sheath and plunged it into her calf. She howled.

The dagger pinned her leg to the floor. I climbed up her body, straddled her back, and held the joints of her wings down so she couldn't move the featherless, sharp bones. Indents were gouged into the bones as if she tried to cut them off like Nash's.

Blood speckled my hands. I swallowed the bile that rose in my throat.

Nash and the others met us in the hallway. Sheetrock dust powdered their dark clothes.

"I got her." My lips tightened into a cruel smile.

Adrianna's eyes were wide. Chandra grinned like she had gotten me to eat a poisoned apple.

Nash approached me and offered me his hand. His face was expressionless. I took his hand, and he helped me up.

Kiran pulled my dagger from the angel's leg. He and Nash grabbed her by both arms and lifted her.

She continued to struggle.

Nash jerked her arm. "Who gave you these cuts?"

She looked at him. "I did."

"Why?"

She stopped struggling and craned her head over Nash's shoulder to look at his back. "Don't you hate yourself?" Her eyes met his. "I do, every day, since I turned into this monster."

Nash furrowed his brow. "There's a place in Hell where you will be punished."

She ground her teeth. "I don't want to go to Hell. I want to die."

"You already have," Nash said, "and now, you have to come with us to die again and again."

"Please, I can't go there. Please."

She begged, begged not to go where Lucifer sent angels, where she sent Adriel. After all he had done for us, I couldn't let him suffer in a place angels begged not to go.

Nash turned away from her.

Her head dropped to her chest, and tears marked the floor. She lifted her head and looked for a savior. Her eyes rested on me. She blinked as if her eyes deceived her. "A human? Who are you?"

She recognized me. Something signaled my humanity and distinguished me from the poor costumes demons wore.

"Don't worry about her," Kiran said. "Are you opening the portal?" he asked Nash.

"What are you doing with demons? You're the girl Michael talked about."

"Michael? The Archangel?" I asked.

"The one and only," the fallen angel said. "He knows Raphael is looking for you."

Nash's face turned dark. "We have to leave. We shouldn't stay this long. We have her, let's go." He let go of the angel's arm and opened the portal. "Lia, come on." He waved me over.

"What's going on?" I asked.

"Just go through the damned portal. We'll talk later."

I climbed through the portal. I waited for the others. Chandra and Kiran stepped through with the fallen angel. Blood ran down the angel's leg where I drove the dagger in.

I don't know what came over me. Was the dagger necessary?

She struggled on the ground. One arm mangled. The other a stump. She would have had a hard time getting back to her feet. I could have easily climbed on top of her without stabbing her through the leg.

Adrianna and Nash followed. The portal blinked out of existence.

Nash's mouth formed a hard line. "Handle the angel. Lia and I need to speak with Lucifer."

I hadn't seen Lucifer in a long time, but I wasn't itching to meet with her again. The chill from our first meeting never left my bones. But another Archangel was after me, and the thought of that left me colder.

The world is a drum, and its song is thunder.

Two

HE skyscraper disappeared into the clouds. Lucifer was at the top, the highest point in Hell. The smell of burned leaves tickled my nose. The air grew misty and cold close to the building, colder than other parts of Sheol, at least, colder than the parts I had seen.

Other darker, deeper parts of Sheol existed that I hadn't visited, like the Circles and the depths of the Pit. I had no intention of seeing either.

But with two Archangels after me, I might not have a choice but to visit the deepest and darkest places of my nightmares. It made sense that Michael and the other Archangels would come after me. They had to stop Raphael from doing what they believed was against God or their inaction would condemn them.

Nash walked with me through the sliding doors.

"Is he working against Raphael?" I asked.

"I know as much as you do," Nash said.

At the welcome desk sat one of Lucifer's clone secretaries. They weren't mirror images of each other, like identical twins. But they dressed alike, had the same wide smile, and wore their hair in the exact same way. They walked to the same rhythm, like they listened to the same song in their heads too. However, I doubted the clone secretaries ever listened to music.

The secretary's hair was pulled back so painfully, it stretched the corners of her eyes toward her hairline. She gave us a toothy smile as Nash and I walked to the elevator.

I didn't look back at her. I feared that she turned her head to follow our movements. I didn't want to see her staring back at me with that creepy smile plastered on her face.

"We should have questioned her," I said. The fallen angel may have known more than she told us, right? What motive would she have for giving us the whole story?

"We couldn't do that at that house," Nash said. "Besides, if I chose to keep this from Lucifer for any longer than the time it takes us to get here, she'd have my head."

Lucifer had her thumb on Nash. But, at the same time, she trusted him. He was the only fallen angel she allowed to roam around the Outer Region. But why? What was it about Nash that none of the others had?

I made a mistake and looked back.

The secretary's grin took up half her face as she leaned over her desk to watch us. Her hands clasped in front of her like she was holding onto a fly she caught.

The urge to run zinged through my body like sharp steel.

"Let's not talk about this here." Nash pressed the button for the elevator.

The elevator dinged as the doors opened. I stepped inside, and my heartbeat quickened. The doors closed on her face, and I shut the image away.

My heart sank in time with the sudden drop. It's funny how elevators create that falling sensation when they're going up. *Must I fall first before I succeed?*

"Are you okay?" Nash asked.

I gripped the railing. My sweaty palms made the steel slippery. "Define *okay*."

Ever wonder how a wild horse feels in a pull trailer? A moment of panic when you don't know what's going on and you're not sure if you're going to be okay, when you're not in control of your own life, that's what I felt. But I had some degree of power over my own destiny.

"I don't think it's hit me yet," Nash said, "what that fallen angel told us."

"What do you mean?" I asked.

The elevator stopped.

Nash pressed the button for the top floor, but the button wouldn't stay lit. Nash jabbed it a few more times, but it didn't glow at all.

"What's going on?" I tried the button myself.

"I don't know."

"Are we stuck?"

The elevator moved up again.

Nash furrowed his brow. "I guess it was nothing."

The elevator zoomed ahead twenty more floors and jolted to a stop. This time, the doors slid open.

Nash paused. "Strange." He pressed the button to close the doors, but they remained open. "Well, I guess we aren't being given a choice."

"There's always a choice," I said. "I could get on your shoulders and pop the top to the elevator shaft. We could climb up or down."

Nash narrowed his eyes.

We entered a hallway. The walls were cream-white with ornate arches evenly spaced. Candle-lit chandeliers hung from the ceiling and lush, white carpets rested against the dark, hardwood floors.

"Where are we?" I touched a statue of a cherub that sat on a pedestal. The cherub was a fat baby with curly hair and wings that reached the top of his head.

Cherubs don't look that way. They are full-sized angels with four faces. I guess they needed all those faces to guard Arcadia, the place in Heaven humans went to when they died.

"Bob lives here." Nash strode to the door at the end of the hall.

I followed him. "Bob? I wonder why the elevator stopped here."

"I wonder the same thing." Nash opened the door that stood three or four inches below the tall ceiling.

The door opened to a dining room. Burgundy red paint colored the walls. To my left was a floor to ceiling depiction of a forest painted in dark greens and pale yellows. To the right was an archway that led into another room. On the ceiling hung a chandelier. A red lampshade covered each light.

In the center of the room was a table for ten. The table was of a dark wood, and the chairs were padded with white fabric. On the table were platters of food: a roast turkey, slices of bread, cheese, a rack of lamb, a whole roasted pig, sausages, biscuits, gravy, mashed potatoes, pasta, and fruit. No part of the table was untouched.

At the head of the table sat Bob, or should I call him, *Beelzebub*, the demon of gluttony and right-hand man to Lucifer.

A white napkin was tucked into his collar. He held a fork and knife. He wore his traditional black, fitted suit and red tie. His hair was slicked back with a thick layer of grease. His Rolex watch gleamed in the light.

Was he going to eat all this food by himself?

He smiled at me and Nash. "Good morning."

I narrowed my eyes. You have to be careful when snakes slither on the ground.

"You've made quite a feast for yourself," Nash said.

"Well, you know I didn't make this myself," Bob said. "You should invite me for dinner sometime."

"I'm afraid I don't have enough food in the kitchen to sate your appetite." Disgust laced Nash's words. I wasn't sure if the disgust was over the meat or the excess.

Bob grinned. "You probably don't. I suppose you're looking for Lucifer."

"The elevator malfunctioned," I said. "You should get that fixed unless you're trying to scare people to death."

"You're the only one in Sheol, we could scare to death, my dear." He smiled.

"It wasn't a malfunction." Bob put down his utensils and removed his napkin. He wiped his mouth. "Lucifer has rerouted all initial contact to me."

Was Lucifer getting too many Jehovah's Witnesses at her door?

"So, you'll have to convince me it's something worth her time," Bob said.

"It's Michael," Nash said.

Bob's mouth tensed.

"We have a source who says he's looking for Lia," Nash said.

Bob stood and approached Nash. "Is that so? Michael. He's a feisty one. Follow me." He smoothed down his suit jacket and strolled past Nash through the door.

We followed Bob to the elevator. The doors slid open, and we stepped inside. Bob reached into his pocket and pulled out a key. He tapped the elevator control panel. Below the buttons was a keyhole.

"Newly installed," Bob said. "It's the only way up past my floor."

A whole floor! Each floor of this place could house ten midsize apartments. My house could fit inside one floor of Lucifer's skyscraper three times.

Bob turned the key, and the elevator bucked upward as if resuscitated.

My fingers played across my palm. Couldn't Michael wait until I killed my parents' murderer? I could face him after that, after I did what I needed to do.

The elevator doors opened. A mild, burning odor weaved through the air like someone had blown out a candle in front of me. We followed Bob down the hall and into one of the many rooms that stood in a line down the hallway.

I recognized this room, the same room where Lucifer told me my birth mother sold my soul to her. The white sofa was the same one Nash and I sat on. I remembered Lucifer's long nails as they bit into the back of the chair she stood behind.

A clone secretary nosed the corner of the room. A bun pulled back her dark hair. Her long legs ended in black heels. She turned as we entered the room and approached us with a wide grin. "Can I get you anything?"

"Coffee," Nash said.

"Never mind that." Bob put up his hand. "Tell Lucifer Nash needs to speak with her about the Archangel Michael."

The secretary blinked. "Michael." Her smile remained, but her face tensed. She hesitated, perhaps hopeful Bob would say more, but when he didn't, she moved along and shut the door behind her.

Nash sat on the couch and put his arm across the top, the way he sat when I first met Lucifer.

"Nash…" I frowned.

"What?" He looked at me as if I had the results of a cancer screening.

"Can I sit there, where you're sitting?" I asked.

He raised an eyebrow. "You want me to move?"

"How can I sit there if you don't move?"

"You could still sit here." His lips curled into a smile.

My face warmed. Definitely flirting. Should I flirt back?

"Scoot over." I nudged his shoulder. Not flirting.

He moved over to where I sat last time, and I took his seat, but that subtle change didn't put me at ease.

The door opened behind us. My skin crawled like it wanted to run away from my bones.

Lucifer entered. She was dressed in a tight, red skirt with a fitted black, business blazer. The heels she wore had her towering over Bob.

The secretary scurried in behind her and handed Nash his coffee. She clasped her hands together and bowed her head toward Lucifer. "Can I get you anything, Morning Star?"

"Leave." Lucifer waved the secretary away.

With that smile, Lucifer didn't look worried that this conversation involved Michael, but Lucifer could put on a damn good performance when she wanted to. A smile didn't mean a thing.

She sat across from us in one of the padded, leather chairs. She crossed her legs. Her featherless wings fanned out on either side of the chair. "You have something to tell me about Michael."

Bob stood not far from where Lucifer sat. What I couldn't read on Lucifer's face, I could read on his. His brows knit together, and his face slumped into a frown.

Michael was not a good topic for them.

Nash opened his mouth to speak when one of the clone secretaries with the wide smiles came in. Her heels tapped across the marble floor as she approached us.

"Morning Star." She bowed to Lucifer. The smile plastered on her face spoke that she wouldn't be in trouble for interrupting the Devil's meeting, but that was far from the truth. "31,855 souls funneled in an hour ago."

Lucifer narrowed her eyes. "We received our quota this morning."

"I know, your Greatness, but 31,855 more were received after the original quota."

"I'm busy. Offer them the standard contract." Lucifer waved her away.

"We have, but 28,111 have refused it."

Lucifer's eyes darkened, and her lips curled. She stood. "Then, throw them into the Pit!" Her voice bellowed. A voice echoed behind hers like she wasn't the only one who spoke, but another deeper voice repeated her words.

Goose bumps erupted on my skin, and a chill settled so deep in my bones, I would never be able to shake it.

Since I met her, in all the times I thought of Lucifer, knowing she was the Devil, my heart had not shuddered at the thought until that moment.

The secretary still smiled, but the corners of her lips twitched, and her eyes spelled alarm. A bead of sweat trickled down her forehead.

Nash, who was sipping his coffee, gulped down his last swallow.

Lucifer smoothed out her skirt and sat back down. She sighed. "Pick out one third of them and make them the offer again. Call their names one by one in earshot of the others. It'll have more effect. The others will wonder why they haven't been chosen. They'll panic and beg to take the deal. If they don't, chuck them into the Circles."

The secretary nodded and left the room. Her heels hurriedly clicked down the hallway.

Lucifer turned back to me. The way her face became so calm so fast sent a colder chill down my spine. I saw why she had a reputation for being a good liar. I bet she would have made an amazing poker player.

"Peter isn't letting people in like he used to," Lucifer said.

"Peter?" My voice shuddered. That surprised me.

"The gatekeeper to Heaven, my dear," Lucifer said.

"Oh, right," I said.

From what I'd read in Nash's library, Peter was one of the Twelve Apostles of Jesus. Jesus gave him the Keys to Heaven. "I knew that."

Nash took a loud sip of his coffee. He was usually a quiet drinker. Was he signaling for me to shut up?

I didn't plan on saying too much more anyway. I didn't like how my voice wavered. It made me sound weak and afraid, and I didn't want Lucifer to think I was afraid.

"We have a problem." Nash put his coffee down on the table. "We hunted a fallen angel this morning. She told us that Michael has his eye on Lia."

Lucifer smiled, but didn't show teeth. She settled back in her chair, and the bones of her featherless wings crackled. "I thought this might happen. Where's the angel?"

"She's in Sheol," Nash said.

"Good."

"Well, what are you going to do about it?" I asked, not able to catch my words before they tumbled out.

She glanced at me. "You might need to make Michael fall."

I gulped. I didn't need another angel in the way of my getting to Raphael. I felt remorse for the others. I would feel none for him.

"You are strong, stronger than when I met you, but you will need help." She spoke to me, but she looked at Nash. She made it his responsibility to protect me.

"She can't." Nash leaned in. "You and I know that, Lucifer. You can't ask her to do something you know is impossible."

Lucifer laughed. "I can ask, but it's not worth my time. My interest is in Raphael. I can't have her killing herself going after Michael."

She didn't want me to attack Michael, but if he attacked me, I'd be on my own. Killing him was my responsibility, not hers.

Nash settled back against the couch. Worry painted his face. He expected Lucifer to do something, but I wasn't sure what. Fight Michael herself maybe.

Did he think the Devil would stick her neck out?

A dark thought crossed my mind.

"Could Michael and Raphael be working together?" I asked.

Lucifer squinted at me. "I doubt it."

"Then why is he after me?" But I already knew. Raphael wasn't the only one who needed to be stopped.

Lucifer clicked her fingernails together. "Because, my dear, he wants to destroy you before Raphael can use you against him."

Three

ASH drove fast. I wanted to talk to him about what Lucifer said to us. The Archangel Michael had his eye on me because he wanted to kill me. Not a pleasant thought. But Nash took the turns at such high speeds, I couldn't bring myself to start a serious discussion while he drove like that.

At this rate, it wouldn't matter if Michael was after me, I would die in a car crash.

"Slow down!" I screamed.

He slammed on the brake, and my seatbelt cut into me and knocked the breath out of my lungs. It took me a moment to catch my breath again. "Nash, what the f—"

"She's not doing anything about it." He gripped the wheel.

"She asked about the angel," I said. "Maybe she plans to question her."

"That won't do any good if she can't stop Michael. She expects you to do it. We have to get home." Nash pressed down on the accelerator, and the car zoomed ahead.

He slowed down a little, but still sped along. He didn't look at me. His mouth formed a hard, thin line. His eyes focused in front of him. I hoped he was looking at the road and not looking past it, lost in his thoughts.

I wished I could have spoken with Lucifer first. She wasn't the most delicate person. I could have sat down with Nash and explained it to him in his own home where he wouldn't have to drive after the news.

I knew this wouldn't be quick and painless, but I didn't need to add another warrior angel on the list of angels that wanted me dead. I had taken the wings from angels who would be happy to see me in the Seventh Circle of Hell, but never an Archangel.

I remembered the first Archangel we tried to take down: Uriel. That hadn't gone too well. I feared for Nash's life that day.

Today, Nash feared for mine.

Or, at least, I hoped he did. It could also be that he feared Lucifer. If he failed to protect me, there was no telling what she would do to him.

He pulled up to the house, and I jumped out of the car.

Nash didn't say anything to me. He went straight to the front door and walked inside. I hurried after him into the house.

I was ready to tear him up for driving like that and shutting me out when he should have been talking to me. I was the one who should have been panicking, not him. My life was in danger. He stole my anxiety and made it his own.

"Nash, can we at least talk about this?" I asked. I wanted him to say something to me, anything that might bring me hope. Raphael was an Archangel, and he was after me too. I didn't get what was so much worse about Michael. Well, besides the fact that Raphael wanted to *use* me while Michael wanted to *kill* me.

But either way I was screwed. Raphael wouldn't let me live past his agenda anyway, not if he didn't need to. The thought of me touching him and taking his wings would scare him too much. Even if he needed to keep me alive, I'd be a prisoner for the rest of my life.

Was Michael the angel who told Mary that she would give birth to the son of God? Or was that Gabriel?

Gabriel. He tossed Adriel's sword into the Pit, all because Adriel had helped me. His eyes were so empty when he did that. If Michael was anything like Gabriel, maybe there was reason to worry.

Paranoia hit me like a boulder rolling down a steep hill. I had experienced it before, many times. I never knew when it would hit me, but every time it did, something bad would happen.

I felt it right before my parents died, before the day I nearly drowned in the school pool, and the day I met the Devil.

Warmth suffused my back as if someone stood right behind me, whispering in my ear what was to come. Only I couldn't hear it because the message wasn't in words but in feelings.

It happened more often now. The only trouble was I didn't know what to connect it to. I didn't know what or who it warned me against.

Nash marched down the stairs to the armory. He opened the door and gathered weapons in his arms. He pulled the weapons down from the wall and piled them onto the table by the door.

He went back and forth from the wall to the table. The angel weapons hung against the back wall. I helped harvest those weapons, not for the weapons themselves, but to lure angels to me so I could touch them and take their Grace away. I wondered where the fallen angels were now.

"Nash, can you please stop for a minute and talk to me?" I pleaded. My voice cracked. At first, I wanted to talk to him for the sake of my own curiosity and my need to be comforted. Now, it was more about grounding him.

"What's there to talk about?" he asked. "Michael is after you. We need to train."

"I don't understand. What makes Michael, a single Archangel, any more of a threat than Raphael and his entire army of angels?"

Nash stopped and looked at me like I had grown two heads. His tone grew grave. "Michael defeated Lucifer single-handedly after taking on an army of demons without breaking a sweat. That's why she's too afraid to do anything herself. If he comes for you, we won't be able to stop him. *I* won't be able to stop him."

I remembered once again, as I had many times, that I was in a world where I didn't know all the rules. What was more, I didn't understand the complexity of Nash's feelings for me, but I did know something. He wanted to protect me.

I put my hand on his arm. "It'll be okay, Nash."

"You should be scared. You don't sound scared."

"You want me to be scared?"

Nash turned to me. His dark eyes hardened to black crystals. "I don't want you to have a reason to be, but I want you to be scared when you should be. Being scared might keep you alive. Being scared might make you fight harder. It might make you think clearer. It could mean the difference between life and death. So, yes, I want you to be scared."

"I am," I said. "But we'll beat him."

"Maybe, a slim maybe, if we stay on top of this." He moved the weapons to the table and packed them away in a bag.

He shut me out again, focusing on something physical. Something tangible, something he could control. But I could tell his mind couldn't let go of an image of me. Was he thinking of my death? Was he playing out all the many ways we could fail?

I drew him away from his task, placed my arms around his neck, and hugged him. It took a moment for him to realize I wasn't letting go.

He wrapped his arms around me and pulled me in. His breath warmed my neck, pushing the cold away until it receded in ripples across my skin. Goose bumps erupted in the places he didn't touch, but they made me appreciate the warmth more.

I was glad I was the one comforting him. It had pushed the apprehension to the back of my mind. On the way back to Nash's car, after we left Lucifer's skyscraper, there was a moment when I thought I might cry. I wanted so badly not to cry. I wanted to feel strong.

Nash had given me something I didn't know I needed.

Before Micah and Alexandria Hebert adopted me, I dreamed my mother or father or anyone who might love me would show up and whisk me away from the strangers who could never be my real family.

But I didn't want someone to save me. I wanted to save myself. If someone else was my hero, I would survive the situation, but if I was my own hero, I would survive the world.

"What's going on?" Chandra stood in the doorway of armory. I wondered if she still wanted to be in Nash's arms.

We dropped our embrace and put space between each other. Nash cleared his throat. "We talked to Lucifer."

Adrianna, Tom, and Kiran wandered in.

"What did she say?" Adrianna asked.

"Not much," Nash said. "We're on our own."

They all wore their training attire. Chandra wore a tank top, tight pants, and arm bracers. Kiran strapped his sword to his side. The hilts of Adrianna's daggers protruded from their sheaths. Tom wore an old t-shirt and jeans and carried his short sword. They assumed whatever Nash had to say meant they would have to fight.

"He's coming to Sheol?" Kiran's shoulder twitched as if a chill settled there.

Nash nodded. "He wants to get to her before Raphael does."

If he doesn't, Raphael would use me as a weapon to force Michael's hand into closing the gates of Heaven to humans. Michael's mission was noble. I cringed. *Had I called my murder noble?*

"But we won't let that happen," Nash said. Those were the words I wanted to hear from him. "We're going to fight him. We're going to up our training starting today." He motioned to the pile of silver weapons on the table.

Adrianna shook her head. Her eyes were distant as she spoke. I never saw a look of hopelessness in Adrianna's eyes, not even when Kiran, Nash, and Chandra had to pull her into the Circles to save her life. "Michael can't be hurt by Arcadian Steel."

"That's a rumor." Nash looked at me as he spoke. He tried to reassure me that I wouldn't die by Michael's hand. "All angels can be cut by Arcadian Steel. Michael can be hurt just like the rest of them."

My eyes darted back and forth. "But how can he come here?" I asked. "Bob warded Sheol, right?"

After the angels attacked, Bob warded Hell against intruders for three years. He explained that no angel, unless fallen, could get in, not even through a portal.

"He couldn't ward all of Sheol," Kiran said. "If Michael goes through the Circles, he could get in. The Circles are harder to ward because no one, not even Lucifer, wants to go down there."

Lucifer wouldn't go into the Circles? How could she control what went on down there if she never visited? That would be like a manager who never checked up on his employees.

"But someone should," I said. "What are the odds that Michael will try to get in through the Circles?"

"It depends on how much of a threat he thinks you are, Angel Killer," Chandra said.

ANGEL Killer.

Chandra was right. *That's what I am.*

My head leaned against the headboard of my bed. My guitar cradled in my arms, I strummed a few notes. The notes warmed me like the sun in winter.

I hadn't seen Adriel since the battle a few weeks ago. There was so much I wanted to say to him. But I knew that Nash wouldn't want me to see him. I wasn't sure why Nash didn't like Adriel. Maybe the two of them crossed paths before?

Whatever the reason, the last thing Nash had to know right now was that I wanted to find Adriel. But maybe he didn't have to know.

I knew someone who could help. And I knew right where to find him. I unhooked the amp and placed my guitar in its case.

Tom sat in the armchair in the library and read. He looked up from his book when I entered.

"You hear me every time," I said.

"I'm used to the quiet," he said. "I notice when it's disturbed."

"Sorry," I said.

"No problem." He closed the book. "I have an eternity. I'm afraid I'll run out of books."

I tried to imagine myself in Tom's shoes. He loved reading. What would he do if the world stopped making books? But that would never happen, not unless the world ended, but would that end Sheol?

"I have a favor to ask," I said.

"Ask away, but I can't promise I'll oblige." He smiled.

"I want to see Adriel. Where can I find him?"

My question hung in the air for a while, long enough that I felt awkward for asking. I wasn't ashamed of the question per se, but the silence was unsettling.

Tom leaned forward in his chair. "There's a special place in Hell for fallen angels."

"Will you bring me there?"

Tom smirked. "I don't think so."

"Why not?"

"Nash won't…"

"I'm not Nash's prisoner. He doesn't make decisions for me."

"Clearly," Tom said. "I guess I don't have much of a choice, do I? If I don't take you, you'll try to find it on your own, and that would be a disaster."

"So, you'll take me."

"If, and only if, you don't say anything to Nash," he said.

"I can't see why I would."

"Okay, but we have to be quick. You're hunting a demon tonight, a Balban. Tough suckers."

"Have you told Nash yet? I don't think he'll want to go. He wants to dedicate every spare minute to training to fight Michael."

"He knows Lucifer won't let him ignore demons while he hunts angels. Hope you don't mind walking. I hate to drive."

"That's fine." I didn't think my stomach could handle anymore race car driving.

The walk was therapeutic. Frustration, fear, and guilt flooded my mind, but the walk brought me some ease. I always walked home from school when I had a bad day. It calmed me.

It was a short moment of sanctuary among chaos. Tom let me have that moment. He didn't say anything as he walked with his hands in his pockets.

He probably had his own stuff to think about. I wasn't immune to the fact that what happened to me would affect others as well, including him. I hoped Lucifer wouldn't banish my friends to the Circles, or worse the Pit, if we failed.

Tom and I stood before a tall, iron gate. Beyond the gate was a city. The clouds above the city were darker than those surrounding it. Neon lights glowed from the buildings, which huddled close together.

Two men stood guard. Giants would be a better description than men. They each stood over seven and a half feet tall by my rough estimate. Their foreheads jutted out above their narrow eyes. They looked like twin brothers with the exact same bulbous nose, high cheek bones, and large lips except one had a swollen eye that made it look like he was eternally winking.

"What's your business?" Winks asked.

"Not business," Tom said. "Pleasure."

The way he said pleasure in a deep cadence made me uneasy. *Had Tom been here before?* Even from a distance the area looked seedy like the kind of place where murders happen in detective movies.

Each twin wrapped a massive hand around the bars of the heavy, iron gates and pulled them open.

I followed Tom past the gates and into the city.

"What is this place?" I asked.

"The Angel District."

Neon lights glowed in the gloom. Buildings stacked on top each other. Loud music assaulted my ears.

There was nothing *angelic* about this place. It was dark, grimy, and smelled like a mixture of vomit and alcohol.

The people, or the demons, wore a range of clothing from suits and dresses to leather jackets and crop tops. The only similarities were the smiles on their faces, the laughter, and the jeers.

But there were also people in chains, not people, angels. Their wings no longer had full white feathers, but were now bones, hanging useless from their backs. Large chains collared their necks, and more chains bound their hands and feet.

A few demons chose not to look like people. Some had red faces with pointed horns. Their eyes glowed yellow in the dark. Others had patchy skin that wrinkled in odd places like across the cheeks and scalp. They had muscled bodies and wielded whips and hammers.

One demon pulled a fallen angel around on his hands and knees like a dog. He barked orders, and the angel was obedient. The angel was once a beautiful winged warrior with white blond hair and soft feathered wings. *Was he one of the angels that I touched?* He ate food off the ground as a horned demon screamed in his ear.

Tears wet my cheeks, and I thought I might begin to sob.

Tom grasped my arms. "Lia," he said. "Stay close to me, and don't look at anybody. There are things down here you shouldn't see."

"I did this to them," I said.

Tom shook his head. "Lucifer did this to them. You think this is bad? Think of how bad the Circles must be, how bad the Pit must be. It's because of her that this is here. Not you. Don't look at anything, and don't meet eyes with anyone. Do you understand me?"

I swallowed and nodded.

I kept my head down and watched Tom's back as he moved through the crowd. The place was packed, and filled back in once Tom pushed through.

"Don't look away!" Someone grabbed my arm and turned me around.

"Don't look away!" the red-eyed demon bellowed as he pulled the chain connected to the angel's throat. Two demons, a man and woman from their figures, pawed each other over their clothes. His hands traveled to her tailbone. She twisted his shirt in her fists and crushed her lips against his. The angel tried again to divert his eyes, but the red-eyed demon grabbed his chin and forced his face forward.

The two demons undressed. I turned my eyes away.

"Look at this," a slurred voice said. "New blood."

A man in a leather jacket stood in front of me with a bottle of beer in his hand. He sounded like he had had a few beers before that one. He was tall and muscular and had the scent of alcohol on his breath.

He took a swig of beer as a woman put her hand on his chest.

"Who do we have here, Sam?" she asked. She wore a tight-fitting knee length dress, like she had come to the bar straight from an office job. Her dark, red lipstick was stark against her pale skin.

"New comer," Sam said. "Look, Delilah, I think she might be scared."

The woman turned her gaze to me. Her eyes widened. She looked up at Sam. "Sam, she's human."

Sam crooked his head back to take another swallow of beer, but when he heard that, he stopped. His bottle tilted away from his lips. "Is she now?" He smashed the bottle on the ground behind him. "What would a human be doing in Sheol?"

"Are you taking a spirit walk or something?" Delilah asked.

I couldn't tell if she was joking or not. She had a slight glint to her voice. She sounded too drunk to be sure.

"How did you know so soon, babe?" Sam asked.

"Look at her eyes. I could tell right off."

My eyes? Something in my eyes showed I was human. But what? Most demons looked like people. Often, I couldn't see any flaw in the disguise. Could demons lift the Veil on each other?

I turned around.

Oh, no, Tom!

I had no idea where he was.

"Hey, hey, wait a minute." Sam grabbed my arm as I tried to leave.

I pulled away from him. I doubt it would have been as easy if he hadn't been drunk.

My heart hammered in my chest as I pushed through the crowd. In the middle of the street people gathered shoulder to shoulder, elbow to elbow. It was difficult to push through.

Despite what Tom had told me and the disgusting things I had seen, my curiosity got the better of me. I could see between the bodies of a few people in front of me.

A tall, black demon with red eyes and curved black horns whipped an angel who stood with his arms spread.

Demons whipped the backs of angels. The people in the crowd threw golden coins at them.

The currency was unfamiliar. The coins looked ancient. I guessed on Earth the money had fallen out of use.

The demon swung the whip. Lashes bit into the angel's back, and black blood oozed onto the concrete. The whip must have been laced in Arcadian Steel. The demon forced the angel's head low to the ground. "Pick them up," he bellowed.

The angel scrambled to pick up the glittering coins from the ground while the others around her did as well.

I searched the crowd for Tom. I dared not yell out his name. I didn't want the attention of the demons on me.

"Lia!"

Far above me, in a window, a pair of darkened eyes gazed down at me.

Adriel.

Pushing through the crowd with more vigor than before, I hurried to the building and tore open the door. I found the steps. *Which room was it?*

A cockroach scurried down the hallway. The wallpaper peeled in curls down the walls. Graffiti marked either side of the hall. My feet pounded against the uneven laminate tiles that lifted from the floor.

Some of the doors were shut with numerous bolts and latches. Others had been torn off their hinges.

Cries echoed down the hall.

I opened a door. This had to be the one. The room was bare except for a twin-sized bed in the corner. No sheets or blankets covered the dirty mattress. The walls were yellowed and brown in the corners where they met the ceiling and floor.

An iron collar hung around Adriel's neck. A chain went from the collar to a bolt in the floor.

He turned his head. His face was pale. His once-shiny, black hair had turned ashy and dull. His golden irises had darkened to black. Thick, black bones grew from his shoulder blades and thinner bones branched from thicker ones.

I destroyed something that was once so beautiful.

Tears welled up in my eyes, and I rushed into his arms. He enveloped me, but his embrace no longer held that intense feeling of warmth. That touch of bliss was gone. It felt no different than if I had been hugged by anyone.

"This place is so terrible," I whispered into his arm.

"I would have come to you, but I couldn't," he said. "I carried my headstone. Then, I had to come here."

"I'm so sorry for doing this to you."

He cradled my face in his hands. "Lia, you saved me."

My breath caught.

"There you are." Tom exhaled. He bent double with his hands on his knees. He looked up at me. "What the hell were you thinking?"

I turned away from Adriel and back to Tom. "I lost you in the crowd."

"You should have stayed where you were. Luckily, I heard him yell your name. Come on, we have to go back to Nash's place."

"I'm not leaving without Adriel," I said.

"What? We can't take him with us. The guards won't let him past the gate."

I wouldn't let Adriel stay another minute in this place, not after all he had done for me. He was my guardian angel for heaven's sake.

"Go," Adriel said. "I'm grateful you came, but don't come back. I can't bare for you to see me in this place."

I turned to him. "But Adriel."

"He's right," Adriel said. "Even if I could get pass the guards, they'll know I'm gone."

"What will they do to you?" I looked from Adriel back to Tom, challenging them with the question.

Tom grabbed my arm. "They'll hunt him down and throw him into the Pit."

four

HE air smelled of burnt leaves. We left the darkness that gathered around the Angel District behind us. Tom strolled silently beside me. The place burned me more than him.

I wanted to slap away Tom's stillness. He didn't care about Adriel the way I did, but no one could be bankrupt of pity after seeing Adriel in that place.

Nash's car sat in the driveway. The car had no license plate upon its sleek body.

Tom and I walked through the front door as Nash came down the stairs.

"Oh, great," Tom whispered in my ear. "Let me do the talking." He shut the door behind us.

I didn't care if Nash knew where I had gone. He knew where they had taken Adriel, and he didn't do anything about it. He hated him, but that place was sick.

"Where were you two?" Nash asked.

"We went to the Angel District," I said.

Tom, looking betrayed, glared at me and ducked into the living room.

"You what?"

"I saw Adriel," I said. "I don't want him there."

"Lia, what were you thinking?"

"He's living in squalor. Worse than squalor. I don't know what to call it. How could you not tell me? I want Lucifer to let him out."

"That's not going to happen."

"Make it happen."

"I don't understand why you have this sense of loyalty to him."

"He saved us. Have you forgotten? He fought with us, and you would let him live an eternity like that?" My voice trembled, and my fingernails bit into my palms.

"No one knows whose side Adriel is on," Nash said. "Before he fell, he might have wanted to hand you over to Raphael."

"He saved your life, Nash. He's protected me for more than half mine. He fought with us against the angels that came to Sheol. What more does he have to do to prove to you that he is on our side? Why would you think he would give me over to Raphael?"

"Perhaps he planned to hand you over to Michael. Michael would have killed you. He still might."

I pressed my lips together. "Adriel had plenty of opportunities to hand me over to anyone he wished, but instead he watched and protected me. Don't you think we might need him to defend ourselves against Michael? Angels can't be harmed by anything but Arcadian Steel."

Nash shook his head. "Fallen angels are different. They are more resistant to weapons than humans or demons, but they can still bleed."

I folded my arms. "We're talking about Michael. If he's really the badass you all say he is, we need as many weapon-*resistant* fallen angels on our side as we can get."

"It's not up to me. It's up to Lucifer."

I marched up the stairs and stopped on the step next to him. "You could help him if you wanted to. You hate him, and that's fine, but he saved us, and he suffered for it in the worse way imaginable."

I continued up the stairs, down the hall, and shut the door to my room.

If Nash wasn't going to help me, I had to find another way.

Adriel was chained to the center of that little room. He should have been able to break those chains. Maybe being fallen made him weaker.

Or maybe he thought it would be useless to run. Tom said they would find him. Could there be some way he could leave Sheol?

Only a few days ago, I made him fall. So, he hadn't been in the Angel District for long. Soon, they would take him down with the others to be tortured and ridiculed.

I rubbed my eyes.

Lucifer was a fallen angel. How could she do that to her own kind?

I needed time to think. I couldn't walk in unarmed and expect to walk out with an angel. I needed a plan, but that would take too much time. As soon as I came up with something, Adriel would have spent days, maybe weeks in that place.

My sheathed sword leaned in the corner of the wall. A dagger rested in my bedside drawer. I could awaken both weapons and tear down anyone who got in my way of taking Adriel out of the Angel District.

But what then?

They'll hunt him down and throw him into the Pit.

* * *

THE road twisted through the trees. Time faded the yellow lines that bisected the street. Naked branches reached over the highway on either side as if the trees tried to embrace.

Light glowed through the fog and caused shadows to stretch onto the road. Crows cawed, and leaves crunched in the distance.

"Tom said we're looking for a Balban." I stood in the middle of the street, which seemed like the safest place to be. Darkness draped the dense trees, but standing water reflected moonlight on the road. "What does one look like?"

"They don't often show their true form," Nash said. "Be careful. A Balban is a demon of delusion. It will try to trick you."

"But I'll be able to see through that," I said.

"Your sight isn't perfect," Nash said.

He was right. I could see demons. Sometimes I saw their full forms, other times I could only see the horns, the tail, or the eyes. I couldn't completely see through the guises Tom, Adrianna, Kiran, and Chandra wore. Maybe I didn't want to.

"The longer we spend with the Balban, the more time it will have to learn how to manipulate us." Chandra approached the tree line.

"Let's go." Nash waved us on.

Twigs snapped under our feet as we moved through the forest. Adrianna walked alongside me. We were a few feet behind Nash, Chandra, and Kiran.

"What do you think Nash plans to do about Michael?" I asked.

"I'm not sure." Adrianna watched the trees. She stayed vigilant as she spoke. "But I don't think he's going to let him near you."

"What if that's the only way to stop him?"

"Nash will find another way."

"He hasn't talked to me about it."

"Nash doesn't like to talk about his plans until he's worked them out completely. He doesn't like to be wrong. If he's going to solve something, he'll do it in private. He'll only talk about it once he's found the solution."

"I need to make Michael fall. That's the only—"

Adrianna grabbed my arm, and I stopped.

Nash, Chandra, and Kiran had their weapons drawn. Ahead of them stood hooded figures among the trees.

The cloaks the figures wore were dark and tattered at the hips. Their faces were shadowed. The legs looked strange like they were bent backward at the knees.

Ten figures stood at varying distances. The mist made the figures who stood further out look small and gray. They waited for something.

It wasn't one demon, but many. Tom was wrong again.

I drew my sword, and Adrianna drew her daggers.

Nash leaned in and spoke to Chandra and Kiran, but I couldn't hear what he said. Chandra and Kiran darted in opposite directions away from Nash.

Nash raced to me and Adrianna. "We have to go."

"What about Chandra and Kiran?" I asked.

"It can only follow one group at a time. It will choose the larger," Nash said.

"But," I said, "there's more than one of them."

"I don't have time to explain." Nash grabbed my arm and ran.

What was Nash up to? Did he want me to figure it out for myself? I ran with him and Adrianna. I couldn't hear footsteps behind me.

What if Nash was wrong and the demons chose to follow Chandra and Kiran instead? They were separated and would have to fight alone. If they were overwhelmed, they would die and go to the Pit like Chandra's brother, Alex.

But Nash knew what he was doing. He had sent thousands of demons back to Hell.

So, why did Adrianna set her teeth and tense her forehead? Was it possible that she was worried Nash's plan, whatever it was, wouldn't work?

"Put your weapons away," Nash said. "If it shows itself, we need to be ready to run as fast as we can. Having our weapons drawn will slow us down."

As I ran, I turned to look. I shouldn't have. The ground shuttered. A demon ran behind us. It stood twenty feet tall with muscled arms and legs. Four backward curved horns grew above its far-spread eyes. Its skin was gray and splotchy.

"What in the world is that?" I asked as I ran.

The thing made the ground quake as it knocked down trees in its path.

"The hooded figures we saw in the forest," Adrianna said.

"But they were many," I said.

"No," Nash said, "they were one."

"It's gaining on us," Adrianna said. "Nash, what do we do?"

The ground rippled. Trees crashed in the forest. The crows were silent.

"Nash, say something," I said. "It's going to catch us."

"Keep running," Nash said. "Our ultimate duty is to keep you safe. We have to keep going."

But where? What would happen when that thing catches us?

"Lia, keep your eyes forward," Adrianna said. "You'll trip."

"I don't understand," I said. "We came to fight. Why are we avoiding it now? Is this not the demon we were looking for?"

"Just follow orders," Nash ground out.

No. I had a sword of the strongest metal that ever existed. I had the power to make angels fall. Why did I still depend on other people?

I drew my sword.

"What are you doing?" Adrianna asked. "Lia, you can't fight it."

I clenched my teeth. How was I supposed to avenge my parents if I wasn't brave enough to do what needed to be done? No running, no hiding. I'd faced my demons. I'll face this one, and when Raphael comes, I'll be ready for him too.

"Think about what you're about to do," Nash said. "You should listen to someone with more experience."

"I can't run anymore," I shouted and turned with my sword drawn.

The Balban raised a massive fist, ready to bring it down on me, but it didn't get the chance. Kiran and Chandra jumped from the trees onto the creature's shoulders. It screamed as they stabbed it. Black blood oozed down its chest.

I stared wide-eyed as Kiran and Chandra cut the flesh between the demon's neck and shoulders.

Nash had a plan all along, and I almost ruined it. Why couldn't he have just said something to me? Why doesn't he trust me?

Nash and Adrianna rushed forward and cut at the beast as it swung its massive arms. The demon looked down at Nash, like it recognized him.

"Nash, look out," I screamed.

The massive hand gripped Nash around the chest and waist and brought him up into the air. It squeezed. It would kill him. It wanted to kill him.

I ran around to its back. Its legs were exposed. With my blade, I sliced the tendons behind one of its knees.

The creature howled and knelt on that knee.

I repeated the same to the back of the other knee and got the same result.

Adrianna jumped off the beast's chest and leapt onto its forearm. She hacked at the demon's fingers until it dropped Nash.

Nash scrambled on the ground, gasping for air, but it wasn't long before he was back on his feet. He leapt and plunged his sword into the Balban's chest. He dragged the blade down, using his weight as leverage.

He pulled his sword from the body and backed away as the demon fell face-first to the ground. The forest shook. The body of the Balban faded like a hologram, leaving only an impression of what had been.

I sighed and put a hand to my chest as it pounded.

Nash shook some of the inky blood from his sword. The ground absorbed the blood like water. He glared at me before he raised his hand and opened the portal.

The others put away their weapons and climbed through. I sheathed my own blade and approached the portal, but before I could enter, the portal closed.

Nash lowered his hand. "I told you to run."

"My legs were growing heavy," I said. A lie.

"If you can't follow my orders, you won't survive Michael."

How quickly the focus shifted from Raphael to Michael. I didn't care about Michael. He wasn't the one who killed my parents.

"If you're so concerned about Michael, you'd make sure Adriel gets out of that terrible place. He's my guardian angel. He'll do anything to protect me."

Nash laughed.

"What's so funny?"

"He wasn't tasked to be your guardian. He named himself that."

"How do you know anything about it?"

Nash's lips formed a hard line. "You need to start following orders."

"What if I don't?"

"You're stubborn."

"You're controlling."

"I'm the leader of this team."

"You're not a very good leader if you don't see things."

Nash narrowed his eyes. "What are you talking about?"

"Someone's trying to kill you, Nash. In Venice, those demons attacked you and now this. That monster looked at you. It wanted to kill *you*. It didn't go after the rest of us."

"That's because it spotted me first and hadn't finished killing me yet."

I pressed my lips together and folded my arms.

"I see what you're saying," Nash said. "But it could be a coincidence. Then again, a lot of demons want me dead. I've sent plenty of them back to Hell."

"You say that like you didn't want to."

"Why would I? Do you think I'm that cruel? I do it because if I don't, Lucifer would send me to the Pit."

"But demons are evil."

"Are Tom and Adrianna evil? Are Chandra and Kiran?"

I'd never thought of that before. All the demons I had encountered before I met Nash whispered horrible things they wanted to do to people. They crouched on people's backs and murmured to them. Sometimes the people they spoke to did bad things.

"Things aren't that black and white," Nash said.

How could someone with so much ink spilled into his soul see things clearer than I could?

"So why is there a Hell?" I asked.

"Because a mistake was made."

"What mistake?"

Nash looked away.

I grabbed his elbow. "What was it?"

"A mistake I made. That's all you need to know." His eyes locked on mine.

I squinted at him. "That's why you're in Sheol. That's why *you* sawed off your wings."

"I sawed them off before all the feathers burned away." His face was tense, pained.

I wanted to erase that pain, to burn it away. Something inside me vibrated like the string on a guitar. It was silent, yet I could *feel* the music. I touched the side of his face and brought my lips up to his.

As our lips touched, he backed away from me. His breath wavered, and his eyes trembled.

Had I made a mistake? I struggled to find words to fill the gulf between us. But I didn't need to.

Nash rushed toward me. His hands cradled the sides of my face, and his lips pressed urgently against mine as if he had been fighting himself the whole time, fighting not to kiss me. And now, he was.

My hands ran through his hair. His fingertips grazed my neck, and goose bumps erupted across my skin. I didn't want him to stop, but he did.

I pressed my lips together. They were still warm from his touch.

Nash backed away from me as if I was a rattlesnake.

"We should go." He opened the portal.

"Yeah, I guess so." I tried to meet his eyes before I stepped through, but Nash's eyes were to the ground. His hands were clenched. He acted like he graffitied a building rather than kissed a girl.

five

I shredded the main riff of *The Devil's Orchard* on my guitar. The music brought me to a place of power. Power I didn't have.

Hard notes flowed from me, but the commanding sound wasn't *of* me. I wasn't going to let others play me like a chess piece anymore. I wasn't going to let things happen *to me*. I would *make* things happen.

I wasn't anyone's knife. I was the butcher. Nash and Lucifer would have to understand that.

As I hit each chord, I thought of Raphael's feathers becoming ash in my hands.

I felt eyes on my back. My fingers skipped the next few notes and tumbled onto the ones following.

If something was watching, I had to keep playing. That way it would think I wasn't on my guard, but I was. I finished the song and put the guitar on the bed.

I eased the bedside drawer open. Breathing, low and guttural, made my hands twitch. I withdrew my dagger in a flash and turned on my heels.

A dark corner faced me. Eyes peered at me from that corner. The light from my bedside lamp shrank away from the darkness.

Not there. Not there. Not there.

I couldn't get the mantra out of my mind. Those words had helped me ignore the monsters I thought I saw in my head. But it hadn't protected me because they were real.

I grabbed the curtain, keeping my eyes on the thing as it stared. I yanked the curtain back, bathing the room in overcast light.

A sigh rose from me.

Nothing crouched in the corner with its eyes on me.

I rested my dagger on the bedside table. My hands trembled.

The air was still and cold. My locket and Dad's cross necklace dangled in front of me as I leaned over my knees. My hands clenched into fists.

I faltered. When I faced Raphael, I wouldn't have time to deliberate. But seeing a demon in its full form would make a rabid dog hesitate. Raphael was different. My hate for him would drive my blade, and he wouldn't be safe from my touch.

I took longer to get dressed than usual, choosing my outfit carefully. Nash would be downstairs, and he would see me. That mattered more now than it had before.

The kiss changed something in me. I didn't know the full extent of how much I liked Nash until that moment. I needed to impress him. But nothing I owned would astound him.

I'd have to wear something from the closet, but those clothes weren't me. I grabbed a pair of jeans and put on my sleeveless Alice in Chains t-shirt. The front of the shirt depicted a giant rooster attacking a city.

Now, I'm ready to woo someone.

I walked into the kitchen. Nash, Adrianna, and Tom stood around the kitchen island. Kiran was behind Adrianna with his hands on her shoulders. Chandra leaned against the opposite counter with her arms folded.

"What are you guys doing?" I took the orange juice out of the refrigerator. Nash had a hot pot of coffee on every morning, but I wasn't much of a coffee drinker.

"Nash asked Lucifer about our angel friend," Kiran said.

"You did?" I put the juice carton on the counter and looked at Nash. *What had made him come around?*

I glanced at Nash. Everything I did around him felt unnatural like I was acting out a play. I poured the juice into my glass.

He nodded and took a sip of his coffee. "We're going to get him today. The gatekeepers won't like it, but we have this." He took a piece of paper from the breast pocket of his jacket and unfolded it. It had a dark red seal, a circle with the image of a dragon curled into its center. "It's an official decree from Lucifer."

"How did you get her to do it?" I asked.

"We have an agreement," Nash said.

"What agreement?"

"Never mind that."

Why was he being so secretive? Maybe he didn't want to talk about it around the others. Knowing Lucifer, I hoped it didn't have anything to do with torture, but I knew Nash wouldn't do that for Adriel.

"So, when do we go?" I asked.

"Have breakfast first," Nash said.

"I'm not hungry." I drank the orange juice to give myself something to do while I tried not to think about the kiss Nash and I shared. The more I thought about it, the more I wished I could hide under a pillow.

Nash narrowed his eyes. He tucked the paper back into his pocket. "Alright, get ready. We'll leave in half an hour."

I was ready in less than five minutes. After I laced up my boots, I sheathed my sword and took the dagger from my bed-side table.

I settled down in the passenger's seat next to Nash. "What made you change your mind?" I asked.

"You," he said.

"Because of what I said about Adriel saving us."

"No, because if you don't do this with me, you'll try to do this without me." Nash backed out of the driveway, and the car zoomed ahead.

Behind us, Adrianna drove a red Lexus. Chandra sat in the passenger's seat, and Kiran and Tom were in the back. Tom leaned in and whispered something to Kiran. Kiran grinned but turned away from Tom.

Are they joking around at a time like this? At least, Kiran was ashamed of it.

Nash drove like a normal person for the first time. He was in no rush to free Adriel from his chains. But at least he was saving him from that place.

I should say something about the kiss? No, that would be weird. Why would I bring it up like that? Should I ask him about us? Now's not the time, Lia.

A relationship with Nash would be complicated. He and I were from different worlds, and one day I would have to return to mine. But I could accept the challenge.

It would be a demonstration of my commitment, plus I could make an arrangement with Tom to use his portals every now and then to pop in unannounced. I could bear Sheol if it meant see-ing Nash time and again, temporarily of course. Sheol would be my summer house.

I scratched my head and glanced over at Nash.

His eyes were glued to the road. His mouth was a thin line, jaw tense.

I felt like a polar bear in a rain forest. I tapped my fingers to my palms to give them something to do. Never before did I wish Nash would drive faster.

Demons passed on the streets. One crawled on all fours like a lizard. My lip curled, and I stopped moving my fingers against my palms.

How could Tom, Kiran, Adrianna, and Chandra look like one of those things?

Nash parked the car, and Adrianna pulled up alongside us. The sky was darker in this part of Sheol, and the air held the faint smell of smoke.

We approached the gates of the Angel District. Neon lights glowed from among the clustered buildings. I cringed at the thought of what went on within the city itself.

Adrianna's hand was on the hilt of her dagger. Chandra wore her brass knuckles.

"If we have the decree, why do we have to bring weapons?" I asked.

"Because here, they like to ask questions second," Nash said.

Winks approached us, but remained close to the gate. His twin brother was nowhere to be seen. I wondered if demons got lunch breaks. "Nash, nice to see ya again. Seems ya never come around anymore."

"That's because this place is a hell-hole." Nash smirked. "But my friends wanted to partake in the city's pleasures. So, being a good host, I'm happy to oblige."

Winks raised his eyebrow, but his face settled into a grin. He wrapped his beefy hands around the bars of the gate and opened it.

We marched down the path into the city. The trees tried to grab us with their spindly branches as they reached over the path.

"Have fun, Nash," Winks shouted. "Don't stay too long. We might just keep ya."

Winks pulled the heavy, iron gates closed with both hands.

That exchange between Winks and Nash was a little too friendly.

Nash had been here before. *Was it to watch demons torture his kind? Did he enjoy watching fallen angels like Adriel suffer? Why did Lucifer exempt Nash from such punishment?*

My nose stung with the scent of alcohol, sweat, and rust. I couldn't imagine being drunk in this place. The neon lights made me so nauseous I wanted to puke. The narrow streets were packed like tunnels in an ant farm.

The music was loud and erratic. It moved like Skittles in a blender. The odd mix of sounds made my stomach hurt.

Shouts and jeers mixed with cries and screams of disgust, but I didn't dare to look this time. I kept my head down and hoped no one would try to pull me away from my friends.

A strange feeling of hopelessness wafted all over Hell, but it concentrated in some places more than others. The Angel District held a heavy sense of hopelessness, the heaviest I had experienced in all Sheol.

"I hate this place," Chandra said. "Remind me why this angel is so important."

I gritted my teeth, and glanced up only to look at the buildings before I lowered my head again.

"Come on," Nash said. "And don't look anyone in the eyes."

Because the demons will recognize me as human, but how? And what would they do to me if they found out?

With a larger group of people, moving through the crowd was easier. Nash and Kiran were in front of me while Adrianna walked alongside me. Chandra and Tom were at my back.

My palms sweat. I bit my lip. *Why did there have to be so many people here?* Fingertips tapped my palm. *What was going on with me?* I'd been to several Metal concerts with crowds packed as tightly as this one.

Demons didn't crowd those concerts, Lia. Maybe. At least, I didn't see any.

I recognized a building. Adriel no longer stood in the window, but I remembered the large set of steel doors and the peeling paint.

"It's that building there." I pointed.

"Okay," Nash said. "Hopefully they haven't moved him."

Angels were tortured in this place and made to feel shame. Adriel had just arrived, but it wouldn't be long before horned demons paraded him down the streets in chains, whipping his back.

My face flushed, and teeth clenched. If they moved him, I would find him and would fight any bastard who treated him like an animal.

I was ahead of the group now. I pulled open the steel door and raced up the stairs. The footsteps of the others reached my ears, but I didn't turn to make sure they followed. My actions were set to one purpose: to find Adriel.

My heart beat so fast, I thought it might pop out of my chest. I tore open the door, and there he was.

Adriel turned to look at me. Fastened to the floor, the thick iron chain still collared his neck.

"Lia?"

I rushed into the room and grabbed his hand. "It's alright. I'm getting you out of here."

"I told you not to come back."

"And you thought I'd listen? How long have you watched me? Ten years? You should know me by now."

I stood on tiptoe. No locking mechanism or clasp adorned the iron collar. Someone must have soldered it around his neck. I knelt on the ground and looked for a way to unlink the chain from the floor.

"You should go," Adriel said.

"Not without you." I couldn't find a way to free him from his chains.

"Lia, get out of the way." Nash walked into the room with the others.

I got up from the floor as Nash held his sword above his head.

Nash swung his broadsword against the iron chain, and it snapped. Heat rose in the air mixed with the scent of blood as the metal sparked.

Five feet of chain still hung from Adriel's neck, but at least he wasn't chained to the floor anymore. His eyes had ink in them like Nash's. His skin no longer held its glow, but was flat and pallid.

Footsteps thundered up the stairwell.

"We have company." Chandra removed her dagger from her side.

Five demons burst through the door, weapons ready. They wore sparse armor. Some only had arm bracers or leather padding around their stomachs.

Their bodies were muscled and large. Nothing covered their gruesome faces that looked like beaten leather mixed with a barrage of severe under bites, curved horns, and narrow eyes that ranged from inky black to fiery red.

Adriel grabbed my arm and pulled me behind him. Steel flashed, blades met blades in a thunderous cacophony. It all happened so fast.

Adrianna managed to slice through the belly of one of the assailants, but he got up again and leaked a trail of inky blood across the floor.

I withdrew my sword, but Adriel tightened his grip on my arm. "Let me go."

Adriel's teeth clenched.

"Adriel! Let me help them!"

"No," he said through his teeth.

Tom lost his sword as a demon with large, curled horns forced it from his hands. As the demon charged him, Tom grabbed its horns and tried to push back.

Kiran and Chandra fought back to back. Blood dripped from the end of Kiran's blade and across Chandra's brass knuckles.

Before he could utter a word, Nash met swords with the tallest and largest of the group. The demon stood roughly seven feet tall and probably weighed as much as a mountain lion. His skin was dark red.

Nash ducked as the demon's heavy broadsword nearly cut his head off. Nash slashed through the demon's exposed stomach.

I jerked forward, instinct willing me to help Nash, but Adriel had my arm in a vise grip.

The demons had strength as an advantage, but they didn't seem as trained as Nash and the others. I doubted they were warriors. They seemed more like nightclub bouncers to me, but they really threw their weight around.

Nash gritted his teeth as the large demon bore his sword down against Nash's blade. His feet slipped from under him, and Nash was on the ground.

The demon raised his sword, ready to bring it down upon Nash's body. Nash had enough time to roll away, but he didn't.

What is he doing?

Nash pulled the paper from his breast pocket. "Wait," he bellowed. "It's a decree," Nash said. "From Lucifer. The angel is coming with us."

Swords hung in the air.

"Let me see that." The large bouncer demon grabbed the letter from Nash's hand.

"You sure you can read it?" Chandra smirked.

"It's got her seal," the demon said. "What do you want with a fallen angel?" The demon looked down at Nash. "You already got one."

"We're just the messengers," Tom said. "We don't have any right to ask questions of the Morning Star." Tom's lips twitched into a smile, and his nostrils flared.

The demon considered the paper again. "Whatever," he grumbled. "Take him. We have enough entertainment for tonight."

The demon tossed the decree onto the floor, and the five of them left the room.

Nash reached over and grabbed the paper. He crinkled it in his fist.

Kiran offered Nash a hand and helped him to his feet.

"They've been working in the Circles too long." Tom grinned. "They've forgotten how to be civilized."

"They should be happy to get out of there," Adrianna said. "It's unfortunate to say, but this is quite a promotion."

I stepped forward, but Adriel seized my arm.

Nash narrowed his eyes.

"It's okay," I said.

Adriel let go of me, and I joined Nash and the others.

A smear of blood streaked across Adrianna's face, and Tom held his arm as it hung limp at his side.

Nash approached Adriel. His eyes darkened. "If you're using us to leave Sheol, I'll throw you into the Pit myself."

six

DRIEL was safe. Well, as safe as he could be in the service of Lucifer. But at least he was out of the Angel District.

He stood outside the house as Nash faced him.

"You're with us now," Nash said. "You'll do as I say. I'm the leader of this team."

"The team that hunts angels," Adriel said.

"That's part of the deal I made with Lucifer to get you out of that torture circus," Nash said. "It's done. There's no backing out now."

"Is that what's in my contract?"

"Lucifer doesn't make contracts with fallen angels," Nash said. "You either do as she says, or she will throw you into the Pit."

I cringed and wondered if I saved Adriel after all. He'd have to betray the angels who were his family for millennia. I had my reasons, but that didn't mean I wanted to pull Adriel into my problems.

"I'm doing this for Lia," Adriel said.

"However you want to think about it," Nash said. "But you're working for Lucifer."

"Hey," Tom said.

I tore my eyes away from Nash and Adriel.

"You want to help me get this thing back in." His eyes fell on the arm that hung at his side.

"Sure," I said.

I walked with Tom to the kitchen. He sat and took his hand off his arm. The arm slumped down.

"What do I do?" I asked.

"Relocate it."

"I've never done this before," I said.

"That's alright. Just pop it in."

"Are you sure? Sounds like that would hurt."

"Probably," Tom said. "But I can't go around with a dead arm, can I?"

I gripped his forearm and grounded my other hand on his bicep. I pushed until a pop sounded.

Tom levered the arm up and down at the elbow. "That'll work," he said. "Didn't hurt as much as I thought it would."

"What if I did it wrong?" I asked.

"I guess if I was still human, it might matter. But it'll heal fine. It'll always hurt though."

"Wait. What?"

"It'll heal fine."

"No, you said it'll always hurt."

"Yeah." He rotated his shoulder. "Good thing it didn't break."

"But you'll always feel the pain? Forever?"

"Yep. Forever. Lets me know I'm alive." He laughed.

"So, every injury you've ever gotten, you still feel it."

Tom nodded. "Every injury since I became a demon."

"Does that happen to fallen angels too?" I asked.

"I don't know," Tom said. "The only fallen angel I know personally is Nash, and I've never asked him." Tom stood. "Well, thanks, Dr. Lia." He patted me on the shoulder before he disappeared into the hallway.

I hung my head. The screams of all the angels I had made fall echoed in my ears. The room fell silent, but a voice invaded the space.

"You alright?" Adrianna asked.

"Yeah, I was just thinking about something," I said.

She slinked into the room. "You were wondering if Adriel and Nash can feel it—the pain they felt when they fell."

I nodded. My lips pressed together tight.

Adrianna turned me around to face her. "Most likely not," she said. "Do you think Nash could function in that much pain all the time?"

"But you do," I said.

"I didn't fall all the way from Heaven to Sheol. I didn't saw off my own wings or feel my feathers burn away."

You nearly had your intestines cut out. "I guess you're right."

"Well, then, there you go. You don't even need to ask," Adrianna said.

She yawned. "I don't know about you, but I'm going to sleep for three days."

In less than two weeks, we fought invading warriors from Heaven, battled a giant demon, and rescued a fallen angel from the Angel District. *I doubt I'd fight it if someone tried to put me in a coma for a few days.*

"Yeah, that sounds good," I said.

It wasn't long before I fell onto the cool, white sheets of my bed. The sky was deceptive. It looked like a cloudy afternoon, but it was two in the morning. I stretched against the covers and knocked one of the pillows off the bed. I didn't hear it fall. That was strange. I knew it fell off the bed. I guess the pillow was so soft it barely made a sound.

With that thought, I hugged the remaining pillow against my body and fell asleep.

WE gathered on the field outside Nash's house. Adriel looked better than he had in the Angel District, but the iron collar still clinched around his neck. The chain was wrapped around his left arm. *Was there anyone in Sheol who could take it off for him?*

As usual, Nash had his display of training weapons on the table.

"What's next?" Chandra asked.

Nash stepped in front of us. "We have to make sure we're prepared if Michael comes."

"But what about the angel weapons?" Tom asked.

"It's not safe to go after the angels right now," Nash said. "If we leave Sheol, we'll be more vulnerable to Michael. If we remain here, he'll have to fight us on our turf."

Where my friends can't die. Good. Still, thoughts of the Pit crept into my mind.

Nash picked up a sword from the table. "Adriel." Nash offered Adriel the weapon.

"I'd rather not fight you." Adriel squared his shoulders. His fists clenched.

"Okay," Nash said. "Fight Kiran then, but you're going to need something better than this." He shrugged and tossed the sword back onto the table.

"I can't wait to see what he's made of," Chandra said. "Please tell me we didn't waste our time liberating a mouse from the snake pit."

"Pick your weapons," Nash said.

Kiran patted his sword in the sheath around his waist. Adriel looked back at him, and Kiran gestured with his head toward the table of weapons Nash had laid out.

Adriel approached the table and walked from one long end to the other. "These are angel weapons," he said.

"Not all of them," Adrianna said.

"No, these." Adriel pointed to the weapons at the end of the table, among them were the Chains of Andromeda, the Hammer of Gerriel, and the Whip of Asrael. "These are all the weapons you stole."

I stepped to the side, positioned myself behind Adrianna, and tried to make myself small. I stared at the ground, not wanting to see that look of disdain in Adriel's eyes fall upon me.

"Pick your weapon," Nash said.

Adriel turned to him. "My weapon is not here. It is in the Pit."

I lowered my head.

Nash walked up to Adriel until their chests were centimeters apart. Nash was as tall as Adriel though Adriel's body was broader. "Don't test me. Pick a weapon."

Adriel stood his ground for a few moments, but he turned back to the table and surveyed the weapons once again. He picked up a sword from the display.

I recognized it. It was the first sword I had trained with over a year ago. It was by Nash's estimate a beginner's weapon, lightweight, but without the ability to do too much damage. The blade wasn't entirely of Arcadian Steel, but like most demon weapons was mixed with a lesser metal.

Why would he pick such an inferior weapon? Especially against a swordsman with Kiran's reputation.

Nash shook his head as he stood in front of the table. "Take your positions," he said.

Kiran withdrew his weapon as Adriel stepped in front of him. Kiran gripped his sword. His blade cut through the air.

Adriel stepped to the side and caught the blade of Kiran's sword against his. Steel zinged along steel until Adriel's blade swept off the end of Kiran's.

My hands clenched into fists, and I had to remind myself this was just practice. They weren't really going to hurt each other.

Despite the chains weighing down Adriel's left arm, he was perfectly balanced. He moved as if he was made of air.

Adriel sword met Kiran's again. The steel sparked as their blades met. Adriel rained a parry of blows with such speed that Kiran had trouble matching him. As steel met steel, Adriel forced Kiran to kneel.

My eyes widened. Adriel beat Kiran in under a minute.

"He's good." Chandra's hands were on her hips. She gazed at Adriel as he approached them.

"You have to be to defend the Throne of God," Tom said.

Adriel nodded. He was out of breath, and that seemed to surprise him. He tossed the sword back onto the table.

"Ha, the Throne of God." Adrianna laughed. She looked to Adriel. "Have you ever seen God?"

Adriel breathed through his nose and closed his eyes.

"Well, have you?"

Adriel looked at Adrianna. "I'm not going to talk about God or any of the secrets of Heaven with a demon."

Adrianna frowned and folded her arms.

Adriel wandered off across the field.

"What the hell?" Chandra said. "Did that guy forget that we saved his ass yesterday?"

"Yeah," Adrianna said. "I didn't mean to offend him or anything. I just asked a question, that's all."

"He's like that," Nash said as he approached. "All high and mighty. Don't let him get to you. Okay, Chandra and Lia, pair up."

Great. Another day when Chandra gets to knock me to the ground. I figured I owed her a few more after what happened to Alex.

As soon as I drew my weapon, Chandra attacked. I blocked her blow, but I nearly didn't. Heat and adrenaline surged through my body.

I came at Chandra with a renewed vigor. My sword clashed against hers. I ground my teeth. Chandra's sword flew from her hands.

Did I do that?

"Good," Nash said.

Chandra grimaced. "She *pulled* it from my hand. She used magic."

"I don't know *how* to use magic," I said.

Nash stood next to me. "One thing I noticed. Your posture needs work." His hand reached out to touch me, but he stopped. "You'll have to work on that. I'm going to start dinner." Nash headed to the house.

I narrowed my eyes. He acted like I was fire. What was wrong with him? Before the kiss, he was fine with touching me.

Chandra narrowed her eyes at me.

I walked with the others toward the patio. Kiran was on the field, weapon in hand.

"Come on," Adrianna called to him. "Come inside with me."

"I'm going to practice a few stances," Kiran said. "I'll be there in a minute."

As I got ready for dinner, I chose one of the nicest dresses in my closet, the blue one with off-the-shoulder sleeves. If it wasn't for my dark hair, I might have looked like Cinderella in that dress. Cinderella also didn't have a tiny, silver nose ring around her left nostril.

Dressing up for dinner made me feel like a different person, but Nash liked it.

I tried to do something with my hair, but not even the bobby pins would hold it. The ends of my hair faded from candy apple to dull red. I had the urge to re-dye them.

My heart-shaped locket was an inch above Dad's golden cross, wrapped in silver thorns. I clenched both in my hand and took a deep breath.

Laughter echoed from the dining room. Adrianna and Kiran had a closeted conversation at the other end of the table. I was too far away to hear what they said.

Kiran's face tensed. He still wore his training clothes, which was odd as he was always the best dressed. I guess he didn't have time to change after practicing his stances.

I sat opposite Nash at the end of the long table. He didn't even look at me. *Great*. I got all dressed up just to be ignored.

"Aren't you going to set a place for Adriel?" I asked.

Adrianna and Kiran stopped talking.

Nash twirled pasta around his fork. "It isn't necessary."

"What are you worried about?" Chandra asked. "We don't need to eat. It won't kill him."

"But we still *feel* hunger," Adrianna said.

"Where is he?" I asked.

"He was still on the training field when I left," Kiran said.

I got up from my seat and earned myself a disapproving look from Nash. I didn't care. Adriel was one of us now. We should make him feel welcomed. I doubted Nash invited him to dinner.

"I'll be right back," I said.

I left the dining room and went to the patio outside. I spotted Adriel sitting in the grass several feet away from the house. I lifted my skirt as I walked through the grass.

Adriel sat on the far side of the field, and my arms ached from training. *Oh, screw it!* I let the skirt's hem sink to the ground as I hurried to Adriel.

I crouched next to him. The hem of my dress was green with grass stains.

A sleek, marble wall separated Nash's house from his neighbors. I'd never been so close to the wall before. Leafless vines crept their delicate fingers across the wall like veins.

Trees with bark white like bone twisted their branches into the still air of Sheol. I wondered if everything—the grass, the trees, the buildings—were all illusions in the Outer Region. But why would anyone want to live in a dulled world where colors lacked saturation?

Were colors more difficult to imitate? Or was this Lucifer's distorted version of paradise?

Adriel looked at the sky.

You probably think Hell is below us. I thought that, but Sheol sat alongside Earth, like an alternate reality. So, maybe Heaven isn't above us either. But maybe it was. Maybe that is why angels have wings.

"You miss Heaven?" I asked.

He glanced over at me and then back to the sky. "I wish I would have spent my final days there."

A chill ran up my spine. *His final days.* He said it like he had died.

"Do you think Michael wants to kill me?"

"Most definitely." He didn't look back at me.

I bowed my head. He touched my shoulder.

Adriel looked into my eyes. "Not even I could stop Michael."

"Maybe you could," I said. "You're Seraphim, right? And Michael's an Archangel. So, you're of higher rank."

Adriel shook his head. "Michael used to be Seraphim."

I arched my eyebrows.

Adriel continued. "Michael used to guard the Throne of God alongside me."

"Why did he stop?"

"There had been no attempts on the Throne for millennia and only one in known history. Michael is a warrior. He needed to be an Archangel, a general, and he had the training."

"But, why would God let him do that? To leave his post like that."

"Michael said it was His will."

"And you believed him?" I asked.

"Angels don't lie."

"What about Raphael?"

"As far as I know Raphael hasn't lied."

"But he's disobeyed. He's trying to go against God to shut the gates of Heaven. And what about Lucifer?"

Father, well, Mother of Lies.

"Lucifer isn't an angel anymore," he said.

I looked at the sky. I tried to see past the gray clouds. I wondered if Sheol was closer to Heaven than Earth, and if I stared long enough I might see some semblance of Heaven through the clouds. Most people, I guess, think of Heaven as above, Hell as below, and Earth is somewhere in the middle. But now I knew that it wasn't like that at all. But there was still more I didn't know.

"What is it like up there?" I asked.

Adriel shook his head.

"You won't tell *me*?"

"It's forbidden, but even if it wasn't, it is indescribable. Your soul is in so much peace and contentment. Humans feel it more strongly because they have lived a lifetime never feeling that bliss. It was like ripping the skin from my body when I left."

Seven

I searched under the bed for the pillow I pushed off two nights ago but couldn't find it. Weird. Maybe someone came in and took it?

A yawn followed as I stretched my arms to the ceiling.

Nash had five guest rooms in the mansion he called home. If someone needed an extra pillow, they would have taken it from one of the unoccupied rooms. The unmade bed and random pair of jeans I left across the chair would signal to anyone that my room was taken.

Mom kept a clean home, but Dad's studio was full of empty paint cans, brushes soaking in brown water, the smell of turpentine, and rags crusted with paint. I had developed a mix of the two's habits, but leaned more toward Dad's idea of tidy. I would do the dishes and make sure I didn't leave my footprints on the rest of the house, but my own space always looked like a hurricane came through. *How had my birth mother kept her home?*

A thought flickered at the edge of my mind, something transient, maybe a memory, and then it was gone.

I checked myself in the mirror. A relieved sigh escaped my lips. I had thought for a moment I might be different somehow.

The feeling was surreal. I sometimes got the same feeling when I let my mind wander. Like I watched myself from the outside, but it wasn't me.

Nothing about me had changed. My silver nose ring looped around my left nostril. My skin was still *sun-kissed* although it hadn't been actually sun-kissed in a long time. My long hair was in a mess of tangles that I no longer wished to challenge.

I picked up the brush from the bathroom counter and hid it away in a drawer so I wouldn't have to think about tearing through my hair with it. Instead, I smoothed my hair with my hands. Not much of an improvement, but it would have to do.

Satisfied that I hadn't grown an extra head or a third eye, I opened the closet and put on a pair of jeans and a t-shirt.

The house was quiet, but not like the quiet of other houses. Other houses still creaked, and the air conditioner switched on from time to time, creating a gentle hum. But this place was as silent as a snake before it bites your heel.

I put in my earbuds and cranked up my MP3 player every night to deafen the silence. How could anyone sleep without the blare of the television or the blast of music in the background? The fear of what could break the silence would be too maddening.

I sauntered down the hall. The door to the library was open.

Nash sipped his coffee. He wore a t-shirt, jeans, and a pair of thick socks. His eyes were closed as if he was meditating.

Maybe I should talk to him. No. What would I say? Why had things become so hard?

My feet pivoted. *Rip off the bandage, Lia.* I took a deep breath and stepped into the library.

A cactus sat on the windowsill next to the couch. The cactus wasn't from Sheol. The green of its prickled body was too vibrant.

I perched on the sofa beside Nash.

Nash's eyes remained closed.

"Thank you," I said.

"For what?" He opened one eye and peered at me.

"For helping me with Adriel."

He took another sip of coffee. His eyes were open, but he didn't look at me.

"I know you don't like him, but he did a lot for me. He became my guardian angel after my first one went missing."

Sydriel.

Nash clicked his tongue and looked down into his coffee mug. "That's good, I guess."

I pursed my lips. "I wanted to ask you something."

"What about?" He turned to me like I had stung him.

"When I went to the Angel District the first time, a demon recognized me as human." I wasn't going to tell Nash anything about my encounter with the two drunk demons in the Angel District, but I needed something to keep the conversation going until I gathered the courage to talk about *us*, and I *was* curious. How could that demon have known I was human?

For a moment, Nash looked confused, like he expected me to say something different. But then, his expression grew dark.

"A demon recognized you?" His voice shouted panic. "Are you sure you weren't followed?"

"Yes. Why?"

Nash breathed a sigh. "There are some demons who get bored of Sheol. They try to leave by any means necessary, and the only way besides express permission from Lucifer would be to highjack a human body."

"Highjack a human body? You mean possess me like in *The Exorcist*?"

Nash nodded. "A demon could live in your body and wander the world until he was done with it."

"Yeah, but couldn't a priest just sprinkle some holy water and bam! Exorcised."

Nash didn't laugh. "This is serious."

"They were drunk. I don't think they realized what they were saying."

"They? There was more than one?"

"Two actually, but only one noticed it at first."

This conversation was fast becoming more serious than I intended. I should have picked something light like *I'm practicing a new riff on my guitar. Oh, and did you know I can play by ear?*

Oh, no I wasn't aware of that.

Yeah. It's all great. Now can we talk about the time you kissed me and what we're going to do about it?

Nash sighed again and put his cup on the coffee table. "You shouldn't have gone there."

Maybe I shouldn't have said anything. "They were drunk," I said. "I don't think we have to worry about them."

Nash's eyes darted.

Stop thinking about all the bad things that could happen to me!

"The woman said she knew I was human by my eyes. But how? My eyes look just like yours or Adrianna's or Tom's. How are mine any different?"

Nash clasped his hands together. His long, pale fingers entwined. Even with his dark hair awry, he still looked perfect. It made me mad. If he was as ugly as a monkfish maybe things would be a little easier for me.

"They're not flat," he said.

I furrowed my brow.

Nash sighed. "It's hard to explain. You can't see it like we do. It glimmers and darts like light playing off the walls through a stained-glass window." He clasped my hands in his and looked deep into my eyes. "It dances inside your irises. It's . . . life, and it's beautiful."

My heart thumped in my chest, and without thinking, like a puppet drawn by strings, my lips were drawn to his.

Nash's lips pressed against mine. He pulled away and spoke against my lips. "That was pretty funny about the priest. You know it doesn't quite work that way, right?"

"Aha," I breathed through my parted lips. I didn't care how an exorcism worked in that instant. I kissed him.

In a terrifying and thrilling moment, I realized it would never be enough. I would lose myself in this. I would become someone different and new, and I couldn't control any of it.

I clung to him as the only clear thing in a world where all else becomes fuzzy and transparent.

My eyes fluttered open and focus came back. Someone filled my peripheral vision. I pulled away from Nash.

Adriel stood in the doorway. Those charcoal gray eyes made him look unlike himself. He ducked his head and left down the hallway.

I cursed under my breath. Nash was close enough to hear me.

I stood, and Nash caught my arm. His grip was firm, but not rough.

"What are you doing?" he asked.

"Maybe he came to talk," I said. "I want to see what's up. He shouldn't feel awkward here. He probably thinks he intruded on something . . . intimate."

There was that look again, like I was tapping my head while reciting the National Anthem. What happened between us *was* intimate.

"Sorry," I said. "I meant—"

"He can wait."

"I don't know what the big deal is," I said. "He probably wanted to ask about training or maybe food. It's not like you'd invite him to dinner or anything."

"Is that what this is about? I didn't ask him to dinner? I make those dinners for my friends. He's not a friend. He's a refugee that you asked me to save. Don't ask me to be his friend too."

"Look, I don't know what's going on between you two, but this is ridiculous. The man saved your life. Yet, you treat him like a dog that chewed through your favorite pair of shoes. And why? What did he do to you?"

Nash's mouth was open, and his eyes were narrowed.

I wanted to say more, but anger rose like smoke in my chest. My core was on fire. I didn't want to yell at Nash. So, I left.

"Lia, wait."

Footsteps echoed behind me.

I closed the front door and strode out into the street. Darkness wrapped its dim fingers over the slash of light in the sky. The air was cold, that fresh stagnant cold of Sheol.

I walked with my hands in my pockets. My thoughts raced.

Raphael and Michael were after me, and they both knew where I was. I would be lucky if Michael wasn't halfway through the Circles by now. Nash and Adriel would never get along. Nash acted as if Adriel slapped his mother or something. And I couldn't bring myself to ask either one of them about what happened between them.

I thought about asking Tom or Adrianna, but I wanted Nash to tell me. I wanted him to open up to me. He was being distant again, not in his actions but in his thoughts.

I passed houses smaller but no less smooth and white than Nash's home. All of them had manicured lawns, although the grass wasn't green. It was more of a bluish-green color, dulled by gray, but not true green. It reminded me of swamp water.

The air tasted of burnt leaves. My nose numbed to all but the smell of smoke, as if the ground roasted beneath me but gave off no heat.

Nash and I had known each other for more than a year now. We were *dating* I guess, although neither one of us had made that very clear. We had kissed. Twice. And we had just had our first big fight. I imagined with all the tension around us, it wouldn't be the last.

After fifteen minutes, I came to a bridge that led over a river. On the opposite bank, a building that reminded me of a castle stood surrounded by tall walls.

A man leaned against one of the circular columns that supported the bridge. He wore a rumpled blue suit and smoked a cigarette. I recognized him.

"You're that lawyer," I said. "Ambrose Letchfield."

The streets were quiet and empty. The streets were always empty. Demons must not be the outdoorsy types.

"You need an attorney, kid?" He gazed off in the distance, past the bridge where the castle rose, bordered by tightly packed walls.

"No," I said. "I saw you *defend* someone." Defend didn't seem like the right word.

Letchfield chuckled. He flicked the ashes of his cigarette onto the ground.

"Why does she do it?" I asked.

He looked at me. I didn't meet his eyes. Dressed in his non-threatening blue suit with his thinning hair, I had forgotten he was a demon and that he might know I was not.

"Who are you, kid?"

"Um, I'm new." I didn't want to come up with an elaborate lie. It would be easier for him to discover me that way.

Letchfield took a long draw from his cigarette. "I came here several years back. Used to be a lawyer actually." He laughed.

"Some people say we belong in Hell. Truth is, I stopped trying a long time ago."

"Then, why?" I asked. "Why does Lucifer go through the trouble if the whole thing is rigged anyway?"

"She thinks it's funny. It's not like she was given a fair trial before she was sent down here." He smiled. "This whole place is rigged, kid. What did you think it would be like in Hell?"

I shrugged. "The Outer Region's not too bad, I guess."

"Maybe if you don't hate yourself." He looked at the cigarette almost burnt to the filter. "I never used to smoke. Who does anymore anyway?"

Demons who have no reason to end their vices. "Is it bad for you?"

"Lucifer told me I should take it up," he said. "She thought it would be amusing like in one of those old movies from the '60s. I didn't like it at first, but now I can't kick it. They don't tell you that back home. Being dead doesn't make you better at dealing with the stuff you couldn't when you were alive. That's because the dead still have souls, you know? We're still kicking upstairs. We just have a lot more time with our bad habits."

He tossed his cigarette to the ground. It landed near where the water washed up on the rocks. Letchfield put his hands in his pockets and strolled to the street. His slumped form disappeared around a corner.

I was suddenly aware of how very empty I felt. Not drained or hungry, but just empty, like a balloon without air.

I passed the bridge and walked into town. The buildings were packed together, like a grayed-out city. All the fixtures were there: street lamps, paved walkways, stores, bars, but it was all dead and gray and wrong.

My fingers tingled. Sharp pricks crept up my spine.

I glanced over my shoulder. Peering from around the side of the building behind me, was an eye, and in the shadowy gloom was the outline of a curved antler.

My breath caught.

I thought back to the time I spotted one while in the car with Nash. A Jinn. I was sure of it. One of them followed me. Again.

I felt like I had backed up over the edge of a cliff. I didn't fall, but I imagined I fell and smashed my head on the ground below. Trying to shake the gory image from my mind, I focused on the creature in the shadows.

Maybe it was another spy for Raphael. But that couldn't be. How could it possibly be delivering messages back and forth to Raphael if the wards were up?

I wasn't sure if I should tell Nash or Bob. What would they do? Jinni could *be* anything. The cold enwrapped me. Jinni could be any*one*.

I darted like a deer after hearing leaves crackle.

Behind me echoed the sound of galloping hooves. The stampeding became louder.

Blood pounded in my ears in time with my feet as they hit the pavement. After a few blocks, I wrapped around the side of a building and hugged the wall. I took in gulps of air that tasted bloody in my throat.

Unlatching myself from the wall, I peered into the street. *No sign of anyone chasing me.* I decided to cut through the alley back to Nash's house.

That thing would not follow me home. If Raphael thought he could get away with the same tactic, he was wrong. I would never be fooled by a Jinn again.

I rounded the corner and caught a glow of light. My eyes anchored to the brightness. The gleam tunneled down an alleyway.

A tall figure stood before the light. The glow wrapped around his outline and made him appear taller and thinner, but the black suit, the gelled hair, and golden wristwatch were the signatures of only one person I knew.

Beelzebub, the prince of gluttony.

Bob stepped through the portal and disappeared on the other side. The portal zipped out of existence.

eight

"WE have to get Lia out of Sheol." Adriel stood at the head of the dining room table next to Nash.

Nash folded his arms. His mouth formed a hard line.

I sat at the table between Tom and Adrianna. Adrianna stared at her knuckles, scarred from fighting. She kept them that way although she could change them if she wanted. Chandra and Kiran sat across from us.

Out of Sheol, I thought. *Where would I go?* Lucifer wouldn't let Nash and the others leave me someplace alone. So, did that mean we'd all be going? I imagined us all staying in Jonah's cramped apartment back in New Orleans.

Uncle Jonah probably wondered where I had gone. I left without saying goodbye. All that remained of me were a few spare guitar picks and three slices of American cheese in the fridge. Jonah hated prepackaged cheese slices, but I bet he'd bear them to see me safe.

"He's probably right," Tom said. "Michael knows she's here, and he's most likely plowing through the Circles to get to her."

Nash shook his head. "Lia should stay here. If we leave Sheol, we'll have to fight Michael in unknown territory. There are more people to protect her here, more demons we can call to arms."

Demons were my defenders. The creatures who used to scare me in dark corners would fight angels for me. And the angels, the bright, beautiful, God-fearing beings wanted me in a cage.

"But Michael knows she's here," Adriel said. "If we hide her..."

"You want to *hide* her from an Archangel?" Nash pointed to Adriel. "You're going to get her killed."

"I'm trying to protect her."

"Key word: *trying*. I'm *going* to protect her," Nash said. "You can keep trying."

I frowned. They were using the matter of my safety as a device to funnel out their rage for each other.

"Nash is right," Chandra said. Her eyes were solid black. They had been that way for the last fifteen minutes. "We have more allies here. We'll be on our own out there. At least here, we're warded and protected by the tortures of the Circles. If Michael does try to get through, he would be stuck in the Circles for a long while before he gets to us. He'll be weakened, maybe spent. We can meet him right outside and take him down while he's winded."

Adriel shook his head. "Michael doesn't get winded."

"Look, I think we should all calm down," Adrianna said. "We should keep training. That's the most important thing."

"We could train for millennia and never be as battle-ready as Michael," Adriel said.

Adriel was right. I could train for millennia and never be able to take down a turtle.

"Talk like that doesn't get us anywhere," Adrianna said. "We need to have a little bit of hope, huh?"

"There is no hope," Adriel said. "That's why we should run."

"She'd be running for the rest of her life," Nash said. "I know that's not what Lia wants."

"Lia wants to be alive," Adriel said.

"Hey," I said. "No one knows what I want but me."

The room hung silent. Everyone looked at me.

"I want to stay in Sheol," I said, "for now. Let's train as hard as we can. Later, we can discuss other plans."

At least I was comfortable in Sheol. Out there, I had no place to go except Jonah's, but I couldn't go live with Jonah now. Angels found me the first time. What if they hurt him to get to me?

Sure, I wanted to be home, but I had to make a home first. I couldn't make a home that would be pulled from under me the moment Michael showed his face.

Sheol was temporary. It wasn't home. If Michael or Raphael showed up here, well it wouldn't be good, but at least it wouldn't give me a taste of what I couldn't have, not for a long time yet.

"Alright then," Chandra said. "Let's get out there." She stood, followed by Adrianna, Kiran, and Tom. They left the room.

Adriel put his hand on my shoulder. "You need to get out of here as soon as you can."

I put my hand on his, offering him a thin-lipped smile.

He left Nash and me at the table.

Nash sat next to me. "Lia, I..."

"I don't need you speaking for me." I got up from my chair.

"I know that." Nash placed his hand on mine. "We need to talk."

I sat back down.

"I'm sorry about yesterday." I dreaded talking about it. What would I say? I wanted to know why Nash treated Adriel like some snake that crawled up and bit him. But that paranoia kicked in, telling me in so many whispers that I shouldn't be asking questions, not about this.

Something told me it wasn't Nash's past with Adriel that I had to worry about but other things, deeper secrets Nash kept from me, that would be teased out if I knew the truth about him and Adriel.

"It's not about yesterday," Nash said. "Well, it is, in part."

I narrowed my eyes.

Nash squeezed my hand. "I made a mistake."

"What kind of mistake?"

"The kind I can't take back."

I tensed. "What mistake, Nash?"

He took a deep breath. "The kiss. It was a mistake."

"Which one, the first or the second?" I pulled my hand from under his.

"Both."

"Because of Adriel?"

"What does he have to do with this?"

"Because I pulled away from you when he was in the room?"

Nash, confused, shook his head.

Adriel hadn't upset him. Nash cut off what was between us because it was temporary. I wouldn't choose to stay with him in Sheol. Maybe he resented that. Maybe he changed his mind about my choice, my deal with the Devil to free my soul.

He didn't like that I made my own choices. He said so himself. He wanted to control me like he controlled the rest of his team. He was angry with me because I didn't fold like a deck of cards like all the other girls he had been with.

"I don't need you, Nash," I said. "This doesn't get under my skin. And as I remember, I kissed you. Both times. So, the kisses were my mistakes. I won't make any more of them."

I marched out of the room and leaned against the wall. My head hit the back of the wall as I closed my eyes and counted backwards from ten. If I started to cry, I wouldn't stop.

The world is an oboe, and its music burns.

*   *   *

BACK home, I'd pinned a hand-made calendar to my door. Every year I would make one. School was the most important thing in my life back then, so I would make a countdown for back to school in the summer, a countdown to winter break, and a countdown to summer in the spring.

When I was in fifth grade, Mom watched me as I made one of my calendars. She offered to buy me one, but I shook my head. I liked the catharsis of making one myself as much as I liked marking down the days with a big fat, red X.

In Sheol, time didn't seem to matter as much as it did on Earth. There were no calendars. I came here a few days after I turned sixteen, but I didn't keep track of the days after that.

Once I reconnected with Uncle Jonah, I found out I was nearly seventeen. I tracked the weeks the year before, a tally for each one on a piece of paper I found in the library. So I knew how long I'd been here.

By my rough estimate, I would be eighteen in ten months, not even a full year. But I didn't feel the same excitement I felt on all those mornings. That's because I had gotten out, but still missed that joy. I hoped like hell I could find it again.

After a few deep breaths and fanning my eyes to stop the tears, I unlatched myself from the wall. I wouldn't let Nash see how I felt about his rejection, and I didn't want to talk about it anymore.

Nash's footsteps were behind me as I approached the door to the backyard. His warmth suffused my left side. He had caught up with me. Damn my short legs.

Don't look at him. Chandra had been right. I *was* temporary like all the other girls Nash had taken up with in the past. Why did I think I was so special? Chandra had lasted two weeks. I had lasted two days.

We met the others on the field. Adriel had a sword in his hand. He approached Nash.

"I'll fight you now." Adriel's eyes narrowed.

Whoa, I thought. *He shouldn't fight him now. Not when tensions between them were so high.* But then again, when weren't tensions high between the two of them?

Would Adriel hurt Nash? Why did my lips twitch at the thought? I didn't want Nash to suffer. He rejected me, but I wasn't a monster. So, why did I have to shake myself free of the idea?

"Alright." Nash picked up a sword from the table without surveying any of the other weapons. It might have seemed like his decision was nonchalant, but it wasn't. Nash knew every weapon he laid out and in what order. He selected the Rapier of Ophaniel. Ophaniel was one of the many angels I condemned to the Angel District.

Ophaniel's sword had cut through Nash's flesh and left paper-thin slashes all along his body. Did he still feel them? Did I want him to?

The weapon was light and sharp, light enough that Nash would have the advantage of speed no matter which weapon Adriel chose, and the blade was sharp enough that Adriel wouldn't feel the cuts it made in his flesh. But they would still bleed.

What was I thinking? Nash wasn't going to cut up Adriel like a piece of salami.

"Pair up," Nash said.

The rest of us didn't move. Our eyes locked on Nash and Adriel.

"I gotta see this," Chandra said. "Does Nash really think we're going to train when this is going on?"

"You want me to pop some popcorn?" Adrianna asked.

"He's good." Kiran rubbed the back of his neck. His eyelids were heavy.

Tom glanced at Kiran. "How late were you up last night?"

"He's been practicing his stances every night," Adrianna said. "Staying up after midnight. I tried to get him to come inside, but he won't respond to anything. I mean anything." Adrianna's eyelashes fluttered.

Tom rolled his eyes.

Steel whipped in the stillness.

Adriel's blade danced through the air. He was light on his feet despite his size. If he could beat Kiran, Nash would have his work cut out for him even with the Rapier.

His blade zinged against Adriel's with a sharper higher pitched sound. Nash was on the offensive, but Adriel defended against each blow with ease.

Some of Adriel's movements reminded me of the feverous and passionate way a musician might play a violin. His arms moved with such speed and dexterity. His footwork was elegant and swift.

I tried to focus on Nash's movements too, but I was so captivated by the fluidity of Adriel's presentation that all else faded from my mind, like watching art being made rather than watching a fight.

"Slow down, Nash," Kiran whispered behind me.

My attention darted to Nash. He swung his blade wildly. His face was red, and his eyes narrowed. Beads of sweat formed on his forehead.

Nash swung again, but Adriel twisted, and the blade glanced off the coil of chains around Adriel's left arm. Nash set his teeth.

I pressed my lips together.

Nash pointed his blade. "Hah!" he yelled.

Black blood oozed from the long cut along Adriel's bicep. The blood painted his arm in dark drips.

"What are you doing?" I ran to them. "Nash, what the hell?"

"It's nothing," Adriel said. "I bleed now." Blood seeped from the wound and onto the training ground.

"That doesn't give him the right to cut you," I said.

"I got carried away," Nash said. "Such is the danger of over-training."

Overtraining? He was the one who insisted we train twice a day. By the time Michael got here, we would be so exhausted, it would be like killing a bunch of office workers after two in the afternoon.

"Come on," I said to Adriel. "I'll bandage that up for you." If I didn't, I was afraid the blood would continue to leak out. He didn't seem to mind, but I sure as hell wouldn't watch my friend bleed all through training hour.

I glowered at Nash as I left the field with Adriel. Nash glared in Adriel's direction.

Back at the house, I got out the first aid kit and some towels. "I think I might have to stitch that one up."

"When did you become a nurse?" Adriel asked.

"I've bandaged up wounds for Nash before, and I popped Tom's arm back in. I'm quite a natural."

Hmm. Maybe I should become a nurse. My music career was going nowhere if I didn't practice. I never liked fixing things, but people, healing people was something I thought I might enjoy. I shook my head. I hadn't even passed high school yet. *One thing at a time, Lia.*

Adriel stood at the dining room table.

"You should sit."

As he sat down, the bony wings on his back spread out on either side of the chair. They looked like they got in the way a lot.

I wiped the blood from his arm with a warm towel. Specks of blood dotted the dining room floor and led out the doorway.

Adriel probably trailed blood all the way from the back of the house. I smiled.

At least Nash would have to play maid for being a jerk. Did fallen angel blood stain? Too bad Nash didn't have carpet.

"This might hurt a little." I pierced his skin with the needle and pulled the thread. Adriel didn't even flinch.

"Feels better than Arcadian Steel."

"He shouldn't have cut you like that," I said.

"We were training. It happens."

"I guess you're used to that kind of stuff then?"

Adriel smirked. "Of course."

Adriel still had the iron collar around his neck. The length of chain wrapped around one arm. He remained a prisoner.

"I'm sorry I dragged you into all this," I said. "It was the only way I could think of to get you out of the Angel District."

"It's alright," he said. "I would have helped anyway. Your fight is my fight."

I paused in my stitching. "You don't have to protect me now. You're not my guardian angel anymore."

"I'm still your guardian angel. Just because I'm fallen doesn't mean I'm giving up on my duty."

"But guarding the Throne of God, that's your duty too, right? But you can't do that anymore."

"I guess not."

I continued to stitch up his wound in silence. I clipped the excess thread and wrapped his arm in gauze. "That's it."

Adriel looked down at the bandage. "Usually I would heal so fast there would be no need for this."

"Nash still heals faster than me or the others. You'll be able to remove the stitches in a couple days, but at least this way it won't scar."

"Thank you."

I shrugged. "No problem."

Adriel put his hands on my shoulders, and his fingers trailed down my arms to my hands. He clasped them in his and looked into my eyes. Could he see the same light that Nash saw?

He continued to gaze at me until I felt my face flush. If I'd let it go on for any longer, I would be a puddle of heat and rapid heartbeats. But before I could break the silence, Adriel spoke.

His words made the warmth drain from my body. "When Michael comes, I want you to run."

nine

I was on the ground in seconds. Grabbing Adrianna's ankle and the back of her knee, I tried to regain control from the bottom. She fell to the ground in front of me, wrapping her leg around mine and gripping my shin.

Her feet anchored behind my knees. Adrianna grabbed the back of my neck and in less time than it takes to blink, she pinned me to the ground. I struggled from under her, but I couldn't get out of her hold.

She released me and offered me her hand, helping me up.

"You're getting better," she said.

I didn't see the point in grappling. If I ever got close enough to an angel without him killing me first, a mere touch would send him into a fury of screams and fire. There would be no need to submit him after that.

Adrianna took something out of her bag. "Here." She offered me what looked like an energy bar. "I made them myself."

"No, thanks," I said. Last week Adrianna brought a home-made pie that tasted like dried fruit and cardboard.

"You have to eat something," she said. "You haven't been coming to dinner."

"I am eating." *Just not when anyone is looking.*

"Nash is worried about you."

I shook my head. *Not about me eating. I'm sure he noticed the leftovers disappearing every night.* "I'm fine."

"It doesn't seem that way," Adrianna said. "I'm excellent at reading people."

I sat on the grass and pulled my legs to my chest. "I don't want to talk to Nash." It had been months since Nash broke it off with me. Why did it still bother me so much?

Adrianna sat cross-legged beside me. "Nash has a funny way of showing when he cares about someone. He cares about you a lot."

"Then why can't things between us be like they are between you and Kiran?"

Adrianna looked away. She blinked a few times and rubbed the back of her neck. "Kiran and I have known each other for a long time." Her voice was emotionless.

"How long?"

Adrianna took a deep breath. "Let's go back inside, okay? The weather out here sucks."

When doesn't it?

Adrianna hopped up from her seat. She held out her hand to me.

"I want to stay out here for a little while longer," I said.

"Suit yourself." Adrianna grabbed her bag and headed back to the house.

I tried to make myself scarce around the house during the day. Nash left most nights. I'm not sure where he went, but it gave me time to sneak downstairs and chow down on leftovers.

Was he giving me space on purpose? Anyone who couldn't sense the tension between us was dumber than a monkey taking a swim with piranhas.

I needed to get over it. Nash and I never would have worked out. After I burned Raphael, I would go back home. Nash was stuck in Sheol. What were we going to do? Become pen pals?

I don't think Lucifer would allow sleepovers.

Staring at the not-quite-green grass, I paced the training field. Tom, Chandra, and Kiran would be arriving soon for dinner. I didn't want to be outside in case they decided to pressure me into attending.

My issues with Nash had to end, but in the meantime, I didn't want to be sitting across an awkwardly quiet table from him.

I stopped outside the library door. Adriel faced the shelves and held a book open in his hands.

I approached him. "What are you reading?"

"Oh, um, I wasn't." He closed the book and put it back on the shelf.

Tom walked in with a book under his arm. "Ah, my library is soon becoming a meeting place for witches and angels. What's next? Hobgoblins?"

"I'm not a witch," I said.

"Well, you're no angel." Tom searched the bookshelves. "It should be a crime to be in here without a book in your hand."

"I wasn't staying." I turned to leave, but Adriel's hand was on my shoulder.

"Lia, what's wrong?"

I glanced over at Tom. He focused on reading the titles on the shelves. His hand passed over *The Seven Archangels of Heaven*. Seven! And I worried about two getting into Sheol. If seven Archangels came, game over.

"I've got a lot on my mind, that's all."

Adriel squinted and leaned his head to the side.

I took a deep breath. "I should go."

"Is it about Michael?"

Michael was only one of the many problems circling around my brain, but I didn't want Adriel prying any deeper than that. "I guess."

"You need to run from him. You can't make him fall."

"I can. I'm just afraid." Michael was on the backlist. My real fear and rage was for Raphael.

"No. You *can't*. It isn't right."

"That doesn't matter anymore," I said. "It's not like I'm on the short list for Heaven. I've made so many angels fall. I don't know where I belong."

"If you stop now, God in His mercy will see that you did what you thought was right," Adriel said. "He will forgive you."

Tom chuckled. He replaced the book that he took from the shelf with the one under his arm.

Adriel turned to him. "You laugh at what you don't understand."

"I think I might understand a little better than you. It must be hard for a puppet to cut its strings. If God is so merciful, then why is there a Hell in the first place?"

"Because Lucifer, in her abundance of pride, decided—"

"To go against God, hence the Fall. Ya da ya da… But really, Hell does exist, and the mere fact that it does means you must deny the notion that God wants to save everyone. He wants us to rot, at least some of us."

"God does not control what men do."

Tom tapped his nose. "Huh, so, God wants us all to come to daddy and live happily ever after in Heaven, but he can't make that happen? So, in a world he created, which follows rules that he made, he simply *can't* save us."

"He gave human kind free will, the ability to control their own destinies. Hell is not punishment, it is choice, the choice to be away from God if you wish. You have made that choice, and now you wish you could take it back."

Tom's lips curled into a smile. He enjoyed this. Finally, someone who could match him. "Couldn't God change the hearts of men without taking away their free will? Let's try this one: God is omniscient so he knows the future and the decisions every man will one day make. So, he knows who is going to Hell. He knows who will choose it, even before that soul is created. He could *choose* not to create a soul that he knows will be damned. If he were absolutely merciful, he would make that choice, knowing that creation of such a soul would damn that person to the fires. And I wouldn't have been able to make the choice that I did."

Adriel didn't say anything.

"What's wrong?" Tom asked. "Would the counter-point be one of Heaven's secrets?"

"Stop, Tom," I said.

Tom tucked the book under his arm and left the library.

Adriel set his eyes. "He doesn't understand."

"He doesn't care," I said.

I tallied up the weeks I'd spent in Sheol since I left Jonah's. Back home, mid-April rolled in. The weather would feel like summer in New Orleans, but it wouldn't yet be unbearable to be outside.

I took advantage of those days to be out of the house. When my parents were alive, I explored every inch of our neighborhood and walked through mid-city. The city wasn't the safest place to walk, but where was safe now-a-days?

My physical safety wasn't my primary concern back then. My main concern was my sanity. Demons lurked in the shadows in closets and corners, and they came more times than angels did.

If I told my parents, they would have worried about me and maybe tried to get me help. They wouldn't have stuck me in the loony bin. But I learned long ago, crazy kids don't get adopted.

Alex and Micah Hebert weren't looking for normal. They saw something in me. They never told me what it was. Now, I could never ask them.

If I showed up again on the outside, child services would find me. I'd be tossed from house to house like a game of musical chairs.

I threw the covers off me and set the writing pad on my bedside table. The pen fell to the floor. I pulled on my jacket.

When I first came to Sheol and in the few months that followed, I kept telling myself I wouldn't go back. I mean, there was no way I would volunteer to go back, but also, I wouldn't let them find me.

In eight months, I would be a legal adult. I wasn't worth finding. By the time I turned up, I would have aged out of foster care. I hoped they gave up on me.

None of that mattered. They weren't going to find me because I was in Sheol, and I probably would be for a long time. That thought of finality was like an ice pick to my heart. *Would I die here in Hell?*

I slid my door closed and tried to make myself soundless as I walked to the stairs. Once I stood outside with my back to the house, I breathed a sigh.

I wanted to forgive all the people who had hurt me in my life: Felicia because our friendship was more important than some boy, Uncle Jonah for not being sober enough to take me in, and my birth mother for selling my soul to the Devil.

I spent more time out of the house lately. I needed to get over what happened between me and Nash and start talking to him again.

But I never knew when Nash would be home or where he went when he wasn't. Sometimes, he would leave for no more than a couple of hours at a time. Other times, he would return the following morning.

Despite the soreness in my legs, I rounded the corner and marched along the sidewalk with my hands in my coat pockets.

We were overtraining. Nash had us practicing every day. Unfortunately, I didn't feel like I was improving. Maybe that was because I was always surrounded by trained fighters, and I wasn't one of them. Plus, my body needed rest.

My feet dragged.

I strolled past the bridge, the furthest from Nash's I had ever gone alone. I stopped recognizing the buildings several blocks ago.

My surroundings were like some *Twilight Zone* version of mid-city. The buildings, the shops, and the parks were the same, but a chilly haze settled over the place. Everything was grayed out. Mist swirled in the distance, disappearing as I moved through it.

I pulled my jacket tight across my chest.

What sounded like the bleating of a goat echoed through the streets. I spun around, but I was alone.

I continued up the narrow street. I passed an abandoned playground. A swing set was planted down into the sandy, gray ground. One seat swung as if someone had been playing there only moments ago.

No children lived in Sheol, not that I had come across, but no wind ever rolled through either. Still the swing moved back and forth, seating some ghostly occupant.

The cold invaded my blood, and no matter how tightly I crossed my arms over my chest, I couldn't stop it. Not even fire could chase it away.

Two people smoked cigarettes across the street. Smoke hovered above their heads like a nebulous cloud.

In a moment of pure fear, I recognized the platinum blond hair and leather jacket. The woman wore a tight red dress and four inch heels. Sam and Delilah. They watched me from across the street.

Did they recognize me?

I sank my hands into my pockets and jogged with my head down. My hand grabbed the hilt of the dagger I carried. I turned the corner and looked behind me. The street was empty.

I strolled for another half hour and decided I needed to go back to Nash's. They would start training soon and would wonder where I was. I didn't want Nash to know that I had been taking walks alone.

I didn't want to go back the way I came. If I did, I would have to see Sam and Delilah again. If I continued to walk in that direction, I could circle back to Nash's house.

Tapping sounded behind me.

I whirled around.

The tapping stopped. The air held its usual stillness.

But as I continued, I heard it again. That tapping. Was it heels? Could Sam and Delilah be following me?

I stopped and slowly turned around.

The Jinn!

Its long shadow grew from the base of the wall. The antlers stretched across the pavement. I knew it was there.

My breath came slow. Quiet.

I wouldn't let that thing follow me. I approached the alleyway. There it was.

My hands gripped its throat. Its black eyes widened. It disappeared from my grasp and reappeared to my right.

I withdrew my dagger and slashed at the creature, but it did its disappearing trick again and reappeared a few inches away from my blade.

Its body was thin. It was small, much smaller than the Jinn that had been disguised as Sim, but they could change shapes and sizes. The creature stood a foot shorter than me. The skin was bark-like apart from a thick patch of golden fur that went down in a V-shape to the center of its chest. Its fingers were long skinny branches that were knobbed at the knuckles.

Its face was the size and shape of a deer's, but the face was flatter, and although small, the nose looked human. The eyes were animal-like with no whites in them. Its lips were short and thin.

Antlers grew atop its head, long, crooked, black antlers. From one of its deer ears hung an earring made of a string of jewels and off-white boxy beads.

I held my dagger in front of me. "Are you the Jinn that's been following me? Are you the one working for Raphael?"

The creature shook its head. When it spoke, its teeth were visible. They were short and every one of them came to a point. "No, that was Faluc. My name is Caiduc. But, yes I have been following you." Its voice was light and melodic like it would fly away on the wind.

I blinked. "Why?"

The creature remained silent. Its lips quivered.

It reminded me of a rabbit I found when I was little. I walked in the park with a man, who I always assumed was my dad. I could never quite remember what he looked like, but I remember his hand, warm and enveloping mine. We found a rabbit near the walkway. Its leg was hurt. When I picked it up, its body trembled with fear. It didn't know that we were trying to save it.

"Why?" I repeated, softer this time.

"I know where your mother is."

My breath caught in my lungs. "My mother's here? In Sheol?"
Caiduc nodded.

Of course, she is. She sold my soul to the Devil and gave me this curse. She was the reason for all of this. Part of me was glad that she was down here, but another part of me wanted to know why. Why would she do this to me? And how had she died?

But this Jinn, it could be lying to me. After Sim, I couldn't trust this creature.

"I could take you to her," it said.

You mean you'll take me to Raphael. "No, thanks," I said.

"You don't want to see your mother?" It tilted its head to the side and looked at me like it was trying to figure out a difficult math problem.

I shook my head. "And I don't want to see you following me again. If I do, I'll yank that pretty earring right off your ear."

It reached up to its ear and covered the earring like it was protecting a canary.

I turned and marched off.

Ten

I ran my fingers along the spines of the books. I wanted to find a book on Jinni. One was following me, and I needed to know its weaknesses in case I had to kill it.

It said it wanted to take me to my mother, my birth mother. Yeah, right. It probably wanted to take me straight to Raphael.

None of the titles popped out at me.

My fingers landed on the rough cover of one of the older books in Nash's library. Many of the books had seen better days, but this one was particularly worn. I pulled it down from the shelf and surveyed the title.

The Book of Enoch.

I leafed through the pages. The book was written in a language I couldn't understand. In the back of the book were several hand-written pages, thankfully in English.

And so, Metatron hid the staff for its power could not be trusted in the wrong hands. For if any part of the staff should pierce an angel's body that angel would turn to ash.

"Doing some light reading?"

I looked up from the book. Tom stood in the doorway and held a book at his side. "You better be careful," he said. "It can become addicting." His hand clasped his chin as he searched for his next victim among the shelves.

"Are you going to attack *me* about moralities?"

"Huh?" He turned his head. "Oh, referring to the debate I had with Adriel. You wouldn't be any good at it."

I ate the insult.

"Have you ever read this one?" I lifted the edges of the book from the table and let it drop back down. It exhaled dust.

Tom approached the table and lifted the cover to look at the title. "*The Book of Enoch*," he said. "Not a light read. I didn't know you read Aramaic."

"I don't."

"Well, you'll have trouble with that one then. I used to speak it, but it's been a very long time. Nash knows it, I think."

"Nash isn't here," I said. "I haven't seen him for days."

"Nor have I."

"Do you know who wrote this in the back here?" I pointed to the hand-written pages.

Tom shook his head. "I read it. No idea who wrote it though."

"It talks about an angel-killing staff."

"Yeah, that sounds about right."

I put my hand on my hips. "Well, don't you think something like that would come in handy?"

Tom eyed me curiously. "Oh." He laughed. "That's just a myth. Rumors spread that Metatron was crafting one, but the rumors were probably spread by Metatron to protect himself from the other angels."

I raised my eyebrow. "Why would he need protection from other angels?"

"Because he doesn't have his own angel weapon."

Metatron's Orb. He used it to sense when angel's weapons were near. We used it to find those weapons and lure angels to their doom.

"Yeah, you explained that one, but you never explained why other angels would be after him in the first place."

"That's because I didn't think it needed explanation. He's a Nephilim. Half-angel, half-human."

"Okay," I said in a way I hoped would encourage him to say more.

He kept his back to me as he surveyed the books on the shelf. "Back before Noah's Flood, angels mated with humans, and the Big Man upstairs didn't like it very much. He sent Archangels to kill all the children of such unions: The Nephilim. He ordered all to be killed, but one. Enoch. Enoch was taken into Heaven where he changed his name to Metatron. There are some accounts that say God turned Metatron into a full angel when he came to Heaven, but the truth of that is unknown."

"But that doesn't explain why the other angels don't like him."

"He's an abomination. Angels aren't free of jealousy. Some say Metatron is the only angel, or half-angel, to see the face of God. That's why he is called the Prince of the Countenance."

"So, the angel-killing staff was just some bullshit he spread to protect himself?"

Tom tapped the tip of his nose.

It's too bad the staff isn't real. If Lucifer had the staff, maybe she would let me go. No, she wouldn't do that. Having two angel-killing weapons is always better than one.

I looked down at my hands. But my curse doesn't *kill* angels. An angel-killing staff, if such a weapon existed, would make an angel disappear forever. I thought of Adriel and cringed that such a weapon could be real.

*   *   *

THE silver fluid flowed into my mouth. The thick liquid was warm and tasted of metal. I struggled to breathe as more was fed to me. My arms flailed, but someone much stronger than me held me down.

I strained my eyes to see who did this to me, but shadows blurred my vision. The silver thickness blocked my nostrils. I needed to fight harder, claw fiercer. I needed to get away or I would die.

Adriel's face flooded my vision. White wings surrounded him. He wasn't the one who hurt me. He tried to help me. "Wake up, Lia. Wake up."

"That's not my name," I whispered. *What was my name?*

Lia was the name I had given myself. I sat down with a case-worker, and she opened a book of baby names. "We have to call you something, sweetie."

"Lia!"

My eyes shot open, but I couldn't move. Nash covered me. His hands gripped my arms, pinning them against the pillow above my head.

"Nash?"

"Sorry." He let me go. "Your arms were flailing. I thought you might hurt yourself."

"How did I get here?" I sat up in bed and looked around. I was in my bedroom at Nash's house.

"You were asleep in the library. I thought you might be more comfortable here."

"I had a nightmare," I whispered, breathlessly.

"I figured as much," he said. "It must have been pretty bad for you to fight like that."

My eyes focused on the corner of the room. I thought I saw something outlined in the shadows. I shook my head.

Nash followed my gaze. He turned back to me. "Are you alright?"

I nodded.

He wore his training clothes: a pair of black pants and a t-shirt. Sweat painted his brow.

I must have missed training again. I hadn't thought that Nash would be back so I didn't bother going. Without Nash around, I decided to take a vacation from sparring and sore muscles, but I worried where he had gone.

I wanted to hug him, but I resisted. I was still mad at him, wasn't I? "Where have you been?"

"Nowhere special." He looked down at the bed.

I frowned. "It must have been a little bit special. You've been gone for four days."

Nash's eyes traveled to the bedside table where he lifted a book. The book was about Jinni, the only book I could find in the library on the subject. I hadn't learned much from the book. It was barely an inch thick and discussed theories more than facts.

"Why are you reading a book about Jinni?" Nash asked.

So, I can find out how to kill one. "I was just curious," I said. Nash didn't need to worry about me, not with this. I could handle it. He needed to focus on Michael.

Nash set the book back down on the table and stood from the bed. "I'll let you get some sleep."

"Nash?" I grabbed his hand. His skin was warm, not like the sun, but like the heat around a fire as you neared the flame.

He looked at me.

I wanted to pull him to me, to shake him, to ask him why he had given up on me so easily. I wanted to burn in his fire.

The world is a bass drum, and its music is lost in the sound of thunder.

I let go of his hand. "Thank you . . . for not letting me sleep all night in that chair." I smiled without showing any teeth. "My back would have been killing me in the morning."

ambassador of

paradise

ICHAEL, Archangel of Heaven, flew up to the Ditches of the Eighth Circle. The Ditches were carved into the ground within a large funnel. Ten trenches wrapped around the sides of the hole in a circle. Bridges ran from the trenches to the center of the hole, like spokes on a wheel.

The Ninth Circle loomed below Michael as he left its icy wasteland and burst into the Eighth Circle. From there, all the Circles radiated outward until he would reach the Outer Region.

Chains held the giant lower ridge of the Eighth Circle. The chains being the only things keeping them from tumbling into the Ninth.

He had heard others speak of places even an angel dare not tread. This was not true of him of course. He was no ordinary angel. He was the commander of God's armies. Nothing existed for him to fear. Not even the nine Circles of Hell could bring Michael to his knees.

A giant reached out, his clawed fingertips inches from Michael.

Michael darted in the air, avoiding the titan's grip.

People, urged on by demons with steel-tipped spears, sauntered along the trenches. They coughed blood into their hands. Their bloated bodies moved along, covered in blisters and rashes. Flesh rotted from their bones and fell in clumps as they walked.

Michael soared.

Disgusting sinners.

A demon with a long, brass sword slashed away the arm of a man. The man screamed. The red-skinned demon who chased him cut away his remaining arm. Others ran from the demon. A woman had a long gash down one cheek and over one eye. A second man lay screaming on the floor, his entrails out in front of him.

Michael turned away from the suffers.

Raphael had a weapon, a young girl who could burn away an angel's Grace. Such an abomination should not exist.

A sound like thunder pricked Michael's ears. He turned in the air, a giant shook the ground. He looked like a man who had grown ten feet tall. He wore a loincloth. Fire issued from his lips as if he was a dragon.

With his army of snakes, he chased the people inside the trench. A man yelped. A serpent hissed at him, its teeth bared. It bit into his ankle. The leg swelled.

Demons poured hot lead over men's backs. It dripped down their bodies like molten robes. Some had dried to the flesh, keeping the men stuck in stiff positions as they walked.

"Ready for this stew!" A long-haired fiend bantered with a horned demon. They forced a woman into the pot. Her voice carried on the wind. It wasn't quite a scream, something low and guttural.

Something flew toward Michael. He dodged.

It was a grappling hook. It sunk into the wall behind him. More grappling hooks embedded in the walls around him.

Michael withdrew his broadsword, Soulshatter.

Large with pincer mouths and armored bodies, demons swung from the ropes connecting the hooks. They fixed their bulbous, red eyes on Michael. Spikes trailed along their backs and down their tails. They were known as the Claws, the guard demons of the Eighth Circle.

Michael cut the first one in half, rendering its body to the Ninth Circle below. The others attacked, swinging at Michael from their ropes and holding spears and short swords. Michael cut through them like they were made of paper.

Foolish demons coming after an Archangel!

Michael twisted in the air, lopping off the head of the Claw in front of him. The head bounced off the wall and down the funnel.

They neared the wheel-spoke bridges. Michael crashed through the boards of one bridge as he cut down another Claw.

The heads of the people at this level were painfully wrenched to face their backs. The skin was dough that had been twisted in opposite directions.

Another Claw swung at Michael. Its teeth snapped at him. Michael gripped the Claw by the throat and hurled it down the trenches. It landed in a pot of molten lead.

A Claw attacked Michael from behind. The spear glanced off Michael's Arcadian Steel armor. More flew at him from their ropes. Michael twisted and turned, his sword flying.

The Claws fell.

Flames sparked along the trenches.

Michael cut into the final Claw, and its body funneled down.

He swung his sword, flicking the black blood from his blade. Something crashed into him. Michael hit the wall between the second and third trenches. His wings splayed out.

The creature whipped its tail at Michael.

Michael jolted to the side.

The spiked tail left a thick gorge in the wall. Michael faced the creature. He smiled. *Geryon.*

Geryon had a reptilian body, two legs, and a tail ending in a diamond-shaped tip. It had the wings of a dragon, but the face of a man.

The beast flew at Michael. Michael swiped at the monster with Soulshatter. Geryon whipped its tail, forcing Michael back.

Michael turned, charged at the monster, and sliced its shoulder. Geryon howled. Its teeth were sharp points. Michael gripped the nape of its neck and straddled its back. Geryon bucked, but Michael held fast, both their wings stretched to the sky.

Geryon was under Michael's command. Geryon sped through the Circles. On the beast's back, Michael rode, slicing through demons with Soulshatter as they flew.

part two
scorched

eleven

CHANDRA'S fist flew past my face as I narrowly dodged the blow. The air was stagnant, but a breeze puffed against my cheek as Chandra's fist pushed the air around it.

I brought my fists up to my face. I jabbed at her with one, then the other.

I didn't hit her. I rarely did.

Nash doubled up training to twice a day. Once in the morning and once in the afternoon. I learned to ignore my sore muscles and took a liking to coffee. Well, not really a liking. It was a love-hate relationship, but it was the only way I could stay awake in the morning.

Chandra's fist smacked into my shoulder.

I winced.

I wanted to talk to Nash about the Jinn. I hadn't found anything about its weaknesses in his books. Maybe I shouldn't have kept my meeting with the Jinn from him.

I wasn't sure what the creature was up to, but I thought it best Nash should know. Besides, I had meant to sit down and talk with him, but when could I find the time?

Chandra slapped me in the face. I hadn't seen it coming.

"Focus," she said.

I jabbed at her. Missed.

Nash kept us busy so we wouldn't think too much about the odds of winning against Michael. He couldn't give us hope so he kept us occupied.

Maybe that was my pessimism sneaking in.

I glanced over at Adriel. He sparred with Adrianna and Tom. Two against one. Kiran and Nash fought a few paces down the field.

Adriel's movements were like a dance, smooth and graceful, yet unpredictable.

I felt my feet leave the ground. I landed on my ass.

"Stop staring at your new boyfriend," Chandra said. "You're not helping me, and you're not helping yourself."

Chandra glared down at me, and her lips curled into a smile. She stalked down the field to the weapons table and picked up a long, curved dagger. She gazed lovingly at the knife. She probably thought of how nice it would feel to run it through my chest. I'd deserve it. I killed her brother.

Before I got up, Adriel offered me his hand. He must have sprinted to get to me so quickly.

"Thanks." I took his hand. "I'm a bit off today."

"It's okay," Adriel said.

"No, it's not." Nash approached us. "She needs to stay focused. This isn't a game. Michael is after her. She has to be better."

"She shouldn't be fighting," Adriel said. "What you're doing is wrong. You should know that better than anyone."

"I'm in charge," Nash said. "You need to back off. This is no place for guardian angels."

Adriel stood his ground. "I'm here for Lia."

Nash stepped up to him. "Then where were you when we were fighting angels? You're on our side now because you're fallen. You would have handed her over to the highest bidder given the chance."

Adriel shook his head. "You're the one who did this to her when you decided to go after angel weapons. If you care about her so much, you'd leave Sheol and hide her from Michael."

Nash withdrew his sword. "I think it's time we have a rematch."

"Hey!" I stood in between Nash and Adriel. I looked at Nash. "I'll try harder, okay? I just need some rest."

I laid on the bed and sighed. I wasn't going to training tomorrow morning. I needed a break. My thoughts tumbled over each other. I couldn't beat Michael. He knew my curse. He would slash me in two before I could get close enough to touch him.

Or maybe he didn't care. Maybe he would sacrifice himself and cut me in two anyway after he was fallen. That sounded about right for a warrior of God. The sacrifice would be so beautiful and poetic. There would be a new book on Nash's shelf about how the Archangel Michael saved the world from the Angel Killer and kept the gates of Heaven open to human souls.

Michael has enough gold stars.

I didn't want the gates of Heaven to be closed to humans either, but I didn't want to *die* to stop it.

I rolled over on the bed and looked at the ceiling. It had been three months since I'd found out about Michael. If he hadn't come after me yet, maybe he wasn't coming. *Wait, three months?*

I grabbed the calendar I had drawn and counted the days. *Four months.* That must be a good sign.

Several days were unmarked, but thankfully I kept track in my head too. *I should mark them just in case.* I searched for the pen, but couldn't find it on the table.

On my hands and knees, I peered under the bedside table. I moved the table aside. No pen, but I did find a small, wooden bead. I rolled the bead between my fingers.

Something blurry and dark moved in the corner of my vision. I turned my head, and my skin prickled all over.

The Jinn sat in silence on the edge of the bed. It held my missing pillow in front of it like a child holding up a picture he drew. Except, unlike a child who would be beaming from ear to ear, the Jinn's deer face could not portray emotion. Its black doe-eyes stared at me.

"What the hell are you doing here?" I snatched my pillow from its twiggy fingers.

The Jinn didn't move. It didn't look offended. It sat on the edge of my bed statue-like and stared at me.

"I thought I'd make my offer one last time," it said.

"I told you to stop following me." I crossed my arms over my chest.

"I did. I haven't followed you since the time you threatened me."

"I didn't threaten you."

"The threat was implied." Its eyes never left me. Its body never moved.

"Get out of here." I pointed to the door although I knew the Jinn would not use the door to leave the room.

"You want me to leave?" Once again, it reminded me of a child. Its face showed no emotion, but its voice sounded hurt like the other kids had decided not to play with it.

"Yes. Yes, leave," I said.

"But this might be the last time you will be able to see your mother."

"What do you mean?" I asked.

"Michael is coming. He is past the Third Circle and well into the Second. He is traveling on the beast Geryon."

I don't know how long my mouth hung open before I realized I didn't want to be catching flies. My jaw clamped shut, but my eyes still felt like they would pop right out of my head.

"When did you find out he was in the Circles?" I asked slowly.

"Weeks ago."

"Why are you telling me this?"

"I don't want you to die not seeing your mother," Caiduc said.

"Why do you care? Why would you want to help me?"

It stared at me wide-eyed for a long moment. Its stare had made me uncomfortable before, but now it looked at me like I was the most moving painting it had ever seen. "Because your aura . . . it's beautiful," it said.

"My what?" At first, I thought the Jinn meant my eyes and the light behind them that enabled demons to see that I was human.

"The glow around you. It's so brilliant like a sacrificed soul."

I shook my head and laughed.

"What's so funny?" it asked.

I narrowed my eyes. "I don't know what you're talking about," I said. "But I'm only going to say this one more time: I don't want to see my mother."

The Jinn lowered its eyes and vanished.

My legs wavered, and I plopped down on the bed. What if the Jinn wasn't lying? What if Michael *was* tearing through the Circles?

But then again, what if this was a trap? But how?

We only had twelve angel weapons. Raphael had over a hundred followers, each with their own angel weapon, which by now they had either retrieved or hid somewhere else. So, why would he need to draw us away from the house?

Whatever was going on, I had to tell Nash.

I darted to the door and down the stairs. Ruffling sounded from the living room. I peered around the corner.

Tom read on the couch. My shoulders fell. He looked up from his book and raised an eyebrow. "Can I help you with something?"

I shook my head. "I'm looking for Nash. I thought he was in here."

"Just me," Tom said. "What do you need to tell Nash at three in the morning?"

I left the room. "Nash!" I called. "Nash?" I walked into the kitchen.

Nash leaned against the counter and sipped his coffee.

"Michael is in the Second Circle." I said, combining all the words into one.

Tom followed me into the kitchen.

Nash put down his mug. His expression was grave. "How do you know that?"

"A Jinn told me."

"You spoke to a Jinn?" He furrowed his brow. "Why would a Jinn speak to you?"

Because of my aura or some crazy yogi shit. "I don't know, but it told me that Michael is on his way."

"When did the Jinn find out about this?" Tom asked.

"Weeks ago," I said.

"Tom, call Adrianna, Chandra, and Kiran."

Tom rushed out of the kitchen, and his footsteps faded down the hall.

"Did he say where Michael was weeks ago?" Nash asked. "Which Circle was he in?"

"The Jinn didn't say."

"You didn't ask?"

"Why are you doing that?" I asked.

"What?"

I shook my head. "No, I didn't ask the Jinn which Circle Michael was in weeks ago. What does that matter now? He's one Circle away from ripping out our vocal chords and using them as strings on his harp."

"It would give us a better idea of how quickly Michael moves through the Circles," Nash said. "It would tell us how much more time we have to prepare."

"The Jinn said he is traveling on Geryon."

Nash's face tensed. "Then there's no time. Where is the Jinn?"

"I don't know. It disappeared." *And I never want to see it again.*

Nash sighed. "Okay. We don't know if it's telling the truth."

"You think it could be working for Raphael?" I wrung my hands.

"I wouldn't rule it out, but Jinni lie anyway. They think it's fun to make fools out of us."

"I asked it why it was helping me."

"It won't tell you. It thinks we wouldn't understand anyway."

"It told me it was because of my light. Not the light in my eyes like you were talking about. Light around me, an aura he called it."

Nash let out a short, breathy laugh. "Humans don't have light."

"But you said…"

"That's different," Nash said. "What makes you human isn't the same thing. It was the best way to describe it to you. It shines from inside, but it doesn't shine around you."

"What was it talking about then?"

"It lied to you. Jinni can't be trusted."

"But we're taking its word that Michael is on his way?"

"We don't have a choice. If we ignore the warning, and Michael does come, we'll be on our asses."

"So, what are we going to do?" I asked.

"We have to be ready for him. We'll wait for him outside Limbo."

"What about Adriel?" I asked.

"He's coming with us." As Nash moved away from the counter, he nudged the mug, and the cup shattered to the floor.

I stooped to help him pick it up, but Nash marched to the opposite end of the room.

"Leave it." He hurried to the armory, gathered the weapons, and put them into a bag on the table.

I followed him.

"What do you want me to do?" I asked. "If you can help me get close enough to him, I can make him fall."

Nash put his hands on my shoulders. "I can't have you out there."

"But that's ridiculous. I'm the only one who can stop Michael. You said so yourself."

"You aren't ready."

"Yes, I am. Even if I trained my whole life, I wouldn't be able to defeat an angel in physical combat." I raised up my hands. "This is what I'm good for. I need to be out there with you."

Nash stopped packing the weapons and faced me. "Listen to me," he said. "I was wrong. I shouldn't have kept you here."

"Nash, you're scaring me."

Nash smiled, but the smile didn't reach his eyes. "We're going to go after Michael with all we have because we can't die here."

Nash stood a breath away from my lips. His face tensed. Hesitance.

"You want to kiss me again," I whispered.

"What?"

"You heard me. You want to because you don't think we'll come out of this one. But still you won't. Why?"

"Because we won't die. It's impossible."

No, he wouldn't die, but things worse than death loomed in the bowels of Sheol. One thing he couldn't come back from, even though it didn't mean death. "You'll be so close to the Pit."

Nash nodded.

My eyes grew wide. "Nash, no." I shook my head. "You can't do that. You can't."

"We have to. It's the only way."

"No, it's not. How many demons will have to jump on Michael's back to drag him down to the Pit? It won't work. All I have to do is touch him."

"He's not going to let you do that. I'm not going to let you die."

He kissed me, and in that thrilling moment I realized he still cared for me. His warm hands traced down my arms, and he wrapped his hands around my waist, pulling me deeper into the kiss.

My hands found his neck, and I draped my arms around it, folding into his embrace, pulling him down to me.

His hands caressed mine, taking them away from his neck, and holding them at my sides. The release of his lips was gentle. "This isn't the end. Not yet," he whispered against my cheek.

His heat didn't leave me when he left. I still stood with the fire, but he was gone. My eyes fluttered open.

Nash stood at the door of the armory. When his hands gripped the sides of the heavy metal door, I rushed forward, but I was too late.

"Nash, no!"

He shut the door and sealed me within the Arcadian Steel room.

Twelve

I sat in the corner of the room, my legs pulled to my chest, and my head nestled in my arms. *How long had I been here? Half an hour maybe?*

I hated Nash all over again. He used that kiss to distract me. How could I have been so stupid?

If I didn't do something, Michael would toss my friends into the Pit and tear the door off this steel prison to rip my throat out. *I need to get out of here.*

I took control of my force pull ability when I rescued Adriel from the Pit. Maybe I could use it again to get that door opened.

I focused on the door. Nothing happened.

I held my hand out, fingers spread. Closing my eyes, I concentrated.

The metal groaned. *I'm doing it!*

I focused so hard, my head hurt.

The metal door unfastened with an echoed screech. I opened my eyes.

"Chandra?"

Chandra opened the door wider. "If you tell Nash, I'll kill you."

"But why?" Could I trust Chandra? The only person who wanted me dead more than Michael was her. But her life also depended on keeping me alive.

"I don't like this plan any more than you do," Chandra said. "You're the only one who has a chance at defeating Michael. But do me a favor. Hang back for a while until we chip away at him a little. Don't come at him while he's strong."

I nodded. "Thank you."

"Screw this up, and Nash ends up in the Pit. And I doubt Lucifer would go easy on your angel friend." Chandra rushed out of the room. Her footsteps disappeared down the hallway upstairs.

I wanted to heed Chandra's advice, but I needed to be close to see when Michael was weakened. I had to be ready when opportunity presented itself.

I armed myself with a sword and dagger. I knew I probably wouldn't get a chance to use them, but I felt safer with them on me. If I was going to stop Michael, I would need to make him fall.

I darted outside. Nash's car was gone.

A car pulled up to the curb. "Need a ride, sweetheart?" Bob asked.

"How did you know?" I asked.

"Chandra told me Nash was getting soft."

I got into the passenger's seat of Bob's car. Bob pressed his foot down on the accelerator.

"They should be at the entrance of the Circles," I said.

"In Limbo, I know," Bob said.

"Bob, you can't tell Lucifer about Nash. He did this to protect me."

"I can't make any promises."

"You can't, please! If Lucifer knows that Nash tried to leave me behind…"

"She probably already knows. She won't do to Nasriel any more than he's already done to himself."

I wasn't sure what Bob meant by that, but right now I had bigger concerns than the secrets Nash kept from me.

We crossed a bridge over a wide river. Bob pressed down on the brakes, and the car came to a screeching halt.

A castle loomed in the distance with seven stone walls of varying heights surrounding it. Nash and an army of demons stood outside it and faced a whirlwind across the river into the Second Circle of Hell. From out of that whirlwind yet unharmed by it, came a figure that shone so brilliantly, it took a moment for my eyes to adjust.

Michael's golden hair glowed in the dull light of Sheol. As his feet touched the ground, the earth shuttered. He raised his large, silver broadsword in the air as if it was weightless.

A fallen angel with ashy black hair and even darker eyes separated himself from the crowd.

Adriel!

Michael said something to Adriel, but I stood too far away to hear the words. Adriel roared and threw himself in a leap as Michael flew a few feet above the ground. He and Adriel met swords.

Nash and his army closed in behind them. More than fifty demons stood with Nash. Maybe they weren't doomed.

Adriel would not go quietly. He cursed as his sword smashed into Michael's. I recognized the weapon Adriel wielded, the broadsword of Zuriel.

Michael attacked again. Something was different about the way Michael attacked. He wasn't like the other angels. He was a trained warrior, an Archangel.

But Adriel wasn't a child playing with a wooden sword either. He was a Seraph, guardian of the Throne of God. He may not have seen battle like Michael, but he was ready for it.

Adriel bared his weight behind his sword. But Michael twisted. Adriel launched forward but spun and met Michael's sword before Michael slashed his back. The chain unwrapped from Adriel's arm as he twisted to meet Michael's blade.

Michael didn't fight fair.

Nash and his army hung back. What was he doing? Why wasn't he helping Adriel?

Nash hoped Adriel would die by Michael's hand. That would solve his problem. He wouldn't have to deal with Adriel anymore.

Adriel leapt back as Michael swung his blade at Adriel's stomach. Michael raised the weapon above his head.

The movement was fast. My eyes missed most of it. Metal sparked like the embers off a bonfire. Their bodies moved as if in a dance, a very deadly one.

Michael ducked Adriel's blow and grabbed the end of Adriel's chain. Michael yanked the chain. Adriel's hand was around his collar as Michael pulled him in. The tip of the sword of Zuriel dragged to the ground.

Michael jerked the chain with more force. Adriel's body was thrust behind Michael. Michael watched over his shoulder as Adriel rolled in a heap on the floor.

The blood drained from my face. Adriel didn't get up.

Bob got out of the car, and I followed him to the back. He popped the trunk and took out a sawed-off shotgun. He turned to me. "Arcadian Steel bullets."

A gun that could shoot Arcadian Steel bullets, a rarity. Where had Bob gotten it? But none of that mattered right now.

"Light him up," I said.

I took two rapid steps for every one of Bob's wide paced ones. When he was less than a yard from where Michael stood, he fired two bullets right into Michael's chest.

The spray bounced off the Arcadian Steel armor, but some fragments made it through, sinking deep into the flesh.

Michael grinded his teeth.

Nash's army charged him. Michael kicked off the ground and waved his sword into the crowd.

Blood flew. Someone's head rolled. But Michael wasn't interested in any of them. He swatted them away like insects. His eyes fell on me.

I should have hung back like Chandra said, but fear for Adriel drove me into the open. I had made a grave mistake. I pulled out my sword. My hands trembled, and the blade wavered in the air.

Michael flew and halted in front of me. The gust of wind from his wings knocked me off my feet. The blade fell from my hand. I was in a desperate battle between not wanting to tear my eyes away from Michael and franticly wanting to find my sword.

I decided the sword would be of little use to me anyway. Two distinct voices shouted my name. But they were blended together now in a cacophony of meaningless babble.

Michael had his sword raised above me. One thought entered my mind. *I'm going to die.* No, I didn't want to die. I held my hands out in front of me as if they could shield me from the blow.

Michael stopped, frozen in the air. He lingered for a moment above me as if held back by something equally as strong.

Panic was visible on Michael's face as he pressed his lips together in a grimace. He was no longer stiff, he kicked off the ground and into the air.

He was a dot in the sky.

A flash of steel gleamed as it hit the light that glowed from the tear in the atmosphere. Like an arrow, his sword darted toward me. I noticed it too late. It would impale me.

People say that when you're ready to die, your life flashes before your eyes. When they say that, they mean your past comes back to life, every moment from the beginning of your life until now, the end of it all. But I didn't have a past to remember. Instead, my future flashed before my eyes, all the things I would never get to do: finish school, get my own apartment, skydive, go to Paris, pretend to be a tourist in the French Quarter, have children.

I didn't want to die.

Small, twiggy hands reached for me, and I reached back. In a flash, everything went dark.

Thirteen

I blinked. The air was hot, and my eyes stung like I had gotten soap in them. I tried to stand, but when I placed my hand down on the ground for leverage, I flinched as if I touched a hot, leather car seat.

I laid in a plain of golden sand. Standing was difficult without using my hands, but I managed. The sand swirled around me. The dry air made it hard to breathe.

Where was I? How did I get here?

Ouch!

My arm reddened. I watched as another drop sizzled on my skin.

Rain.

The burning droplets fell faster.

In the distance trees grew. I ran to them, finding it odd seeing them in the desert. They weren't cactuses or other desert plants. They were chestnut oaks. I took shelter under them.

The air was humid. I put my hand against a tree and tried to catch my breath. But as my hand landed, I realized it didn't feel rough like bark. It felt fleshy.

I looked up at the tree.

A man's face twisted in agony.

I screamed and backed away. The faces of many more souls were trapped in the bark of the trees. Their faces twisted in utter despair and horror.

A loud screech sounded in the sky.

Above the trees flew a creature with brown wings and a tail like a lion's. The beast was long and slender. Standing upright, it would have been eight feet tall.

A chill went down my spine when I made out its face, a human face with teeth sharpened to points and hair that grew high on its head and down its neck and left it bald in the front. Its hands ended in long curved claws.

It looked down at me and circled back.

I ran through the trees as the thing that screeched behind me grew closer. I wanted to scream, but I didn't dare. What if more of them came?

I froze.

One foot slipped over a cliff. I threw myself back, avoiding a more perilous fall.

I looked up. The creature no longer followed me. I breathed a sigh and scrambled to my feet.

I knew now where I was. I was in the Circles. I wasn't sure which Circle specifically, but I was in the Inner Region of Sheol, and I had to find my way out. Tom told me this was no place for mortal souls. I understood why. If I stayed here, I wouldn't be mortal for very much longer.

I pushed aside the foliage and tried to ignore the cries of the souls trapped within the trees. I jerked my hand away every time I accidently touched the fleshy trunks.

I stepped upon harder ground. Pools of bright red liquid bub-
bled up from the earth. Mounds of steam shot out from the
cracked floor. I stepped lightly, afraid that, at any moment,
steam would shoot up where I stood and burn me.

I wasn't sure if I was going in the right direction or if I was
sending myself deeper into Hell. I tried to remember the Circles
in the correct order. I studied them for so long when Nash and
the others got lost there, I thought maybe if I could figure out
which one I was in, I could better find a way out.

The First Circle is Limbo, the only one that wasn't dangerous. But I wasn't in Limbo. I was on its outskirts before I was
taken here.

I dodged the spray from one of the gory pools.

The Second Circle had strong winds. I didn't find the winds
to be particularly strong here. The Third Circle was inhabited
by Cerberus, the three-headed dog. I hoped he wasn't around.
But the rain there is icy. Rain where I was, burned like acid.

I looked at the sky. Red clouds mingled with wisps of gray.
They churned as if all the air that was sucked out of the Outer
Region was funneled here. But it kept to the sky and did not
grace my heated skin.

In the Fourth Circle, people were weighed down with stones.
None of that so far. Then there was the Fifth Circle, where peo-
ple drowned in the river Styx. Flaming tombs lit up the Sixth
Circle.

But the Seventh, burning sands, talking trees, and a boiling
river of blood. That's where I was! I wasn't in the Ninth Circle.
There would have been an icy lake. I couldn't be in the Eighth,
I would have seen the Claws, demon guardians of the Ditches.

But then, what was that creature I'd seen earlier?

It must have been a harpy—the creatures that feed off the
souls trapped in the trees.

I'd figured it out.

My excitement faded as the harpy screeched from above the trees. I was in the open now. If I didn't want to be attacked by another harpy, I had to move fast.

At least I knew I was going in the right direction, I was in the Outer Ring of the Seventh Circle. But it was the largest of the three rings. I wasn't sure how long it would take me to get to the Sixth. I kept my hand on my dagger. I lost my sword when Michael attacked me.

I had no idea how I would make it out of the Circles. In all likelihood, I wouldn't make it, but I didn't want to think about that.

No one would come to get me. How could Nash know where I had gone? I didn't know how I had gotten here. The memory of hands, small, branch-like fingers flashed. The Jinn!

What if it sent me here to die?

That didn't make sense. If it wanted me dead, it could have killed me many other times. But then again, maybe it couldn't. Maybe Jinni couldn't kill people directly so it needed a way to indirectly murder me.

But that theory didn't quite work either. If that was all true, the Jinn could have sent me here weeks ago. Why now? Only one thing made sense. Michael would have killed me if the Jinn hadn't sent me here. It tried to save me.

Tried to save me. *Did I . . . die?*

I didn't remember touching its hands. All was black.

My hands went to my mouth, and tears flooded my eyes. If I died, that meant I failed. That meant my friends were doomed to the Pit.

"She's there."

I whirled around.

Caiduc pointed straight ahead of me. His black antlers were striking against the orange sky.

"Am I dead?" I asked.

Caiduc shook his head. "I brought you here."

My hand flew to my chest, and a smile spread across my face as my breath came in short, deep gasps. "Why did you bring me here?"

"Your mother."

It made sense. Caiduc wanted me to see her. So, when the opportunity presented itself, he whisked me off to the Seventh Circle.

"She's in the Outer Ring," Caiduc said.

"Why do you want me to see her?" I asked. "Just take me back."

Caiduc shook his head. "You should talk to her first."

I walked in the direction Caiduc indicated. My face glistened with sweat. My whole body was coated in a thin layer of perspiration. It made my clothes cling to me.

When Caiduc sent me back, I would be in desperate need of a shower. But just the idea that I would be going back sent a thrill through my body.

Caiduc pointed.

A woman knelt on the stone steps, her face strained up. Her long, dark hair tangled like mine.

"Hello?"

The woman slowly and mechanically looked down at me. Her eyes were hooded and narrow. I was at the foot of the steps and approached her with caution.

"Rachel?" Joy leaked into her voice, but it didn't belong there.

Rachel. Was that my real name?

"My name's Lia," I said.

I stepped up to her and studied her face. Her lips cracked like she hadn't had a glass of water in days. Her skin was pallid. She wore black, torn clothes, and had soot smeared on her face.

"Sit with me," she said.

I shook my head. Was this a trick? Did Lucifer have something to do with this? But why? "Are you . . . my mother?"

As the woman smiled, tears flooded her eyes. She nodded her head, fast as a hummingbird's wings.

I wanted to be angry with her, but she looked so . . . miserable, it was hard to feel anger. It was hard to feel anything but pity. Whatever she had done, she paid for it in this horrible place.

She put her pale hand against my face. "You grew up more beautiful than I could have imagined."

I flinched away from her touch.

I didn't know this woman. She looked like me. She gave birth to me, but I didn't *know* her.

"But you're here," she said. "Did you die?"

"No," I said. "I'm here because of you. Lucifer needs me to stop an Archangel from closing the gates of Heaven. You did this to me."

Tears streamed down my face. I wiped them away. I hadn't expected tears. I had been raised by a wonderful woman, Alexandria Hebert. She was my mother, and she loved me. That was all I needed.

The bloodied woman tried to reach for my hands, but I put them behind my back.

"I tried to save your soul by performing a ritual," she said. "That ritual made you what you are. I thought it was the only way that the Devil would offer you a deal to get your soul back."

I swallowed. So, that was it. She wanted to save me, but she was also the reason I needed saving in the first place. *The world is a harpsichord, and its music chimes and crashes.*

"Why are you in the Seventh Circle?" My voice sounded accusatory. I hadn't meant it to be. I wanted my feelings to remain silent. This was about answers, not feelings.

She lowered her eyes. "Because I'm a murderer." She reached up and tucked a lock of hair behind my ear.

The moment she touched me, I felt an ache like I had hit my head against something hard. I put my hand to my temple, a tension headache. My vision went white for a second.

My mother's tears fell onto my head. Across the room was a cage, and inside the cage, an angel lay in a pool of silver blood. The blood matted down the white feathers of the angel's wings. Her head lowered to the ground. Someone else was in the room. A man, but I couldn't see his face.

I blinked, and I was back again in the orange haze of the Seventh Circle. My head rested in my mother's lap. *When had I sat down?* She stroked my hair.

I jolted up.

"The ritual required me to kill an angel," she said.

I backed away from her. "That's impossible."

My mother frowned.

I was looking in a mirror. Her hair, her eyes, her tanned skin. She was me.

"It's time to leave." The Jinn stood at my side.

I turned to him. "But Michael's still after me."

"Time works differently in the Circles. It goes by very quickly on the outside. Minutes become hours."

My mother stared up at me. Her eyes begged me to stay.

"I still have questions for her."

"I'm sorry," Caiduc said. His bark-like hand grabbed my wrist, and the air was cool and stagnant.

fourteen

I knelt in front of Nash's house. Caiduc was gone. The air cooled the sweat on my skin and peppered my arms with goose bumps.

Lights brought my shadow in front of me. A car door slammed. Feet hit pavement.

"Lia!"

Nash dropped to the ground and embraced me. "You're alright." His soft, black hair tickled my face.

I enjoyed his warmth for a moment before I pushed him off me. "You tricked me."

Nash looked as if I had stabbed him. He did care about me, so why was he pushing me away? *Because of a choice you made.*

I chose Heaven, which meant I didn't choose Nash. No wonder he distanced himself from me. We could never be anything.

Kiran and Chandra stood behind him. Though sweaty and out of breath, they didn't seem to be injured. Their swords were sheathed at their sides.

Chandra's brass knuckles were curled into her fist. She must have had mixed feelings about finding me alive. She needed me to avoid the Pit, but she wanted me dead for what happened to her brother.

"The Jinn saved you," Kiran said. "Michael's sword is still in the ground where you laid before you disappeared."

"He left his sword?" I asked.

"He soared away," Chandra said, "like something scared him."

Disappearing girls will do that. But he showed unease before I disappeared. He hovered in mid-air as if frozen. Had I done something to him?

"We have his sword. That's good, right?" I asked.

Nash shook his head. "No one can remove it from the ground. We tried. He'll come back for it."

"He'll come back for me."

"Yes," Nash said. "But not now. Michael knows battle. He'll want to retrieve his sword and recuperate before he attacks again. He might bring an army next time."

An army. Like Raphael. Two armies of angels fighting to rip me out of Sheol.

"Where are Adrianna and Tom?" I asked.

"They are searching for you," Kiran said. "We went in different directions to look."

"But the Jinn could have taken me anywhere," I said.

Chandra nodded. "True."

She hoped the Jinn had transported me someplace terrible. I didn't give her the satisfaction of knowing I was chased down by harpies in the Seventh Circle.

"Where's Adriel?" I asked.

Nash stood up, and I stood with him. "Nash?"

"He's fine," Nash said. "He's lucky. Michael could have tossed him into the Pit."

Because you held back. Because you didn't help him.

"You really think Michael will come back?" I asked. "For more than his sword?"

"He will return," Kiran said. "He must finish what he started."

He had to finish killing me.

"He tore a hole in Bob's ward when he blasted through it," Nash said.

"He broke Bob's ward?" I furrowed my brow. "I thought angels couldn't go through it."

"Not from outside Sheol," Kiran said. "But he destroyed it from the inside. Bob can't fix it for another three years."

"So, we're unprotected," I said.

"As newborn babes in the snow," Chandra said. She and Kiran went inside.

"What are we going to do?" I asked.

"Going to find a safe place for you," Nash said. "I was stupid to think you'd be protected here. You could have died." Nash gritted his teeth. "But you're staying in Sheol until I know where to send you. When Tom gets back, I'll ask him to look into a few places. Then, you'll pack your bags and leave."

"Lucifer will let us go?"

Nash paused.

"I'll have to talk to her," he said. "But she needs you. I can't see her saying no. The only problem is I might not be able to go with you." Nash approached the house.

"Why not? That's ridiculous." I hastened my steps after him.

"I have promises to keep. Lucifer isn't going to let me forgo my duties."

"What duties?" I grabbed his arm. "I thought the only thing Lucifer commanded of you was to train and protect me."

Nash turned to face me. "Lucifer asks many things of us," he said. "You'll be safe with Adrianna, Tom, Kiran, Chandra, and . . . Adriel."

I folded my arms. "I'm not leaving without you. What if Michael comes back, and I'm not here?"

"That's the point of you leaving," Nash said.

"I want to talk to Lucifer," I said.

"You shouldn't be so familiar with the Devil." Tom walked up with Adrianna.

Tom reached out and pulled me into a hug. "Glad to see you're arguing as fiercely as ever."

"We thought we lost you." Adrianna hugged me.

"Don't trust us to protect you?" Tom asked.

"It's not that," I said. "We're a team. I'm not going to leave any of you behind."

"Not even Chandra." Tom nudged me with his elbow.

"Not even Chandra," I said.

"I'll see what I can do," Nash said. "In the meantime, you should rest. You look like you've been through Hell."

I didn't tell Nash that Caiduc brought me to the Seventh Circle. Caiduc didn't mean any harm by it, and telling Nash would only worry him. He couldn't do anything about Caiduc, and he wouldn't have any more ideas about the Jinn's motives than I did. For all he knew, Caiduc brought me from the battle straight to Nash's front door.

I sat on the bed. A chill ran down my spine when I remembered the faces in the tree trunks, the boiling pools of blood, and the harpy's teeth. But the image that was most chilling was my mother's face, a mix of hopelessness, hysteria, and fear.

She was paying the price for killing an angel. But how did she do it? Angels couldn't be killed. They could fall, but they couldn't die.

I rubbed my arms.

I wanted to take a shower, go to bed, and forget that any of this ever happened. But I knew that wouldn't be possible.

I glanced at the glowing digital clock on my bedside table. It was three in the morning. I yawned and closed my eyes against the pillow. I lay there for an hour, trying to drift off, but sleep didn't come back to me.

I sat up in bed and stretched. My body needed more rest. My muscles were sore, and I had a headache, but I didn't want to toss and turn in bed all night. I thought maybe a short walk would wear me out enough to fall back asleep.

I slipped on my shoes and grabbed my coat.

Opening the back door, I wished the soft, temperate air would drift around me, but no luck. It stood as still as time did in Sheol.

I wondered if, because of my time here, I would live a year longer. I guess in the grand scheme of things that didn't matter much. I could die tomorrow.

I hoped that wherever Tom decided we should go, the weather would change often. I missed the rain.

Across the training field was a small dot. Someone sat far from the house. I couldn't make out his or her features in the distance.

But as I stepped closer, I recognized the blackened bones of a fallen angel. How many times had Adriel sat awake on the field outside Nash's house? He had nowhere else to go.

I sat next to Adriel. He stared at the sky. The gold had drained from his eyes. I couldn't get use to the inky blackness that settled there.

I brought my knees up to my chin and folded my arms on top of them. "My mother is in the Seventh Circle. That's where the Jinn took me."

"I'm sorry," Adriel said.

"Don't you want to know why she's there?" I asked.

"Why is she there?"

"She killed an angel," I whispered.

Adriel turned to me. "That's impossible."

"Well, my mother managed to do it."

Adriel's eyes wavered. He looked back to the sky. "How did it feel to see her?"

"Strange. I always thought if I ever found my mother, I would be so mad at her for abandoning me, I wouldn't be able to say anything to her without screaming. But it wasn't like that at all. It was like meeting a stranger, but not a stranger. I had so many questions. And even though I don't know the whole story, I'm still sad she's in the Circles. Is that weird?"

"She's your mother. You love her."

I hugged my legs. *Did I love her?* Adriel said it so matter-of-factly like I was programed to love her. I didn't even know her. But if I didn't love her, why did it bother me that she was in pain?

"You know something?" I asked. "When I got there, to that horrible place, it wasn't the place itself that I was most afraid of. I'm not saying the Seventh Circle isn't the most awful place I've ever seen. Believe me, it is. But, I thought I died. And that thought was what terrified me the most. I thought I would never have a family, live a life, and watch my children grow up. I never thought about those things before. I'm too young to think about those things. But when I thought I lost them…"

Adriel caressed the side of my face. "But you haven't."

His fingertips grazed my jawline, cultivating a trail of warmth. My heart beat erratically as his touch sent ripples through me.

I pulled away and wiped my tears. "Nash says we'll be leaving soon."

"He told me today," Adriel said.

"He *told* you?" I asked. Nash really wasn't coming with us. He only told Adriel in person because as much as Nash hated him, he knew Adriel would protect me when he couldn't.

Adriel nodded. "But he's spending too much time preparing. We should go now while we have the chance."

"I think he has to get permission from Lucifer or something," I said.

Adriel cringed.

"You don't want to take orders from her."

"I'd rather take orders from an insect," he said.

I put my hand on his arm. "You're following me like you always do," I said. "You're not taking orders from her."

He glanced down at my hand.

I quickly removed it and settled down with a thin-lipped smile. "Angels are supposed to do the right thing."

"Yes," Adriel said.

I gulped. "So, what Michael is doing, trying to kill me, it's right."

Adriel shook his head. "He's thinking about the greater good."

"Was Raphael thinking about the greater good when he killed my parents?"

"Raphael isn't what you think he is." Adriel rubbed his forehead.

"What do you mean?"

"I shouldn't be telling you this," he said.

"Adriel, please."

He sighed. "When there was rebellion in Heaven, Raphael fought with us, with Michael against Lucifer. Raphael loved humans, but there was tension in his alliance. I never understood why. He nearly lost his head in the War. He's never been the same since."

"*Nearly lost his head.* You don't mean metaphorically, do you?"

"No. He was cleaved across the neck."

I rubbed my throat. "Would he have died?"

"I don't know," Adriel said. "No one's ever cut off the head of an angel."

It's time someone did.

I stood. "Do you want me to get you a blanket or pillow?"

Adriel looked over his shoulder at me. "No."

"You want to spend the night on the wet grass?"

"I'm okay." Adriel watched the sky as if he expected Michael to break through the clouds.

I turned on my heels and walked back to the house. Adriel's dark form was a dot in the distance as I eased the door shut.

My footfalls were feathers on the marble floor. I jumped and caught the scream before it escaped my throat. My reflection stared back at me, frightened, in the mirror that lined the wall.

Feeling foolish, I grabbed the bannister and tiptoed up the stairs to my room. I slid my door shut and settled down on the bed.

The silence was a living thing that could not be disturbed. I opened the drawer of my bedside table and grabbed my MP3 player. I plugged my ears with the earbuds and turned up the music.

The sound cascaded over me in comforting waves. I felt like a rabbit in its burrow. I leaned back against the pillows with my hands on my stomach.

I stared blankly around the room. Shadows crept in the corners.

What Adriel told me didn't make any sense. Raphael *loved* humans. That idea didn't match the blood-thirsty angel who thrust his staff into my parents' car and watched them die.

I clenched my fists.

If Raphael wanted me, I dared him to come. I wanted to watch all his pretty feathers burn. I wanted to hear the pain in his voice.

I spotted something out the corner of my eye: a long thin form with thorn-like appendages on its head. I jumped.

"Does my form frighten you?" Caiduc asked.

The Jinn had long, twisting, black antlers and animal-like eyes. He was a Frankenstein's monster of animal parts.

"It's creepy," I said.

"I could be anything you want me to be."

I cringed. It was disgusting how Jinn could change form, how they could fool unsuspecting people.

"No thanks."

The Jinn sat on the end of the bed.

"Why do you look like that?" I asked.

"It's my own creation. I took all the most beautiful things in the world and put them together.

"A lion." He touched the full fur on his chest. "Large and bold. A deer—graceful and elegant. A tree—tall and strong. And a touch of humanity." He tapped his nose. "A little imperfection can be beautiful too."

"Do all the Jinni do that?" I asked.

Caiduc shook his head. "Most Jinni prefer their true forms."

"What are their true forms?"

"They look like puffs of smoke."

I raised an eyebrow. "That's it?"

Caiduc nodded.

"So, that must mean you can't be harmed?"

"I cannot talk about the secrets of the Jinni," Caiduc said.

"But teleportation. That's not one of your secrets, is it?" I asked.

"Teleportation?"

"You transported me from the Outer Region to the Circles in a flash," I said.

"Yes," it said.

"Why can't you transport my mother from the Circles?"

The Jinn shook its head. "That is impossible. I could come back, but she can't."

"What if you brought her back to Earth?"

Caiduc shook its head again. "Your mother's soul is woven into this place. It would take someone with great power to rip out the stitches to save her."

"And you can't?"

"No. It is beyond what I can do."

Fifteen

I pushed my food around with my fork. I thought of my mother. Why should I feel guilty? She put herself in the Seventh Circle.

"You don't like it?" Nash asked.

"What?" I asked. *Oh, the food.* "No, it's great." I speared a carrot with my fork and closed my teeth around it.

Adriel had come to dinner. I was suspicious of his presence. Adriel wouldn't have come if serious matters weren't to be discussed. After all, he didn't touch his food.

Adrianna explained that although there was no need for him to eat, he would still feel the pain of hunger. He stared down at an empty plate. The others didn't seem to mind. He did this to himself on purpose, a masochistic penance for what he had become.

I nudged Adriel. "Will you put something on your plate at least?" I whispered.

Adriel took the tongs and grabbed a roll.

"Oh," Adrianna said. "So, you're not above eating with us?"

Adriel froze, the tongs and roll hovered above the plate. "I thank God for his bounty."

"That isn't God's bread. That roll is from Hell." Adrianna smirked.

"It is so good that in his divine justice, your god still graces us with excellent food," Kiran said.

Tom pointed at Adriel with his fork. "What do you think of God's justice?"

I touched Adriel's arm, and he placed the bread on his empty plate. Tom watched Adriel like a cat that had laid a trap for a lion.

Adriel returned the tongs. "I will not—"

"Yeah, yeah," Tom said. "You will not discuss matters of God and Heaven with demons. But surely, even God's yes-man must think that the Circles are a bit too extreme. I mean, since when is justice served by never-ending torture?"

"Hell is not retribution. It is a rejection of God's love." Adriel bowed his head. "To be denied the love of God is torment in itself."

Tom looked at him quizzically. "But souls are punished in Hell."

"Yes," Adriel said. "As they should be."

Tom leaned forward. "And you don't think the punishment is disproportionate to the sin?"

Adriel eyed him.

"Tom," Adrianna warned.

Tom raised a hand to Adrianna. "Humans only have so much time. They can only sin so much in the time they're given. Yet, they are tortured for an eternity."

Chandra leaned back in her chair and smiled. Nash watched Tom and Adriel like a tiger who came to see the lions fight.

"You are still alive to commit more sins," Adriel said.

"Because I have accepted a contract. Those tortured in the Circles did not. If anything, the existence of Hell perpetuates sin. We accept contracts to torment others to save ourselves."

What my mother did, horrible as it was, happened in an instant, yet she would suffer in the Seventh Circle forever. Tom was right. How was that justice?

I slowly chewed my food. I had no taste for it. I pushed my plate away. My silverware clanged as it moved against my plate.

Everyone except Adriel glanced toward me.

"I guess you've found a place to hide me away until Michael gets here," I said.

Tom paused with his fork suspended in the air before his lips. "Well, I wanted to talk about it after dinner."

He must have seen the look of vexation on my face. "But I guess now's as good a time as any," he said, putting down his fork. "The Isle of Kings. I think it's the best place," Tom said. "Angels can't enter. The place is permanently warded."

"So, it's like Switzerland?" I asked. "A neutral ground?"

"Sure, if you want to think of it that way," Tom said. "The bottom line is: Michael can pace back and forth by the door, but he can't enter, and he certainly can't kill anyone inside."

"Okay, so when do we leave?" I asked.

"You have to pack your things," Nash said. "You can take anything in your room. Everything's yours."

"Wait," I said. "What about you?"

Nash shook his head.

I stared at him, opened mouthed. "No," I said.

"Lia, I tried."

I let out a breathy laugh. "So, what, you train me for over a year, you fought angels with me, and now I have to go off to some fortress while you stay and do what? What's more important to Lucifer than protecting her precious weapon?"

I wanted to mention a few other things he had done with me, but I held my tongue.

Nash tossed me aside like bones picked clean. How could he?

"We should pack tonight," Tom said.

"Forget it. I'm not going." I stood and threw my napkin down beside my plate.

Nash rushed to the opposite end of the table where I stood. He grabbed my arms. His eyes were intense. "You have to go," he said. "We can't protect you in Sheol. You saw that. Michael will come for you. You might not survive it next time. If you don't want to end up in Hell for an eternity, you'll go now."

I shrugged him away. "I'm not going anywhere." I left the dining room and marched up the stairs.

What did Lucifer want with Nash? I needed him to come with me. I wasn't sure how long I would be in that place.

Nash and I had some things to work out, but we were still friends. He had saved me on more than one occasion, and he taught me how to fight. I wouldn't to leave him in Sheol to fight Michael by himself.

I needed to talk to Lucifer. I had more than one thing to say to her. My mother was in the Seventh Circle. If Lucifer wanted me to continue playing on her side of the field, she would release my mother and allow Nash to come with me.

I watched from the window as Adrianna linked her foot behind Chandra's heel and yanked. Chandra fell to the ground. I smiled.

Nash and Kiran sparred with swords farther down the field. Adriel and Tom fought hand-to-hand. Adriel frowned whenever Tom's lips moved. I couldn't hear what Tom said, but he was probably talking about Heaven, or God, or the angels.

I put on my coat and raced down the stairs, swinging the front door shut. My feet beat along the pavement as I jogged the distance to Lucifer's skyscraper. The skyscraper rose over the other buildings in the distance. The top of the skyscraper disappeared above the clouds.

After jogging half the distance, I slowed to a walk. The breath in my lungs burned, and my feet felt like lead.

I stopped.

Light flooded the alley as I passed. A tall figure was backlit against the glow. Bob. He had opened that portal before. What was he up to?

I stared as the portal disappeared, leaving the alley dark. Turning away I continued down the sidewalk. I had no time to think about Bob. I needed to see Lucifer.

I strode for hours until I reached Lucifer's skyscraper.

I sauntered through the sliding glass doors and up to the reception desk.

"I'm here to see Lucifer," I said. "I need to go straight to her office, and I don't want to see Bob first."

The secretary looked at me with her painted-on smile. Her eyes were wide. "But you don't have an appointment."

"No, I don't."

The secretary's pupils quivered like she was a machine that went haywire, but the smile never left her face. "Well," she said. "You'll have to make an appointment."

"Alright," I said. "I want to make an appointment for right now, right this instant."

"I'm afraid there are no appointments available for today."

"She might have an eternity, but I don't," I said. "I need to see her now."

"I'm sorry. I have to ask you to leave." The secretary stared back at me. Her lips painfully spread into a smile, and her eyes blinking like a marionette doll.

"Lia." Lucifer stood at the elevator. She wore a tight, red dress and black stilettos. The bones of her wings stretched from one side of the elevator to the other. "Why don't you come up to my office?"

I unhinged my hands from the desk. Lucifer waited inside the elevator, her long hand kept the door from sliding closed. I took a deep breath. I was a robin getting into a box with a rattlesnake.

I boarded the elevator with her. I could sense her behind me. My heart thumped in my chest. "How did you know I was here?"

"Cameras, dear."

The elevator stopped, and a whipping sound swept through the air. Lucifer had folded the bones of her wings down. "Follow me," she said. Her heels clicked as she walked down the hall.

She turned the corner and opened the door to one of the rooms. Inside was a desk in front of a floor to ceiling window. Outside, thick, gray clouds clotted the sky.

On the opposite side of the room was a large couch. A bar nestled in the corner with a shelf of wines and liquor behind it.

Across from the bar in the opposite corner was a secretary. I hated the way they smiled as they watched me. I was glad that the desk faced the window. I didn't want to have my back to her.

Lucifer sat behind the dark brown, mahogany desk. "What shall we discuss, dear?" She gestured for me to sit in one of the chairs opposite the desk.

I didn't sit. I placed my hands on the desk. "A modification of our contract."

Lucifer's smile twitched. "What modification?"

"My mother. She's down here in Sheol, in the Circles."

"That's right."

So, she knew. She knew the entire time, and she had no plans on telling me.

"So, what change would you like to make?" she asked.

"Everything about our agreement will stay the same. I'll still work for you. I'll go after Raphael and his followers. But it's not my soul I want you to set free, it's my mother's."

Lucifer raised her eyebrows. I guessed that she hadn't been surprised in a long time. But if I had blinked I might have missed that gesture because it faded faster than a promise from a politician.

"Your mother is a murderer." She didn't say it in an accusatory way, but more like she had simply stated a fact.

"She did it to save me," I said.

"Oh, it's not me that has a problem with it. It's Peter who won't let her through the gates. An Angel Killer. Tsk. Tsk."

"Aren't there exceptions? I'm an Angel Killer, aren't I?"

I dared her to tell me the truth, that she never planned on freeing *my* soul. She wouldn't even if she could. I was far too valuable to her.

"You are something different, my dear. But I'll see what I can do for your mother. Saving her child might make for a good exception, but you'll be sacrificing your own soul on a gamble."

I hesitated. My mother might not be the best person, but she was my mother. "Okay."

"Draw up the contract," Lucifer said to the secretary.

"Wait!" I said. "I want the transaction completed today."

Lucifer clicked her fingernails together. "You're going to make Raphael fall today?"

I couldn't. But I needed to know Lucifer would keep her end of the bargain. "Put him in front of me. I'll claw his eyes out."

Lucifer's lips curled into a smile. "Eager. I like it. But the bottom line is the transaction cannot be completed without you upholding your end of the bargain."

"At least bring my mother to the Outer Region."

Lucifer narrowed her eyes. "Another soul would have to take her place."

I gulped. "Mine?"

Lucifer's fingernails tapped along the desk, and she sighed. "How can you make angels fall for me if you're trapped in the Seventh Circle, dear?"

"You're going to put someone else there."

"No, *you* are." Lucifer pointed to me.

I shook my head.

Lucifer smiled thin-lipped. "Get me Lia's contract and a copy of the standard contract for the sale of a soul."

The secretary in the corner nodded, and she hurried out of the room.

"There you go," Lucifer said. "I'm a reasonable person even to those who come in demanding my time. But that's not the only reason you came here, is it?" Lucifer sat back in her chair.

She would let me trade my soul for my mom's. That was too easy, I thought. What if she was trying to trick me? But she wouldn't let my mom out of the Seventh Circle, not without a replacement.

"I'm waiting, my dear, but my patience is wearing thin. What else do you want?"

"Nash. I want him to come with me."

"With you where?"

I eyed her uncertainly. "He asked you if we could leave Sheol to escape Michael."

Lucifer twined her fingers together. "He asked me nothing of the sort."

"I don't understand."

Lucifer leaned forward. "I gave Nash full permission to leave Sheol whenever he desires, and that was long before you got here, my dear."

"But he said…"

"I don't know what he told you, but it sounds like he's keeping a lot of secrets from you."

I gulped.

The door opened, and the secretary came back with the new contract. She handed the scroll to Lucifer, and she unrolled it in front of me.

"This contract will void the old one," Lucifer explained.

My head still reeled from the revelation. Nash didn't have to stay. At least, not because of Lucifer.

"Offers can just as quickly leave the table," Lucifer said. "Are you sure this is what you want to do?"

I nodded.

She pushed a golden cup across the table. The cup was shallow and no bigger than a shot glass. A sharp point rose from the center of the cup.

"You have to sign it in blood." Lucifer's teeth were an unnatural white.

I reached for the cup and pricked my finger on the golden point just as Sleeping Beauty did on the spindle. But I wasn't signing up for a long sleep. Mine would be an eternity in Sheol.

Before I could press my finger onto the page, blood dripped and dotted the contract. Lucifer pulled the paper away from me. "Perfect."

"What's her name?"

"Hmm?"

"My mother's name."

"Lydia," Lucifer said. "Lydia Palermo."

Lydia. What had she called me? *Rachel.* Rachel Palermo. My real name.

Lucifer handed me another contract. "This is for you. In case you change your mind." She rolled the white paper between her fingers.

I couldn't let someone else burn. I frowned, took the contract from her, and rushed out of the office.

sixteen

SO, the contract was changed. I would be saving my mother's soul instead of my own. I didn't know what would happen to me now. Would Lucifer chuck me into the Circles when I died? Making angels fall couldn't be defined as murder, not even Biblically, but it had to be a sin. It certainly *felt* wrong.

The sword slipped from my fingers onto the grass. I cursed and snatched it from the ground, hopeful no one else saw.

I tried not to think too much about it. Every time I did, I had to own up to the possibility that I might die sooner than I intended. Not that anyone intends to die, but I guess if I had to think about it, I assumed I would die asleep in my bed of old age.

It would be the same boring death that most people fall to. I didn't want to be a hero. I wanted to be boring.

I hoped that when this was all over, that's exactly what I would be. I hoped to lead a happily uneventful life. I wanted to hear every use of the word normal applied to me.

But the longer I stayed in Sheol, the further from normal I was going to get.

For one, I didn't age here, and every moment I wasn't on Earth was a moment of missed opportunity. I was eager to start my normal, boring life. Even though it should be the furthest thing from my mind, I couldn't help but think about it.

I swung my sword through the air as I practiced my stances.

Tom approached me with his hands in his pockets. "You're getting good."

"Am I?" I smirked. *If I could keep my clammy fingers from slipping on the hilt.*

What if Lucifer didn't keep the deal with my mom either? I needed to get her out of the Seventh Circle. No one belonged there, but that was the catch. Lucifer couldn't, or wouldn't, release her until her soul was traded for somebody else's.

But I couldn't let someone else suffer either. Could I?

What was I thinking? I couldn't leave Sheol anyway, not without telling Nash that I had traded my soul for my mom's. I'd need him to open the portal to Earth so I could scout for some poor soul to trade.

But Nash wasn't the only one in Sheol who could open portals, Tom could and so could Bob.

"I saw something." My sword hung at my side as I faced Tom. "Bob opened a portal behind a bar. Twice."

Tom raised his eyebrows. "Okay."

"I don't trust him. I want to know where he went."

Tom shook his head. "I can only tell you that if you remember the exact days and times he passed through."

That was right. Sheol rotated. It's placement over Earth was different depending on the time in which the portal was opened. I decided to make a note of that the next time I saw Bob go through.

*   *   *

I stirred the cereal in my bowl and sipped the coffee. I still hated the bitter taste, but by now, I thought of it as medicine.

I couldn't sleep.

What had I done to Michael that scared him so much?

Thoughts of Caiduc entered my mind. Was he telling me the truth about why he was interested in me? If he was, it made no sense. He made it possible for me to see my mother, and he brought me to that horrible place to do it.

Nash told me that I wouldn't understand a Jinn's motivations because Jinni weren't like humans or demons or even angels. But I needed to know if he was an enemy or a friend.

I made a face and put down the cup of coffee.

I wanted to sleep. I wanted to forget about the past few days and fall into a blissful slumber. I was tired of drinking coffee to take the edge off.

Someone behind me put a spoon of sugar into the coffee and stirred. "That should help." Nash walked around the table and sat down across from me.

"Thanks," I said, taking another sip of the coffee. It was much less bitter now.

"How are your battle wounds?" I asked.

"They're healing."

I looked down into my cup of coffee. "But will they hurt forever?" I whispered into the mug.

"What?" he asked.

"Never mind," I said. "Look. I know a lot has happened. I want to push it under the rug, to start over."

"I can agree to that." His hand rested on top of mine.

"But first," I said slowly. "You have to tell me the truth."

Nash leaned his back against his chair. "The truth?"

"I know you lied to me about not being able to leave Sheol."

"How do you know that?"

"I talked to Lucifer."

Nash furrowed his brow. "You should be meeting with the Devil as little as possible and especially not alone."

"I can handle myself."

"And she told you that I could leave?"

"She told me that you didn't ask."

"That's a lie, Lia." His voice was firm, and he looked me straight in the eyes.

"Then why would she tell me that?"

Nash shook his head. "Maybe she thinks we're getting too close."

"Why would she care?"

"It doesn't matter."

"Yes, Nash, it does."

The door slid open, and Bob walked in. "Hope I'm not interrupting anything. I need to talk to Lia."

I turned back to Nash and spoke without looking at Bob. "Actually, we were just in the middle—"

"Sure." Nash got up from his seat. He patted my hand before leaving as I glared up at him.

Bob sat in the chair opposite me and folded his hands across his stomach as he lounged. "I heard you changed your contract," he said.

I nodded and took a sip of my coffee as I looked around to see if anyone else was within earshot. I hadn't told Nash about amending the contract. I didn't know when I would do that, if I decided to say anything at all. "Is there a problem?"

"Oh, no problem," Bob said. "I just wondered why."

I put my mug down on the table between us. "She's my mother. I hated to see her there."

"But you do realize that you will take her place."

"I've thought about it. I hoped Lucifer would show some leniency after all my help."

"Sweetheart, offering you your own soul was her leniency. She's going to need someone to patch up that hole she's about to leave in Hell."

And she wanted me to patch it.

I didn't want to talk about this anymore. I wasn't going to change my mind now. I would figure a way out of this, but I wouldn't let my mother rot in Hell even if she did sell my soul to the Devil in the first place.

"Hey, how did you get to Sheol?" I asked.

"Lucifer created me. She splintered herself, and I became whole," he said. "I guess you could say she's my mother."

"I thought only God could create?"

"What? That's ridiculous. Can't humans create? Aren't they making cells multiply in a lab as we speak."

"Sure," I said.

"Then why not angels, fallen angels, or demons?" Bob asked.

"Then what makes God so special?"

"What indeed," he said.

"Because God made all that we see from a blank canvas." Adriel stood in the doorway. "Humans, Angels, and Demons— they don't truly create. They imitate. They put things together in unique ways, but they don't make anything new without a foundation of what has come before."

"Your angel friend has forgotten that he is fallen," Bob said. "He's defending a god who's turned his back on him."

"I'm not defending him. I'm stating facts. God needs no de-fender."

"That's why he created you to guard his throne." Bob's words were thick with sarcasm.

He stood and walked to the door. Adriel moved aside to let him pass. Bob put his hand on Adriel's shoulder. "You need a lesson in logic, my friend. Then you will see how little sense your god makes. There is only one Prince of the Countenance, and he is a liar."

Adriel listened as Bob's footsteps faded. "You shouldn't listen to him," he said, taking the seat next to me.

"Is he wrong? Isn't it true that only one angel has seen God?" I asked.

"Michael has seen God."

"Michael *said* he's seen God," I corrected.

"Angels can't lie," he said matter-of-factly.

"Then why is only Metatron known as the Prince of the Countenance?" I asked.

"Because he gave himself that title," Adriel said.

"But if angels can't lie, he must have seen God."

"Metatron is no angel." Adriel's voice was fierce. I had never heard him raise his voice in anger.

I remembered what Tom said about Metatron being a Nephilim and the other angels thinking he was an abomination. I thought Adriel was free of that prejudice. I was wrong.

I put on my jacket and stepped out onto the street in front of Nash's house. I would catch Bob in the act again, and this time, I would know exactly when he goes through that portal.

Demons gathered across the street from me. One had a tail that whipped back and forth beneath his coat. The other two were females with no flaw in their disguises.

I pulled the jacket's hood over my head and turned my eyes to the sidewalk. The air was still, yet my breath misted in front of me. I stopped outside the bar and peered down the alleyway.

No sign of Bob. This was ridiculous. I'd have to camp out here. I couldn't expect Bob to come sauntering through just because I was watching.

"What are you looking for?"

I spun.

Caiduc. The creature scratched its wrist and looked up at me with haunted eyes.

"Don't sneak up on me like that." I took a deep breath to steady myself.

"I wasn't sneaking," Caiduc said.

"You were sneaking, and you startled me."

"I'm sorry." He scratched his wrist so frantically, flakes of bark floated to the ground.

I grabbed his hand, stopping his self-mutilation. "Stop that. What's wrong with you?"

"It doesn't hurt."

I let go of his branchy arm. "Caiduc, do you think you could try that transportation-thing on me again?"

Caiduc's eyes were wide. "Where do you want to go?"

"Back to Earth," I said.

Maybe telling Tom where the portal brought me would help in discovering where it had taken Bob. The positioning had to be somewhat predictable. If not, Tom wouldn't know where the portals would send us when we hunted demons.

"You're leaving Sheol?"

"No, not permanently. Just for a little while. There's something I have to do."

Caiduc nodded and reached out to touch me.

I leapt back. "Wait. Don't you have to know where Sheol is positioned over Earth right now?"

Caiduc looked at me quizzically. "Why?"

"So, you don't transport us into a volcano."

"Why would I do that?"

"Your powers don't work like portals."

Caiduc shook his head. He grabbed my arm.

I wasn't distracted by anything this time. When Caiduc, transported me, the experience wasn't unpleasant like going through a portal. It was like splashing into a pool and coming up from the bottom.

I gulped in the fresh, moving air.

Wet, crisp leaves covered the black, foggy street. Dark cars sat in driveways and along the curb.

A man sauntered down the road, his hands in his pockets, with his head down. Something small and dark crouched upon his shoulders. Walking in a quick, feverous pace, he turned the corner.

I narrowed my eyes and followed him.

"Where are we going?" Caiduc asked.

I shadowed the man down the next street. He stopped outside a house with a for sale sign in the yard.

He pulled the gate to the fence open and walked into the side yard. I peered through the gaps in the wooden fence.

What was this man doing?

"Why are you following him?" Caiduc asked.

"Shut up," I hissed.

I peered closer. The shadow on the man's shoulder moved. Its fingertips pierced the man's flesh. The creature was dark and spindly like a spider. Its grin was full of yellowed teeth.

The man lifted the door to the basement and stepped down into the bowels of the house. Steel flashed. Was that a knife?

A scream, sudden then muffled, breached the silence.

"It's not safe." Branchy fingers bit into my arm, and I was tossed into the pool, coming out dry on the other side.

I stood in Nash's library. I was alone. "Caiduc," I said in a harsh whisper. He had abandoned me.

Someone was in that basement, and that someone needed my help. But I didn't know where I was, only Caiduc knew where he brought me. I planted my face in my hands.

*   *   *

I fell asleep reading the handwritten pages in *The Book of Enoch*. The heavy tome rested on my chest and fell to the floor, rousing me from my sleep. I picked up the large, leather-bound book and placed it on the table beside my chair.

I didn't learn much from its pages, and I surmised that it was at best vanity writing. From listening to Tom and Adriel, Metatron seemed like the type of guy who wanted to be more than he is and tried hard to convince people that he was more.

I was thirsty so I decided to go down to the kitchen to get any beverage other than coffee. As I walked down the stairs, I noticed a few bags at the landing.

Adrianna and Chandra talked in the foyer.

"What's going on?" I asked.

"Nash told us to pack for you," Adrianna said.

"Really?" I raised an eyebrow. "Because I didn't plan on going anywhere today."

"You have to leave sooner or later," Chandra said.

"Later then," I said. I grabbed the handle of one of the bags and started hauling it up the stairs.

Nash came into the foyer. "What are you doing?"

"I'm bringing these bags back up to my room," I said.

"Lia, everyone's ready to go."

"Are you ready to go?" I asked.

"I won't allow you to stay in this house," Nash said.

"Fine," I said. "I'll sleep on the damn training field with Adriel."

I didn't care if my words stung. I couldn't believe he tried to force me to leave without him. I didn't like the secrets he kept from me. I turned my back on him.

"Tom's opening the portal to the Isle tonight," Nash said. "You can either go with or without your bags. But you're going. I'm not letting you stay."

I whipped around and marched down the stairs, letting my bag thump behind me. On the second step from the bottom, I was eye level with Nash. "I sacrificed my soul for my mother's. Isn't that what you wanted? For me to stay down here with you!"

Seventeen

I slammed the door to my room, leapt onto the bed, and buried my face in the pillow. The downy softness muffled my scream.

I wondered if they would drag me kicking and screaming through the portal. They probably would.

I embarrassed myself enough by acting like a child in front of Nash. I had two choices. I could walk through that portal on my own two feet as irked as I was or avoid the situation altogether and run.

Avoiding the situation wouldn't get me very far. I was pretty sure Bob had a tracker on me, as he always seemed to know where to find me.

After a few more screams into the pillow, I decided to go with them. Nash wasn't joining us, and I wasn't sure why. I wish he would at least give me a reason for his absence, but no reason would be good enough. It would just start another fight between us.

Nash wouldn't let Lucifer toss me into the Circles when I finally kicked the bucket. After all, now we *would* have a possibility of a future together. That was part of the reason I wanted him to come with me. Now, we had a chance. Maybe Sheol wouldn't be so bad after all.

I glanced over at the clock. It was a couple hours until what would be nightfall if the skies ever changed in Sheol. I needed to get out of the house. I figured I'd walk this off, and then hop into a portal that would take me far away from Sheol, to a place that would supposedly protect me against Michael.

But I couldn't go downstairs. They all waited for me down there, and I didn't want to face them just yet. As grown up as I wanted to be, my anger was still too fresh to show my face.

I opened the window to my room and climbed out onto the balcony that stretched from the study. The ground wasn't far below. Maybe nine or ten feet at most, but I couldn't jump from that height unless I wanted to come out of it with a broken ankle.

The building's plaster was smooth with no sign of a ledge or crack in which to wedge my foot and climb down. The window was set into the wall of the house so that the lip came over two feet or so. If I grabbed onto it, I could lower my body far enough to close five and a half of the nine or so feet from the ground.

I did so and allowed my body to drop onto the grass below, hoping I wouldn't break a leg. If I did, there would be plenty of time to rest up. I was going somewhere where my only responsibility was to hide and wait.

I rolled onto the grass, uninjured. I stood up and hurried toward the street. Once I was a good distance away, I slowed to a walking pace and took in a gulp of stale air.

I hoped the island had good walking trails so I wouldn't be cooped up in some building all day. I turned the corner, keeping careful account of how many times I turned right. Sometimes I would let my instincts guide me, but I wanted to be back by to-night so Nash wouldn't worry that I had run away.

I wondered if Caiduc would still visit me on the Isle. The Jinn showing up at the end of my bed became a regular occurrence, and I imagined that I might miss it.

"What are you thinking about?" Caiduc appeared alongside me.

That man, the one who went down into the basement with screams echoing before him.

"You have to take me back," I said.

"Back where?" Caiduc asked.

"To where you brought me last night." What if Caiduc couldn't visit me once I left? If Archangels were forbidden to enter the Isle, maybe Jinni were barred too. This would be my last chance to save whoever was locked up in that basement.

Caiduc shook his head slowly. "Too dangerous."

"He could have been hurting someone down there."

"That's why it's too dangerous."

I grabbed Caiduc's tree-limb wrist. "Take me back."

Caiduc looked at me with fear in his wide eyes as they twitched. "If I take you, will you promise to be careful?"

"Yes."

"Alright. Hold on."

My body was brought through the water, and I came up on the other side.

I stood in a dark room. Light peered in through a long slit above. I rushed to the light, which came from two sets of wooden doors.

I tried to open the doors, but when I did, a heavy chain rattled from outside. "Damn it, Caiduc."

"Who's there?" A voice came from the darkness.

I turned. The slant of light ran across the face of a teenage girl. Her hair was dirty and stringy. Her clothes were unwashed.

I approached her as one would a frightened rabbit. "I'm going to get you out of here."

In her arm was a needle. The needle was attached to a clear, plastic tube, ending in a clear bag that filled up with her blood.

I pulled the long needle out, and the girl winced. A large, brown bruise colored the crook of her arm where the needle had gone in.

"Can you stand?" I asked.

The girl nodded.

I helped her to her feet. It was like making a deer stand on its hind legs, but finally she stood.

The chain rattled outside. I held the girl so she wouldn't fall. "We have to hide," I said. "We can dart out while he's looking for you."

"It's too late," she said.

The doors creaked open and fell back on either side in a cloud of dust.

The man was long bodied like a snake with limbs. His eyes were wide and his cheeks sunken. He climbed down into the basement.

He approached us. He looked more surprised and concerned than angry.

The creature clenching his shoulder grinned from its perch.

As the man got closer, I thought to pull my dagger and warn him to stay away, but the girl had taken the dagger from my side.

She plunged it into the belly of the man and ran for the moonlight. Adrenaline carried her body away.

The man was on the floor. He clenched his stomach in one hand, the other hand reached for the blood bag. He chewed it open with his teeth and crushed it against his mouth, drinking it like a thirsty man in the desert. When he drained the bag, he tossed it aside.

The demon crawled into the corner, disappearing into the darkness.

I made for the exit, but stopped. This man was dying, and he had done terrible things. If anyone should take my mother's place—

I pulled the contract from the pocket of my jeans and knelt beside the man as he bled on the floor. "Sign this," I said.

The man looked at me, quiet, knowing he was dying. Blood painted his pale lips.

"Sign it," I repeated.

"What is it?" His words were whispers in the musty air.

"Something that will take you where you belong. You need to sign it in blood."

The man grinned. He dabbed his finger in the blood that dripped from his mouth and brought it to the page.

"No." I grabbed his bony arm. "*Your* blood."

He moved his hand from his bloody wound. Blood gushed out on the floor like a broken water fountain. He painted the bottom of the contract in a smear of blood and grinned again.

He thought this was a joke. I wondered if it still counted. The blood crusted the bottom of the contract.

The man grabbed my arm. His grip was tight for a dying man. "You'll never get away," he said. "Not in your dreams."

I yanked away from him, and my arm slipped from his blood-slick fingers.

Caiduc stepped out of the shadows. "Can we leave now?"

A bruise formed on the crook of my arm where the man grabbed me. "Yeah," I said, "I hope that girl can find her way to a hospital. I'm not sure how much blood she lost."

"What girl?" Caiduc asked.

"You didn't see her. She ran."

Caiduc quivered when I approached him. Warm blood trailed down my arm. His fingers gripped my hand, and I was lost in the cool waters.

Caiduc disappeared. I stood alone on the dim-lit street. In my hand was the rolled up contract. Tucking the contract into my coat pocket, I folded my arms across my chest and walked.

Footsteps tapped behind me. Maybe someone else had the same idea, a quick walk before dinner perhaps. It wasn't Caiduc, I would have recognized the clogging of his hooves against the concrete. This sounded more like heels.

As the footsteps grew louder, my suspicions swelled.

I turned around in time to see the flash of a red dress slink behind a building.

"Nice night, isn't it?" A deep, firm voice said.

I faced forward.

Sam stood before me, and in his hand, was a knife. He grabbed my arm. "I got her," he called.

The heels approached, and I strained my neck to see who it was.

Delilah.

She grabbed my other arm. "Walk with us," she said.

They walked on either side of me, grasping my arms.

"Where are we going?" I asked. "My friends will expect me back for dinner. I hope it doesn't take long."

"Oh, it won't take long," Delilah said. "You'll be back with your friends in no time."

"I know what you're trying to do, but it won't work," I said.

"Oh, yeah, what are we trying to do?" Sam said.

"You want to possess me."

Sam and Delilah laughed.

"Isn't that right?" I asked.

"Well, we call it taking a ride," Delilah said. "Possession sounds so . . . formal."

"You can *both* do that?"

"It will be woefully temporary," Delilah said.

"But since your friends are planning on leaving tonight," Sam said, "what better time than to *hitch a ride?*"

"How did you know that?" I asked.

"We've been watching you." Delilah tapped my nose, like an adult might do to a child.

I felt like a child. Why did I need to leave Nash's house? A few more screams into my pillow would have done the trick just the same. Now, I had to deal with two demons wanting to take over my body so they could escape Hell.

I struggled, but Delilah's fingernails dug into my arm.

"Hold still. Even if you could get away, it wouldn't take much to catch you."

She was right. Even untrained demons were stronger than me. If I had a weapon, I might be able to get a few lashes in, but I doubted that I could outrun them.

We turned the corner into a dark alley. Like the Angel District and Lucifer's skyscraper, the sky was darker in this part of Sheol.

"Tie her down," Delilah said.

Sam pushed me against the wire fence at the back of the alley and took off his belt. He tied the belt around my arms and through the fence links. The links he picked were high up, and I had to stand on my tiptoes to keep the belt from rubbing against my wrists.

As Sam tied me to the fence, Delilah set out several large candles in a semicircle from either end of the fence and into the alleyway. She went to each candle in turn, whispering something as she lit each one.

Sam removed the knife from his jacket along with a small bowl barely large enough to hold a cup of water.

I was eye level with his chest. I looked up to see what he was doing.

Using the knife, he sliced into my thumb.

I gritted my teeth as he squeezed the thumb, allowing the blood to pool into the small bowl. He dipped his finger into the bowl and etched something onto my forehead. He knelt to the ground and drew a circle with lines through the center on the cement in front of me.

The metallic scent of blood stung my nose. Cooled blood dripped from my thumb and tickled my arm as it trailed down.

"What are you doing?" I asked, but I already knew. They were going to perform a ritual to take over my body. But I struggled for what to say. I had to say something. I could feel it. It felt as if talking would save me. It would make them realize I was a living being with feelings.

What do demons care about your feelings?

I had to try. "My friends will know it isn't me."

Sam brandished the knife in front of my face. "Oh, you'll still be you," he said. "But you'll keep your mouth shut because if you say anything, we *will* take over. And we'll make you so much stronger."

"Not strong enough to kill them," I said.

Delilah walked over to me. Her eyes were solid red like blood had spilled into them. "No, but they won't want to fight you. They'll know that fighting you would mean killing you. Sure, they'll try to restrain you, perform an exorcism perhaps. But in all that time, you know who will be on his way."

Raphael. I needed to be me so I could make him fall.

"You could save a lot of time by keeping your mouth shut and letting us along for the ride. When we get to Earth, we'll let you go."

"But you can't roam around without a host." *Not unless they had a contract.*

"I could think of a lot of people I'd rather be than you," Delilah said.

"So, you're going to infect someone else?" I asked.

"Oh, don't act all high and mighty," Delilah said. "You're no angel, love."

Delilah knelt beside the bloody circle. She chanted words in a language I didn't understand.

The air was no longer stagnant. It moved around me like piranhas around their prey. The wind blew my hair across my face.

I struggled in my bonds, but Sam, grinning, just watched as I fought to free myself. I wasn't going anywhere. All I did was make the skin on my wrists raw. I twisted my body against the chain-linked fence.

Sam's face changed. His forehead wrinkled like a big, drooping frown above his eyebrows. His eyes were black holes. When he grinned, his mouth displayed a set of sharp, brown teeth.

"Hold still." Sam forced me back around.

Twisted, black horns grew from Delilah's head. She continued to recite the incantation. The winds picked up. The candles' glow dimmed.

As the flames died, the marking on the ground glowed, and my forehead warmed. I strained my eyes upward.

Light glowed above my eyes, burning into my forehead. I closed my eyes, hoping it would be over soon and the pain would go away.

"What's taking so long?" Sam asked.

"I don't know," Delilah said. "It's like something is pushing me back." She continued to chant, louder now.

I heard a grunt like someone had the wind knocked out of him. Delilah stopped reciting the incantation.

My eyes shot open.

Delilah stared off to the side, her lips quivering. Sam was pushed up against the building, and hands were around his neck.

Someone stood in front of him. The featherless wings of a fallen angel adorned his broad, muscled back. His ashy black hair had been cut shorter.

Adriel slammed Sam's back against the brick wall of the adjacent building.

"Continue the ritual." Sam spit out blood.

Adriel glared at Delilah. "Say one more word, and I'll sling both of you over my shoulders and toss you into the eternal depths."

Delilah scrambled to her feet and ran, knocking over one of the candles. All the candles in the semi-circle went out.

Adriel removed his hands from Sam's throat and backed away, giving him a chance to run.

Sam didn't run. Instead, he stooped to the ground to pick up his knife. He pointed it at Adriel. "Come on," he said. "If it's a fight you want, we'll fight."

Adriel reached for him, and Sam sank the knife deep into Adriel's chest. Adriel didn't flinch. He grabbed Sam around the neck and cracked his head against the brick wall.

Sam's body slid down the wall as blood dribbled down his chin.

Adriel approached me and untied the belt securing me to the fence.

I rubbed my wrists. "Thanks."

"Are you alright?" He took my hands in his and looked down at the redness that encircled each wrist.

"Are you?" I asked, glancing up at the knife in his chest.

Adriel looked down like he hadn't realized it was still there. He pulled it out without a word or a shutter of pain and tossed it on the ground.

"Did it hurt?" I asked.

"No."

I knew he was lying. He was ashamed that it *did* hurt. The blade wasn't made of Arcadian Steel, yet it hurt him because he was fallen.

"Nice haircut," I said. "I didn't know there are barbers in Hell."

"I cut it myself."

"Maybe that could be your new calling."

Adriel frowned.

"Sorry, that was—" I trailed off.

"I'll walk with you back to Nash's," he said.

"I think that would be a good idea."

Nash stood outside the house. I had been gone for hours. I would have been back sooner had I not run into Delilah and Sam or asked Caiduc to help me save that girl. But I couldn't leave her with that man, not knowing if I'd have another opportunity to help.

Nash's eyes fell on me. His expression was a mixture of anger and relief. He rushed forward and embraced me. Pulling away, he asked, "What happened?" He glanced down at the marking on my forehead.

"Parasites," Adriel said. "They were looking for a host."

"I'm ready," I said. "I'm ready to leave."

"I sent everyone home," Nash said. "I didn't know where you were. I figured you'd run. I can't force you to do anything, not even if it is in your best interest."

"I know that was a shot at me," I said.

"Maybe it was," Nash said, "but you deserved it." He winked. "Come on. I saved us some dinner. I'll wait for you to get cleaned up."

I narrowed my eyes. I thought Nash would confront me about changing the contract, but he hadn't said anything about it. Maybe I was right. He wanted me down here with him, and I had given that to him. Perhaps he wasn't in any rush to get to the Isle now because he knew that if I died I would end up right back here.

The three of us ate in silence. After the meal, I went up to my room, leaving Nash and Adriel alone downstairs.

I placed the signed contract in the drawer beside my bed. The bruise the man gave me had purpled. It ached when I curled my arm.

I had washed up before dinner. I scrubbed the sigil off my forehead before I got into the shower. I paused before climbing into bed when I heard the door slide open. I expected it to be Caiduc, but Jinni don't open doors.

"I hope I'm not intruding." Adriel stood in the doorway.

I hesitated. I wore the white tank top and shorts I usually wear to bed. I realized this was the first time Adriel saw me this underdressed. Then, I realized it wasn't. Adriel watched me for years after my first guardian angel went missing. He'd probably seen me in various states of dress and undress. The thought made me blush.

"I'm sorry. I shouldn't have…"

"No, come in," I said.

Adriel nodded. He eased the door closed behind him. Without turning back around, he said, "I heard you. I heard you say you changed the contract. Did you say that in anger, or is it true?"

"It's true."

He faced me. "Lia, you should be saving your own soul. Don't you understand what this means?"

"It means my mother can go to Heaven, the place that you miss so much. You look up at the sky, hungry to see it again."

"And you'll never get to see it."

"Isn't that better? Wouldn't it be worse if I had seen Heaven first?"

He grabbed my arms and pulled me in close. He tucked my hair behind my ear. "I should have known you would do such a selfless thing."

Why did he look so much like Nash? But he wasn't Nash. He didn't want to control me. He wasn't selfish or cruel.

In that moment, I didn't care that Archangels were after me or that my soul would be trapped in Hell for all eternity. I wanted only one thing. And something whispered that it was right.

I stretched up to meet him and pulled him into me. The warmth of his body against mine sent chills up my spine. Our lips touched.

He didn't crush his lips against mine. His kiss was soft, un-rushed. His fingertips brushed my arms.

He took his time because he wasn't going anywhere. He didn't have to bruise me with his urgency and fly away from me as if we would burn.

eighteen

I reached for the coffee pot reflexively, but stopped. Nope. No coffee today. I was as peppy as a squirrel that drank a soda.

Sleeping through the night will do that to you. Not one bad dream haunted my rest.

At training, I couldn't stop myself from stealing more than the occasional glance at Adriel. Once, I caught myself full out staring, and my eyes darted away.

I felt a little guilty about what happened between me and Adriel, but I wasn't sure why I should. Nash treated me like a movie rental.

I shook my head. I was so new at this. None of it had any permanence if I died tomorrow. Michael could come back with an army of angels, or Raphael would come with his army. I should be focusing on staying alive, not thinking about my complicated love life.

Nash hadn't said a word to me about last night. He didn't argue with me about the contract. He didn't try to march me up to Lucifer's tower to change it back. He didn't ask me about the demons who were after me, and there was no more talk of me leaving Sheol.

I fell on my ass again right as Nash passed.

He looked at me, but no glare marred his eyes. "It's okay," he said. "Stand up, and try again."

Adrianna offered me her hand. I took it, and she pulled me to my feet.

Nash circled around to Adriel and Kiran. He stopped them in the middle of their sparring and talked to each of them in turn. I was too far away to hear the words, but it looked like he was giving them advice. His hand was on Kiran's shoulder. He didn't glare at Adriel when he spoke to him.

"Why is he going so easy on us?" I asked.

Adrianna shrugged. "He isn't doing us any favors. We got lucky last time. If Michael rolls through town again, he will have our heads on pikes."

She was right. Why was Nash being so passive? My mind could only summon up two possibilities: he was trying to give me some space because he could sense that he was losing me, or he didn't care what happened to me in life because he would have me in death.

I cringed that it might be the latter. I was afraid to ask him despite my curiosity. We were growing apart, but I didn't like to think that he could be so selfish.

After training, I took a nap. When I woke up, it was two in the morning, and I missed dinner. My stomach grumbled. Leftovers were scarce when Nash cooked, but I managed before.

I crept down to the kitchen and opened the refrigerator. There was rice and stir-fried veggies in a container. I pulled it out and heated it on the stove. I walked into the living room with my plate full of food.

Nash sat on the sofa, sipping his coffee.

"Hey." I walked into the room. "I didn't know you were up. Don't you ever sleep?"

He looked up at me. "It leaves you vulnerable. So, no, I never sleep."

I had said it half-jokingly. I didn't expect that answer. He never sleeps? Maybe he was exaggerating. "You mean you haven't slept in a couple days?"

"I mean, I never sleep."

"In your whole life? You would have died."

Nash laughed. "I can't die."

I kept forgetting that Nash wasn't human. None of my friends were. "That's why you drink so much coffee."

"It dulls the pain of a sleepless night and gives me more willpower."

"Why don't you ask someone you trust to watch over you while you sleep?"

Nash shook his head. "You shouldn't trust anyone."

That hurt a little.

"What enemies do you have in Sheol?" I asked.

"Everyone in Sheol is an enemy."

"What about Chandra, Adrianna, Tom, and Kiran?"

Nash nodded. "They are demons, and demons do for themselves."

"They're your friends."

"For now."

Why was he being so melodramatic all of a sudden?

Nash leaned forward with his arms against his knees. His eyes were on the floor. "We should go to Lucifer tomorrow and get her to modify the contract again."

"To what?"

"To save your soul."

And there it was. So, he hadn't planned on letting me make my own decisions. That part made me angry. But then again, he still cared about me. He wouldn't let me skip out on Heaven. I felt guilty for thinking he might be that selfish.

I shook my head. "I'm not changing the contract again. I'm getting my mother out of here."

"That isn't your mother, Lia!"

"What?"

"Lucifer lies. That's what she does. She could have sent that Jinn to take you to her."

"If she's not my mother, who is she?" I asked.

"Some random woman pretending to be her. You haven't seen her in years. Lucifer must have offered her a deal to trick you."

"Why would Lucifer do that?"

"Because she wants your soul," he said. "You're a good person. Having you down here would be a gold star on Lucifer's record."

But that couldn't be true. She was my mother. I remembered her now. She looked like me, and she hadn't aged a day since I'd last seen her.

"How do you know that's true?" I asked.

"I don't, but doesn't it make sense?"

"Maybe. Or maybe you're feeling guilty about what I said to you last night. About you wanting me to be down here with you. I'm sorry I said it. But you lying to me isn't going to get me to change my mind."

"You think I don't know that?"

"You don't know anything," I said.

I turned and walked back up the stairs. I closed my bedroom door.

Could he be right? Was she really my mother? Caiduc. Did Lucifer ask him to work for her? No, this was all Nash. He tried to convince me of something that wasn't true so I would change the contract.

Lucifer couldn't draw up a contract for something she couldn't offer. If my mother wasn't in Sheol, Lucifer couldn't make a promise that she would release a soul that didn't belong to her in the first place, right?

I shook my head. I didn't know anymore. I didn't like to make decisions that weren't based on evidence. But I took a lot on faith lately. It made me uneasy.

I was back to coffee the following morning. I drank it down in two gulps without sugar, and I still yawned afterwards.

I hadn't yet had an opportunity to talk to Adriel about what happened between us the night before. I thought something had to be said about it. I would tell him that I just wanted to slow down. After all, my mind raced with things I had not yet sorted out. Nash was one of them.

I wanted to figure out one thing at a time before deciding whether I should move onto the next. I had to admit that Adriel made me feel things that Nash didn't, but I wanted to let those things develop more before anything serious happened.

Plus, it would be easier to think more clearly about where I would go next if this wasn't clouding my mind. I let my feelings for Nash dictate whether I should leave Sheol. I wouldn't let that happen again.

Nash said demons do for themselves. Well, it was time I did for myself too. I might as well start getting some practice. I would be one of them soon.

The thought was surreal. I mean, I didn't think I could become a demon. Although I wasn't on board with Lucifer tossing me into the Circles. I was trying to protect myself from the truth, but the mind can only do so much when you know you're damned to Hell.

I passed the living room. Chandra leaned against one of the columns in the entry way.

"I saw who went into your room last night," she said.

I stopped in mid-step. "You what?"

"That angel, Adriel. I think I could guess what you two were up to."

"We were just talking," I said. "You shouldn't let your imagination run wild. You might start dreaming up things that aren't true."

"You could have talked anywhere," she said.

I shook my head and started down the hall, but she darted in front of me. Her movements were so flawless. I was a little shocked when I saw her standing opposite me.

"I'm not going to say anything to Nash," she said. "I wanted to give you some advice. That's all."

Chandra and I got along with each other like a bird gets along with a cat. We were never friends. I was guessing her motives the moment she told me she saw Adriel enter my room. Did she think she would use it to break up whatever Nash and I had going on? Did she think she could use it as leverage for something else? But what did she think she could gain from me?

"I don't need your advice," I said.

I tried to move around her, but Chandra blocked my path with her arm, which she had pinioned against the wall. "I'm going to give it to you anyway: Don't let guilt stop you from going with your gut."

"Eloquently put," I said.

Chandra grinned at me. "Just because Nash was your first, doesn't mean he has to be your last."

I pushed past her. That must be it. She wants Nash for herself again, and she wants me out of the way for good.

Chandra told me a year ago that Nash was like that with girls. He dated them for a while and then let them go. I couldn't imagine an eternity with anybody. I couldn't imagine an eternity.

The transitory nature of life makes some of us pick comfort over adventure. I imagined given the opportunity to live forever that things would get boring. Nash might like me, but I doubted that *I* could ever break his heart.

CAIDUC and I stood outside Lucifer's skyscraper. Staring at the clouds surrounding the building, I clenched the signed contract.

What if Nash was right?

"Are you lying about my mother?" I asked.

The Jinn looked at me. "I showed you your mother." His voice had an edge of defensiveness to it.

"Was she really my mother?"

The Jinn's forehead wrinkled. "Of course. Who else would she be?"

I shook my head. If the Jinn was lying to me and it was working for Lucifer, it wasn't going to just come out and tell me.

I had two choices: I could flat out assume the Jinn was lying to me and disregard everything it told me, or I could find out more and determine whether it was telling me the truth.

If my mother wasn't in Sheol, Lucifer's contract would make no sense. How could I save the soul of a woman that didn't need saving?

"Is there a way you could prove she's my mother?" I asked.

The Jinn shook its head. "Not in any way you could understand."

This was bad. Now the Jinn knew I was suspicious. Would it change its tactic? Maybe there was some other way I could find out if it was lying. There wasn't time to think, and I wasn't going to ponder in front of it like this for much longer.

Everything Nash said was speculation. This woman looked like me. As distant as I felt from her, I could sense she was my mother, and I had to save her.

*   *   *

I slammed the contract down on the table. Bits of dried blood flaked off the page.

"Nice," Lucifer said.

"This is enough to replace her, right?"

Lucifer flashed a thin-lipped smile. "Yes. I'll make the arrangements."

"What arrangements?" I asked.

"That's none of your concern. First, you have to retrieve her from the Seventh Circle."

"Because you won't go down there?"

Lucifer shook her head slowly. "And I doubt you'll get Nash to do it. Even though he did come out alive the first time."

I narrowed my eyes. "You don't think I can do it. That's why you made this deal in the first place."

Lucifer grinned.

"You don't think I'm capable of getting my mother out of there anyway." Which meant Lucifer didn't send the Jinn to trick me. If she had, she would know the Jinn could transport me straight to my mother. Caiduc was telling the truth. Or maybe this was all part of the act.

Lucifer leaned forward on the table. She searched my eyes. "If you go down there and get yourself killed, you, your mother, and everyone you've ever known will be down here with me. You can't pull her out."

I slowly lowered my face to hers and met her eyes. "Watch me."

I whirled around and marched out of Lucifer's office. Outside, I met Caiduc. "I'm ready."

"It isn't safe."

"It's the last time," I said.

Caiduc ambled over to me. His twiggy fingers entwined in mine.

I splashed into heat. Wet pops of bloody bubbles filled my ears. The humidity stuck to my skin like cling wrap.

My mother, Lydia, rested on the hot steps of the Seventh Circle beside pools of boiling blood. Her hair was in wet tangles matted to the sides of her face. She looked like she melted into the stairs.

I approached her, stepping around the bubbling pools. The red water splashed onto the hem of my jeans. The liquid ate through the fabric.

"Rachel." Her voice was like a puff of smoke, dissipating into the air.

"I'm getting you out of here." I offered her my hand.

Lydia shook her head.

I grabbed her arm and hauled her from the steps. Gritting my teeth, I heaved. Her skin pulled from her back like taffy.

Thick ropes of flesh splayed from her body. I pulled. My hands slipped from her blood-slick arms. I fell back.

I leapt up. The ground was hot like I had touched a pan straight from the oven *with my entire back.*

I wiped my bloody hands on my jeans and grabbed her arms again.

Caw!

A harpy circled the sky. Its wings cut through the tumultuous clouds. The lion's tail trailed behind it, and its stringy hair whipped in the wind. It cawed and displayed a mouth of sharp teeth in a jaw that opened too wide on its semi-human face.

"Rachel, stop!" my mother screamed. One of her fleshy tethers snapped.

I tugged for all I was worth. *Snap. Snap. Snap.*

No resistance. I staggered back and found my footing. Lydia stood, shaking and covered in blood.

"We have to go." I cupped my hands around my mouth. "Caiduc!"

Caiduc stood at the bottom of the steps, scratching his wrists. I grabbed Lydia's hand and pulled her to Caiduc.

"Get us out of here," I said, offering him Lydia's arm.

Caiduc nodded and took both our hands. The hot, dry heat changed to cool, dry air. Lydia panted.

She knelt in the middle of the road. Her palms touched the concrete. Caiduc was gone.

We were a mile from Lucifer's skyscraper. Getting to Nash's house would take hours.

Hopefully, Nash had some leftovers in the fridge. Lydia was painfully thin. She hadn't been that way when I first saw her.

I reached for her arm to help her up. "Let's go," I said. "You can rest when we get to Nash's."

"She's coming with us." Two lanky demons stood in front of us, wearing tight-fitting black suits. They tried their best to look like men, but their solid, black eyes gave them away.

They approached us. One of them pushed me aside. They each took one of Lydia's arms.

"What are you doing?" I asked.

The demons dragged my mother between them.

"You're not taking her back!" I drew my sword, but rough fingers wrapped around my arm.

Caiduc's hands trembled as he cowered behind me.

"Let go!"

Caiduc shook his head. "They're taking her to Lucifer. They won't let you see her again until you've completed your task."

"We'll see about that." I tugged, but couldn't release my arm from his branchy fingers.

"It won't do any good. If you fight them, Lucifer will send more."

"Fine." I shrugged away from Caiduc. At least, she was out of the Circles. But wherever Lucifer kept her, I would find her and free her from that place too.

I awoke to my mother shaking me.

"Wake up, Rachel. I need you to do something for me, sweet-heart."

I rubbed my eyes. Sleep had not yet released me from its hold. I blinked, trying to adjust my eyes to the light.

I glanced over at the open window. The moon and stars were out. The warm night breeze brushed against my cheek.

My mother looked the same age she was in the Seventh Circle. She was roughly thirty years old. She wore jeans and a t-shirt. She hadn't changed for bed.

I wondered what she had been up to so late at night.

"Come on, baby." She offered me her hand.

My hand was so small in hers. I looked down at my Bugs Bunny nightgown stained with purple jam and the smallness of my bare feet.

She helped me out of the bed, and I walked with her into the hallway. We stopped outside her bedroom. The door was closed.

My mother gave me a container of salt. "Make a circle around the room," she said. "Make sure you don't leave any gaps, and keep your head down, okay?"

I nodded as I gripped the container in my small hands. I made a circle with the salt. Out of the corner of my eye, I could see cage bars and a warm, glow, but I dared not look.

My mother took things out of the room, the nightstand, a lamp, and several paperbacks. When she finished, she returned with a large leather-bound book. She sat with the book near the center of the room and reached for me.

She pulled me into her lap. "Now close your eyes and don't peek. It's just a game."

My mother chanted feverously. It sounded like one of the Romance languages, maybe Latin, although I'd never heard it before.

My hands were clammy, and my eyelids tickled. I had to see what was happening.

The room was bare except for a steel cage a few feet from where we sat. It reached the ceiling.

In the Arcadian Steel cage was an angel with long, flowing blonde hair. She looked at me and mouthed the words, "I'm sorry. I couldn't protect you."

My mother had tears in her eyes, but her lips continued to spill out the words.

The angel screamed a high-pitched, unearthly scream, almost like a song. She smiled at me as silver blood sprayed from her neck. "I love you," she whispered. *Sydriel, my guardian angel!*

My mother continued to chant as if she couldn't see or hear the pain she caused.

A figure stood in the corner of the room. Darkness shadowed his face. He stood outside the salt circle. He made no move to help the angel. He stood and watched.

The silver blood raced toward us as if the house was being tipped like a tea kettle. My mother held me in her arms. She scooped up the silver blood and fed it into my mouth.

I jolted up from bed. My forehead was sticky with sweat, yet I shivered in the cold room. My mother killed my guardian angel, Sydriel, the angel Adriel left his post to find.

"Bad dream?"

My skin tingled, and my heart leapt. My body remained in that state of anticipation until my eyes focused on the form at the end of my bed.

The Jinn.

"What are you doing here?" I asked.

"Sometimes I come to watch you sleep," Caiduc said.

I wanted to tell him how that was one hundred times past creepy, but I figured he wouldn't understand anyway. "You shouldn't watch people sleep."

"Why not?"

"You're invading on their privacy," I said.

"But you have no privacy. Everyone is watching you, always."

My skin crawled. "What do you mean by that? You mean Raphael and Michael?"

The Jinn shook his head. "Raphael and Michael are puppets. They just don't know it."

"Look if you're going to be cryptic, you might as well leave now."

The Jinn lowered its head like a dog that had been scolded.

A question burned in my mind, one that I never thought to ask before. It wasn't something that would help me separate truth from lies, but it was something I had to know.

"Is my father down here too?" I asked.

The Jinn shook its head.

"Is he in Heaven?"

The Jinn's eyes glowed in the dark. "Robert Palermo is alive."

The price of a human soul

THE image of the house reflected in the dark waters that touched the street. A bare twisted tree grew on the front lawn. The moon had an orange cast.

The street was quiet and empty. The windows of the house were dark.

Across the street was a gated playground with a rusty swing set and a flooded sandbox.

The Redeemer strolled along the dark, wet street. He wore a long, black coat. His skin prickled against the cold, but he didn't feel the chill as humans did. The cool air could not overcome his fire nor could the coat stoke it.

The Redeemer stepped up to the front door and swung the brass knocker. The woman wouldn't answer. The house was supposed to be empty, but a lot of things weren't as they were supposed to be.

The Redeemer knocked again and waited. When no answer came, he banged on the door with the ball of his hand. *I'll kick it in if I have to.*

The door opened a crack.

"Hello?" a timid voice answered, a woman's voice. A dark, narrow eye peered through the crack.

"Lydia." The Redeemer's mouth curled into a smile. *She won't run this time.* She had taken the bait with the Archdemon. "May I come in?"

"No."

"Why don't you open the door a little wider? I won't come in if you don't want me to, but I brought you this." He showed her the thick leather-bound book he carried. "I won't be able to fit this through that little crack."

Lydia inched the door open. She wore a long, cotton nightgown. Her dark-brown hair was tangled down her back.

The Redeemer passed her the book, and she flinched. "Go on. Take it."

Lydia's hand trembled as she reached for the large tome.

"Both hands," the Redeemer said. "I won't have you dropping it."

Lydia took the book in both hands. The book had been preserved like a mummy, taken from the author as soon as it was written.

"Everything you need to know is in there," the Redeemer said. "You can save her."

Lydia looked up with appreciative eyes that glistened.

"Mommy, who's that?" A little girl stood in the hallway and rubbed the sleep from one eye. Her hair was dyed red to disguise her from her father.

Her father had called her mother crazy. He tried to take the girl, but only she could fix what she had done.

A glowing form stood beside the young girl. *Sydriel.*

"It's okay, honey." Lydia rushed to her daughter and knelt in front of her. "He's a friend of Mommy's. Go back to bed."

Sydriel glared at the Redeemer, and her wings flared. Her golden hair hung in curls around her face and neck and matched her eyes. *She won't get in the way. She wants this for the girl. It might be the only way to save her.*

Sydriel was going to help the process along, though she might not know it yet.

The little girl nodded to her mother and turned back down the hallway. *What mother sells her daughter's soul?* Sydriel's hand was on the girl's shoulder as she led her down the hall back to her bedroom.

Lydia turned back to the Redeemer. "You're sure this will work?"

A muscle in his face twitched. *Not the first thousand times.* "Yes," the Redeemer said.

Lydia pressed the book to her chest. "I will try it."

The Redeemer smiled. "You'll need help. Read the book. Prepare for what you'll have to do. It won't be easy. I'll come back same time tomorrow."

"So soon?"

If I give her too much time to think about it, she might lose her nerve. "You did this to your daughter," the Redeemer said. "I'm sure you'll want to make it right as soon as possible."

Lydia nodded and kept her eyes to the floor.

The Redeemer had done many awful things in his life, but he could still make this woman feel shame.

She provided him what he needed, yet he still couldn't understand why. She didn't know his plans.

I shouldn't be surprised. How many mothers have I come across who were willing to save the souls of their children on a demon's promise? Too many.

Lydia smiled weakly, clasping the book to her chest.

The Redeemer turned his back on her and moved toward the cold, dark street.

part three

scorned

nineteen

I laid awake in bed feeling tired. I had slept on and off the night before. It was difficult getting back to sleep after the dream, especially knowing Caiduc liked to watch me in my sleep.

The dream brought me a mix of comfort and dread. Dread for the obvious reasons. My mother killed an angel and made me drink that angel's blood. Comfort because my memories were coming back.

Throughout the night, I remembered bits and pieces of the past I had forgotten. They were small things that might seem insignificant but meant a lot to me. I remembered my childhood home, the smell of my mother's perfume, and drawings I did when I was little.

Most significant was the memory of my father's face. I could see him. He was no longer the faceless man from my dreams.

His hair was dark and his eyes blue. He had a big nose and crooked lips when he smiled, but he did smile a lot.

I wondered what happened to him. He wasn't in the house the night my mother murdered an angel.

But who was that shadowy man?

No, he wasn't my father. I didn't know who he was, but I could sense that much. My mother left my father the year before.

I remember her packing her suitcase as she cried. I stood in the doorway, confused and frightened.

Would I ever see my dad again?

I thought about what Nash had said.

How was I supposed to figure out if the Jinn was lying or not? Did I save my mother? Or did I save some random woman Lucifer commissioned to lie to me?

The return of my memories was a good indication. How could I remember a woman I never knew? She had to be my mom. Her touch brought back my past, a past I thought was gone for good.

Still, there was a predicament.

I didn't want to stay in Sheol. What if Lucifer chucked me into the Circles? Just because I'm helping her now doesn't mean that it guaranteed me a place in the Outer Region. I didn't like the idea of missing out on Heaven either. I'd seen the look in Adriel's eyes when he talked about it.

I never believed in Heaven before, but now that I knew it was real, I didn't want my soul to be stuck in Sheol when I could be in eternal bliss.

Nash said that Heaven wasn't all it was rumored to be, but maybe Nash was bitter because he couldn't be there. How had Nash fallen?

But more importantly, Mom and Dad were in Heaven. If I didn't go there, I'd never see them again.

Could Lucifer's contract keep me out?

Wasn't there a loophole for saving the world? I mean, if I stopped Raphael, it would be kind of shitty that the girl who saved everyone had to spend eternity in the Underworld.

I went down to the kitchen and poured myself a cup of coffee. I dreaded it, but it would help me stay awake. Lying in bed and kicking the sheets around wasn't very productive so I figured if I couldn't sleep soundly, I wouldn't sleep at all.

I wondered how Nash filled his nights.

We sleep so much of our lives away, it's a wonder what we could do with all that extra time.

The dark brew was bitter on my tongue, but the mug warmed my chilly hands. I settled down in the armchair in the library. I tilted my head back and closed my eyes. I knew that sleep wouldn't come to me, but it was comforting to shut everything out.

After a few minutes of peacefulness, I heard footsteps approaching. I opened my eyes.

Tom walked in. Sweat gleamed on his forehead.

"What are you doing here so early?" I asked.

He jumped before looking in my direction. "Oh, it's you. Sorry I didn't know you were in here."

I took a sip of coffee. "Couldn't sleep. What are you up to?"

"I helped Nash deliver a weapon to the armory."

"An angel weapon?" I raised my eyebrows. No one told me about another weapon.

Tom shook his head. "No. It was forged here."

"Oh. Okay." I found it odd that Nash and Tom had decided to get the weapon in the middle of the night, but I guess it wasn't too weird for Nash since he never sleeps.

Tom plucked a book off the shelf. "Sorry. I'll read upstairs."

"Wait, Tom."

Tom paused in the doorway. "Yeah?"

"Why did you choose Sheol?"

Tom raised his eyebrow. "Why do you ask?"

I shrugged. "Just curious."

"It's not that bad, Lia," he said. "She's not going to throw you into the Pit."

I shook my head. "That's not why I'm asking. I'm just curious, I swear."

Tom sighed. "You really want to know?"

"Sure."

"I'm Doubting Thomas."

I laughed, but Tom didn't join me. "You're serious. From the Bible?"

"Yep. I'm the one. He showed me his hands. Holes through here and here." Tom pointed to the center of each palm. "The good book says I believed." Tom threw his hands up like he was at a Christian revival.

"But you didn't, not even after you saw his hands?"

Tom shook his head. "I put my fingers through the holes, but I thought there must have been another explanation. I went to my grave thinking someone must have slipped me some hallucinogenic mushrooms or something."

"Really?"

"Yep."

"So, they wouldn't let you into Heaven because of *that?*"

Tom shook his head. "No one stopped me at the gates. I turned my back on them. I didn't feel like I deserved to be in Heaven because of the doubt. So, I came here. Lucifer offered me a deal: a hundred years of possessions and hauntings, and here I am."

"You never stepped foot in the Circles?"

"Nope, and I never plan to. My soul has been demonized."

"What does that mean?"

"I can never enter Heaven now, and when the Rapture comes, my soul cannot be reunited with my earthly body."

"But you have your body."

"That's your perception. This body is only what I want you to see, when you're not piercing my Veil that is. We can manipulate how humans and other demons experience us. Angels see us quite differently."

"What do angels see?"

"You should ask Adriel that one."

"So, is Nash's soul demonized?"

Tom shook his head. "The process to demonize an angel's soul is . . . complicated. You would know if Nash had become a demon."

"How would I know?"

"Fallen angels aren't able to change their appearance at will like demons do. That's why Nash cut off his own wings rather than disguise them."

That's why I couldn't pierce Nash's Veil. He didn't have one.

"So, if Nash was a demon, I wouldn't know because he would look the same, right?"

"No, he wouldn't."

"But I thought you said…"

"I said that fallen angels can't change their appearance at will. I didn't mean that their appearance can never change. The process by which an angel demonizes his soul changes him. It makes him look like we do, but without the ability to disguise it."

"Can you show me?" I gulped. "Can you show me what you really look like? I've never been able to see *completely*."

Tom smirked. "I don't think you'd want to see that. Once you do, you'll never get that image out of your head."

NASH carried a weapon, a staff. I had never seen it before. It must have been the weapon he and Tom brought the night before.

Nash tossed me the staff.

It ended in a point that could be driven into the ground or into the body of an opponent. It had markings on the sides. It was clearly an angel weapon of some kind.

But Tom said it was forged here? Had he lied to me?

The detail was remarkable. The markings were depictions of humans in the arms of angels. I turned the staff around. On the other side were images of angels in armor with their weapons held above their heads. Below them were infants swaddled in blankets.

I looked more closely. It was as if the angels were coming down to attack the babies. I turned my eyes away from the weapon.

I wanted to ask Nash where he had gotten it, but he stepped in front of me and pointed a less ornate staff at me.

"Ready?" he asked.

I nodded.

I blocked his first blow and the second and the third. I could see every move before it happened. It made me dizzy.

I looked down at the staff.

"What's wrong?" Nash asked.

"It's this weapon," I said. "I don't like it."

"You have to get used to it," he said.

"Where does it come from?"

"It was forged here. It will help us fight Michael. We all must train with it."

"But there's only one."

"True."

"It's making me dizzy."

"Alright." Nash took the staff from me. "Let's use the swords." He handed me one of the swords from the table.

"Ready?"

I nodded again.

Nash moved slowly, far too slowly.

It wasn't the staff, I realized. Nash was going easy on me.

I dropped the sword to my side.

"You need a break?" he asked.

"No," I said. "You're clearly going easy on me."

"I wanted you to get the feel for it."

"I've practiced with this sword a thousand times. If you're not going to train me for real, I'd rather have another partner." My eyes betrayed me as I glanced toward Adriel.

The gesture wasn't missed by Nash. But instead of hate, defeat settled in his eyes.

"Train with Adriel," he said. "Choose your weapons."

"I won't fight Lia," Adriel said.

"She could learn a lot from you," Nash said.

"I am not a teacher," Adriel said. "If she wants to learn, she can watch."

"This is ridiculous," I said. "I'm going back inside."

"You have to train," Nash said.

"What's the point?" I asked. "The only thing that's going to save me from Raphael or Michael are these." I put my hands out in front of me, fingers spread. "Every time I've fought an angel it was the only thing that saved me. I can't fight. It's been luck every time."

I could sense the others watching me as I left, but I didn't care if I caused a scene. All I wanted was for Nash to stop looking so defeated and for Adriel to quit treating me like a delicate flower. Neither one of them was helping me.

I went up to my room and plopped onto the bed, hugging the pillow against my body.

"It wasn't luck." Caiduc's voice came from behind me, and I knew he sat on the end of my bed. "Luck isn't real. It was your light."

I groaned. "Why don't you just go away? I don't like you spying on me."

"The light protects you," the Jinn said. "Powers are awakening inside you like memories. The staff invoked one."

I turned my head to face him. "I don't know what you're talking about, and I don't care right now. I'm tired of hearing your riddles."

"You want to go back home."

"Yes. I had a job and a life. I had a normal boyfriend. I should have stayed."

"But Raphael will find you."

"Maybe," I said.

"Definitely," Caiduc said.

"Is there a way to reverse what my mom did?"

The Jinn shook its head, which was its response for everything it didn't know. It didn't like saying the words, like by acknowledging out loud that it didn't know something would be acknowledging that it was lesser in some way.

It said it liked watching me when I sleep. Does that mean that like Nash and the others, it didn't need to sleep?

I wondered if Jinni could feel pain. Nash didn't need to eat or sleep, but he could feel the pain of hunger and sleep deprivation. Still, Jinni were different.

I wish I knew more about them, but I had failed to find anything in Nash's books. But there were so many, I hadn't gotten through them all yet. Maybe I could find one tomorrow. I needed to know more about this creature and why he was helping me.

I walked back out onto the field. Chandra was the only one out there. She wielded a weapon, but I was too far away to tell which one. I wondered if it was the staff Nash brought to training that afternoon.

My face grew hot then cold.

I shook my head. I shouldn't be acting this way. Nash was only trying to make amends. He wasn't going easy on me because he wanted me dead. That was clear from the way he demanded I go to Lucifer to change the contract back.

He was trying to apologize in the only way he knew how: by giving me my space.

The problem was I wasn't sure space was what I needed right now. I didn't want to think about Nash or Adriel. After all, there were more important things to think about. But I didn't know how close Raphael or Michael were. I wasn't sure if they were coming tomorrow or ten years from now. Angels lived for an eternity, twenty years would be the blink of an eye for them.

This problem I was having with Nash and Adriel was more immediate. That's why my mind kept wandering back to it.

I couldn't stop thinking about the kiss. Should I feel guilty? I found myself feeling guilty that I didn't feel guilty about it.

I hadn't spoke with Adriel since it happened. A kiss wasn't something you ignored, but Adriel didn't seem at all bothered by it. Did he not like me that way? I was pretty sure he was kissing back.

Chandra practiced her fighting stances on the field.

"Can I join you?" I asked.

Chandra shrugged.

I picked up a sword and practiced alongside her. "I was thinking about what you said the other day, about going with my gut."

"It's good advice, you should take it," she said.

"But what if my gut is pulling me in two directions?"

Chandra paused, then continued. "That's impossible. Your gut isn't pulling you in two directions. It's pulling one way, and your guilt is pulling you in the other."

"How do I know which one to choose?" I asked.

"That depends on what type of person you want to be," she said. "Do you want to lie to someone to make yourself feel better, or do you want to take what you desire and be honest with yourself?"

"That's easier said than done."

Chandra stopped and glowered at me. "I didn't give you the advice so that you could shit all over it."

"Jeez. Sorry," I said.

Chandra turned away and sighed.

"Hey, are you okay?" I asked.

"Better than I deserve."

Was she thinking about Alex?

"I lost someone," she said. "Someone I loved, and when I came here Lucifer told me he had chosen Sheol. But that wasn't the truth."

"He's in Heaven."

Chandra nodded. "In hindsight, I should have known. He was a good man. My gut told me he was in Heaven. My guilt told me neither of us belonged there."

"So, how did she fool you?"

"We were mercenaries. We killed a lot of people. Him more than me. But they were thieves, murderers, and rapists. Still, a priest told me that murder was murder, and only God could choose who lives and who dies. So, when Lucifer told me that Dillon was in Hell, a small part of me believed her. Yet the pull was strong in the opposite direction, I should have chosen differently."

"Are you mad at Lucifer?"

Chandra pursed her lips together before she spoke. "No. There's no point in being mad at Lucifer. It's like being mad at the wind for blowing. She lies. That's her nature."

She crinkled her nose like she smelled something that died a long time ago. "I was the fool for believing her. There were so many times I could have told him I loved him. We could have raised a family together long ago. Now, I will never be able to say my peace."

Twenty

DRY heat wafted against my face as I stared out into the red plain littered with erupting pools of boiling blood.

"Mom?" I called, but my voice didn't echo. It didn't carry on the wind across the plain.

I walked, flinching as the boiling pools sprayed my legs with blood.

Lydia struggled to keep her head above the blood that filled the river. Despite my disgust, I reached in and grabbed her bloodied arm. The blood scorched my hand, urging me to flinch back, but I didn't. I pulled my mother from the river and helped her crawl onto the bank.

Her skin was pink from being in the hot bath of blood. She tried to wipe the dripping red liquid from her face, but that only smeared it.

"Are you alright?" I asked.

She took in deep gasps of air before she could speak. "Yes, now I am." She patted my arm and left blood there. I tried to ignore the sticky feeling on my skin.

"Why are we back here?" I asked.

"Because this is where you see me," she said.

"I don't understand. Is this real?"

Lydia nodded. "I'm real."

Was this a dream? I'd never been so aware in a dream before. "I have something I need to ask you." Blood sprayed across my cheek. "What happened to my father?"

Lydia shook her head, and blood spewed onto the stone steps. "I don't know."

The words fell on me like a death sentence, so much finality and yet so little resolution. There had to be more she could tell me.

"Why did he leave?" I asked.

Lydia hung her head. "He thought I was crazy," she whispered. "One night, he decided to leave. He wanted to take you. I couldn't let him do that. So, I took you and ran. I didn't want to, but he couldn't help you. Only I could. He didn't believe you were in any danger."

"Because you made me drink angel's blood."

She shook her head. "No, I did that to protect you." She touched my cheek. "Before that, before you were born, your father was dying. He was the love of my life. I didn't think I could love anyone more than him."

She looked into the distance. "A demon offered me a contract. To save your father, I had to give up the soul of my unborn child. But I didn't know I was pregnant at the time. After I made the deal I wasn't going to have any children. You were born several months later."

So that's how it happened. The price of my soul was my father's.

"As you got older, I worried more and more about what I had done. I told your father. He didn't believe me. He thought I had gone crazy. I knew I was the only one who could fix it."

"And you thought that making me into an Angel Killer would do it?" I asked.

"He told me it would," she said, staring into the distance as if someone stood there.

I turned my gaze to see what she was looking at, but there was nothing there, only miles and miles of red plains and pools of blood.

"Who told you?" I asked.

She turned back to me. "The Redeemer. He told me he could get an angel to do it. I couldn't see her, but he assured me she was there. He told me you could see her because you were still young. Even the damn cat could see her, but I had to take it on faith. He told me if I performed the ritual, you would have meaning to Lucifer, that she would make a deal with you."

She was talking about the man in the corner. The man who watched the horrible thing without flinching. I couldn't see his face.

"Did he tell you his name? His real name?" I asked.

Lydia shook her head.

"You could see him?"

"Yes," she said.

"How could you see him but not the angel?"

"I practiced witchcraft, and he wanted me to see him. I knew a few incantations. One in particular that I had practiced for a long time."

My eyes widened. "You could push people back without touching them."

"How did you know that?"

I tried to explain to her I could do it too. I had so many questions, but the edges of my vision became dark. I was pulled from the Circles and jolted upright, gasping for air.

"Caiduc?"

Long branch-like fingers crawled up from the end of the blanket, and Caiduc's head popped up from over the edge of the bed.

"Bring me back," I said.

"Back where?" Caiduc cocked his head.

"To the Circles."

"You shouldn't spend so much time there."

"Why not?"

"Because you are alive. You could die there."

"Then, why do you keep bringing me back?" I asked.

"I did not bring you back."

"Yes, you did, and somehow you brought my mom back there too."

Caiduc shook his head. "I did not. You were dreaming."

That didn't feel like a dream. Why was the Jinn lying to me?

"You want answers," Caiduc said. "I'm trying to give them to you."

But I wasn't getting the answers I needed. There was still a missing piece that had nothing to do with what my mother did to save me. It had to do with my identity. I didn't know him, but he was part of me.

"I want to know where my dad is."

Caiduc shook his head.

"You said he was alive. How could you know that if you don't know where he is?" I asked.

"I have searched Heaven and Hell. He isn't here, and he isn't there. So, he must be alive," Caiduc said.

"You guessed." All this time, I thought the Jinn knew something I didn't. I thought it knew my father was alive when it had merely guessed by process of elimination.

"There are only three places a human soul can go."

I popped out of bed and pulled on my jeans. Its doe-eyes followed me as I moved across the room.

"Where are you going?" Caiduc asked.

"I need to clear my head." I walked to the door and shut it behind me.

I had gathered a nice little stack of books from the shelves and leafed through a few of them, hoping to find a mention of Jinni. The few I had pulled from the shelf didn't seem relevant from their titles. But none of the titles mentioned Jinni. I grasped at straws.

My fingers run over the titles on the shelves. *Seven Princes, Nine Circles*. Nostalgia. I read this one when Nash and the others were lost in the Circles.

I pulled the book from the shelf and leafed through it. Lucifer had separated herself into seven distinct personalities. That's what Bob must have meant by splinters, her seven vices: Pride, Gluttony, Envy, Greed, Lust, Sloth, and Wrath. But they were all Lucifer, parts of herself that had become separate and whole.

I fell asleep with the book in my lap when I was awakened by the door shutting. Startled, I picked my head up and glanced around the room. I expected to see Tom, but it was Nash.

He walked over to me. "That's quite a stack you have there," he said.

"Sorry." I gathered the books into my arms.

"No worries," he said. "Let me help you with that."

Memories of when I left Sheol flashed in my mind. I remembered when a boy asked to help me with a stack of books. My life was so normal then.

"No, I've got it," I said, balancing each book atop another. The stack of books touched my nose as I slid my feet toward the shelf.

I heard Nash snicker behind me.

I tried to look over my shoulder as I balanced the books. "Now, I know you're not laughing at me." As I said that, I took another step and felt the weight of the stack shift.

One book slid off the top and four more joined it on the floor. I knelt and started to pick up the books.

Nash knelt beside me, taking one of the books in his hands. A wide grin spread across his face.

"What's so funny?" I asked. "I could have damaged one. They're very old."

"They're just things," he said.

"Where did you get all of them?"

"I stole them," he said, "from libraries around the world."

"You stole books," I said.

He nodded.

"Did you steal jewelry or, I don't know, money?"

"Nope. Just books. You'll find there are a lot more valuable things in these pages than money or jewelry. Tom could tell you that."

"I don't know," I said. "I might find more value in a diamond necklace than I would in…" I squinted and read the title slowly . . . "*Three Men in a Boat.*"

"It's great for anyone who's ever wanted to go on a boating holiday," Nash said.

I raised an eyebrow. "A boating holiday?" Well, at least I knew I could scratch that one off my list of books with no mention of Jinni.

"Yeah," Nash said, "it has very practical suggestions like why you shouldn't bring cheese with you on a boat."

"Why not?" I asked.

"Because it gets everywhere, all over the boat, and makes all the rest of the food taste like cheese. And then, everything smells like cheese."

I laughed. "That seems very practical, but you don't eat cheese."

"Now you see why."

"No, not really."

We laughed together, and weight lifted from me.

The laughter died, and Nash gazed at me with a hungry look in his eyes. His hand reached up and touched the back of my neck, easing my face closer to his.

My heart beat in time with my racing thoughts. I had to tell him now.

I bent my head low, and my hair fell over my face.

"Sorry." He pulled back.

I looked up. "I can't do this anymore."

"I know. I'm sorry."

I furrowed my brow and looked down at my hands. "What's going on with you, Nash? You told me the kiss was a mistake, but how many more mistakes are you going to make?" I wasn't angry anymore. I was confused.

Nash's hands rested on mine. "I..." He shook his head.

The words burst from my lips. "I kissed Adriel."

My heart clenched as his hands left mine.

"You want him?"

I shook my head. "I don't want anybody. I want to go home. This is too much, Nash. A year ago, my biggest worry was passing a history exam. Now, I have two Archangels after me. I don't have any time for anything else. I barely get any sleep and when I do, I have those terrible dreams. I'm not ready for any of this."

Nash was silent.

"Please, say something."

Nash stood. He lowered his eyes. "You're right." He began to walk away.

"Nash." I grabbed his hand. It was balled into a tight fist. I let him go. Out of the corner of my eye, his figure was blurred as he left the room.

I closed my eyes and took a few deep breaths, but that didn't stop the tears. I wiped them with the backs of my hands. I hadn't expected them.

I stood. I needed to talk to Adriel too before I lost my nerve.

ADRIEL walked nearest the road. I strolled alongside him on the sidewalk. I didn't know how I was going to start. What I had said to Nash wasn't perfect, and it was far from easy. Although, I thought that talking to Adriel would be easier. I was wrong.

"You said you wanted to talk to me about something."

"Yeah," I said. "But it's . . . I don't know how to say it."

"You want to talk about the moment we shared."

Had he been thinking about it too? My head swam from the thought of it. I opened my mouth to say something when light erupted from the sky.

"What was that?" I asked.

Lightning cracked the smooth sky. The brightness stung my eyes, and I looked away.

"Angels," Adriel said. "I have to go."

"I'm going with you." I followed his feet as I shielded my eyes from the light.

"It's not safe."

"I'm your greatest weapon. I'm coming with you. But we should warn the others first."

"There's no time."

Darts of light zoomed from the skies down upon Sheol.

"It looks like they're headed for the Angel District," he said.

We made it to the gates of the Angel District. Winks and his brother had abandoned their posts. Shouts and screams issued from inside.

I touched Adriel's arm, and he turned to look at me. "What are we going to do? You don't have a weapon."

Adriel grabbed one of the bars of the heavy gate and pulled. With a screech, the bar was freed. "Stay behind me," he said.

I nodded. "Give me an opening when you can."

Demons ran through the streets. Blood stained the buildings as the angels wielded their weapons, cutting down demons like they were blades of grass. The angels pulled open doors and flew through windows.

"What are they doing?" I asked.

"They're looking for something," Adriel said.

"What?"

A horned demon ran past us. Adriel turned and cleaved him in the head with the heavy iron bar. The demon fell face down amongst the stampede. Adriel knelt and took his machete from him. It gleamed in the neon light. Arcadian Steel.

Adriel stopped. His eyes rested on an angel who wore silver armor. His hair was braided down his back. He stabbed a horned demon in the chest with a long, silver staff. His face was expressionless.

"We have to leave," Adriel said. "I should have never brought you here."

"What?" I asked. "What did you see?"

Adriel met blades with one of the angels. As the angel bared down on Adriel, I reached out, grasping a fistful of feathers. The white feathers turned black and smoldered in my hand. From the angel's lips bellowed a long, haunting scream. I backed away as the heat of the flames touched my skin.

I turned back to Adriel. His face paled, and his mouth twisted in a frown.

"Adriel, watch out!"

Adriel whirled around moments before another attacker's sword fell upon him. "Run, Lia! Go to that building and hide."

He glanced at a tall building across the street.

"I can't leave you here," I said.

The angel's back was to me as he and Adriel fought. My fingertips only grazed him, but his wings burst into flames. He ran through the streets, feathers turning to ash in the air.

Adriel grabbed my hands. "Don't," he said. "Please, just go. I can't die here. I want to find out why they've come."

Why was he asking me to stop? Could it be that he was afraid my actions would draw attention to me? Or was he so disgusted by my ability he couldn't bear to see me do it?

I slowly nodded. I turned away from him and ran to the tall building. The screams sounded distant behind me as I yanked the door open and took the stairs two at a time.

Why did they come here, to the Angel District? They were looking for something, but what?

I breathed in short gasps by the time I made it up the stairs. Adriel's fear was infectious. I didn't know why I was so afraid, but my hands wouldn't stop shaking.

I tore open a door. The room had bare walls and no furniture. Chained to the wall in the back of the room was a fallen angel. I approached her.

"Andromeda?"

Andromeda's once clear eyes were now black. Her wings were only bones, hung useless on her back.

"Angel Killer," she hissed.

It was true. I had put her here. For an angel, this was death.

"I'm sorry." I lowered my head. A spatter of black blood was on the floor below where Andromeda hung.

She glared at me. "I don't want your pity."

"What are the angels looking for in Sheol?" I asked.

"You, of course."

No, that couldn't be right. Why would they think I'd be in the Angel District? They would have come to the Outer Region as they had before.

I shook my head. "I wasn't here when they came. What are they looking for?"

"If I knew, why would I tell you?"

"Because they're not just hacking up demons down there."

"They have no loyalty to us. I wish they could kill me."

"You want to go to the Pit."

"That is not death," she said.

A crushing feeling came over me. I wanted her to know I was backed into a corner. I wanted her forgiveness.

"I didn't have a choice. My deal with Lucifer..."

Andromeda sighed. "You can't trust the Devil. She is a deceiver."

"Yeah, I've been hearing that a lot lately."

"Lucifer ordered you to do this to me."

"I had to. You were working for Raphael."

Andromeda laughed.

"I don't see what's so funny," I said.

"I'm not working for anyone but God. I've never spoken to Raphael."

"But, why..."

"Is that what she told you? That she wants you to attack Raphael and his followers? So that all of humankind won't be shut out of Heaven? Oh, how noble of her to care so much."

Andromeda spit on the floor. She looked me in the eyes. "Lucifer wants you to make all the angels fall so there would be no gatekeepers in Heaven. She could take over Heaven and Hell in the blink of an eye."

I shuttered. That certainly seemed like the kind of thing the Devil would do, but wasn't there one person who would surely step in if Lucifer tried to take over Heaven? It was the same guy who stopped her before.

"God wouldn't stop her?" I asked.

Andromeda leaned forward until her face was inches from mine. The chains on the wall rattled as she moved. "No one has seen God for millennia."

Twenty One

DRIEL burst through the door. "They're leaving," he said.

"What? Why?" I asked.

"They either found what they were looking for or they gave up," he said. He walked up to where I stood next to Andromeda.

Andromeda looked up at him, studying his face. "Adriel? She got you too."

Adriel stepped forward and caressed the side of Andromeda's face. He could look upon her without pity. His gentle, reserved smile was one that might grace a man who is looking upon the rolling hills of the quiet countryside with the breeze against his face.

He turned away from Andromeda. The smile faded from his lips. "We should go," he said. "When I look at them, I want to liberate them all. But I know if I do that, they will be tossed into the Pit."

Andromeda looked from Adriel to me and back to Adriel again. "You're with her. You're working for Lucifer." She narrowed her eyes. Her mouth sealed shut, and I imagined she was working up some saliva, but this time, I don't think she planned to spit on the floor.

Adriel grabbed my arm and pulled me to the door.

"You're a traitor, Adriel," Andromeda yelled. "You were always meant to fall."

Adriel kept his head low as he marched down the hall and to the stairs. Andromeda still shouted, but I could no longer make out the words.

Outside the streets were brighter. A bright, round patch of light glowed in the sky where the angels had descended. I wondered how many more of those patches of light the angels would dot around Sheol. The place would have so much light, it would cease to be Hell.

Blood was splashed against buildings and along walkways. It was black and silver, but mostly black. It was the first time I had seen the streets so empty, except for the demons who were too wounded to walk and the fallen angels that were chained to the outside of the buildings. Everyone else left the city.

Doors were torn from their hinges, and windows were smashed. The Angel District had been looted.

"They didn't come here to spill blood," Adriel said.

"Are you sure?" I asked. I tried to avoid the blood that ran through the streets like they were arteries.

"They were looking for something," he said.

"What?" I asked.

"I don't know." Adriel's eyes were distant. "But whatever it was, Michael must have believed it was of great importance. He went after it before coming after you."

"Michael was here?" I asked.

"No."

"Wait, that angel you were looking at, the one with the braid. Was that Raphael?"

I didn't recognize him. If I had seen his eyes...

But he had a silver staff. I didn't recall the large, silver cross at the top, and I remembered the weapon being broader, but I only caught a glimpse before he plunged the staff into my parents' car.

I expected him to be more terrifying. I had been running from him for over a year now. I'd seen a flash of him when he killed my parents and in nightmares he had fangs for teeth and razors instead of feathers. But this man looked angelic. I shook my head.

He was my enemy, but he was no monster. He was an angel, one of the good guys. *I* was the big, bad wolf.

And I was.

But I didn't care if my parents' murderer was an angel or a demon. I still wanted him dead. I wanted him to suffer in flames the way they did.

I wiped the tears from my eyes.

"That wasn't Raphael. That was Phanuel. Michael must have sent him."

"Phanuel doesn't follow Raphael?"

"Michael chose Phanuel to replace Ramiel after Ramiel's betrayal. He would never side with any angel over Michael."

Andromeda hadn't worked for Raphael. How could we get that wrong? But *we* didn't. Lucifer was the one who sent us after those angels. Had she lied to me about her true motives?

Maybe what Andromeda said was true. This wasn't about Raphael. Lucifer wanted to rule over Heaven and Hell, and taking down all the angels was the best way to do it.

It didn't seem like God was too keen on showing his face. So, there would be no one to stop her.

But she didn't plan on me finding out.

"I have to go," I said as we left the abandoned gates of the Angel District.

"Where?" Adriel asked.

Cuts and bruises patterned his arms, and one nasty laceration was above one eyebrow. I should've stitched it up for him.

"I'll be back soon," I said. "It's better if I go alone."

Adriel shook his head. "I'm not letting you out of my sight."

"I'm going to Lucifer's tower," I said. "She won't hurt me. She needs me. But she won't like me bringing a fallen angel. Well, one with which she's not well acquainted."

"She knows me."

I put my hands on my hips. "You know what I mean."

Adriel nodded. "Alright. But I don't like thinking of you in the company of the Devil."

"Believe me. I don't either."

Twenty Two

"I want to see Lucifer," I demanded.

The secretary grinned, but I could see past her smile. Her eyes were wide, and the corners of her lips twitched. "You need an appointment."

"I don't care. I need to see her now."

The secretary dialed a number on the phone. "Bob, I have Lia down here. She wants to see Lucifer. Okay. Yes." The secretary hung up the phone and turned to me. "You can go up now."

The elevator wouldn't go fast enough. I rushed out of it as soon as the doors opened to Bob's apartment.

"Bob!" I shouted. "You're going to give me that key right now."

Bob stood in the doorway to the dining room. "Demanding today."

"I need to see Lucifer."

The large, silver key hung around Bob's neck. "Do you now?"

"I'm not in the mood for games."

"Well, neither am I, but I have a job to do."

"I'm calling her out on a lie. That's all I'm telling *you*."

"That's a shame because," he said, "I'm what's standing be-tween you and her."

I withdrew my sword.

"Oh, this is a mistake, sweetheart."

I swung my sword at him.

Bob folded back like he was in *The Matrix*, but my blade cut the cord around his neck. I slid across the marble floor and caught the heavy key as it fell.

I turned and raced down the hallway. Bob's feet stormed be-hind me. I swooped into the elevator and jabbed the key in the hole, turning it.

The elevator doors closed on Bob's face as his lips curled into a smile.

My heart pounded as the elevator ascended. The doors slid open, and I darted down the hall.

I stormed into Lucifer's office. She read over a document on her desk, acting as if she hadn't heard the door slam behind me. She wore reading glasses, which I might have found amusing under different circumstances.

"They weren't all Raphael's followers," I said.

Lucifer didn't look up from her work. "What are you talking about?" she asked.

"I'm talking about the angels you had us attack."

Lucifer laced her fingers together and put her elbows on the table. "I didn't make the battle plans. How do you know they weren't Raphael's followers?"

"Andromeda, she told me."

"Andromeda's down here? Pity."

"I think you *want* all those souls to funnel into Sheol. That you want to make the angels fall so you can gain control over Heaven like you always wanted."

"I told you," Lucifer said. "The maintenance would be a nightmare. Why would I want to put that much pressure on myself?"

"Then why would you send us to fight angels that aren't on Raphael's side?"

Lucifer sighed and took off her glasses, resting them on the desk beside the snow globe and the bowl of apples.

"I asked you to make his followers fall," she said. "Do you think I have time to work out the minute-to-minute details? That's why I put Nash in charge. You'll have to ask him."

Nash? Why would he lie to me about this? Why would he waste our time on angels that weren't our enemies?

As awkward as things might be between us, I needed answers. He had to have a good reason. Maybe he misidentified Raphael's followers? That was probably it. How would he know for sure who was with Raphael? But there must have been some way to rule them out.

Tom. Nash put him in charge of researching the angels. He would know what method Nash used.

Nash didn't do it on purpose. What reason would he have?

A dark thought clouded my mind. What if we got them *all* wrong?

NOT there. Not there. I chanted, but the mantra brought me no comfort.

I was in Hell. I was asked to do the impossible, and I failed.

Lucifer played with me the way she did with Letchfield. There was no winning, only the game. *The world is a fiddle, and its music tricks.* I was destined to lose.

That's Hell. It's not fire and brimstone. It's offering hope and then ripping it away, burning it away, and cauterizing the wound.

A demon eyed me from across the street. My eyes flickered to the solid black eyeballs and to the tail whipping behind its back. He wore a dark trench coat.

We stood, facing each from across the quiet street. He smiled, pointed teeth cramped in his mouth. Our standoff was over. Challenge accepted.

He approached, closing the distance between us.

The demon glared at me. "A human."

I pulled my dagger. The demon put his hands up. His tail whipped behind him.

A sting hissed. I dropped the dagger. Smoke rose from a slash across the back of my hand. The demon's tail settled back behind him.

I lunged for the dagger, but the demon plucked it from the ground. I reached to take the blade from him. He jabbed.

Pain lit me on fire. I grabbed my side where the dagger had gone in.

"You ran into it. What a waste."

I hemorrhaged blood.

The demon smiled cruelly. He approached me with the dagger. I held out my hand, and the air rippled in front of me.

The demon's feet left the ground as a force pushed him backward. His body skidded across the concrete.

I ran.

But the demon didn't follow. I was nothing to him now. A waste.

Blood dripped from my wound. I couldn't keep life inside my body. I knelt in an alley. The blood spilled around me.

I woke to chirping. I touched my temple. My head hurt.

I felt my side. Blood, but no pain. I lifted my shirt. A jagged tear ripped the fabric, but my side had healed. Not even a scar.

How did I—?

"You're awake?" Caiduc perched with his knees bent on a dumpster in the alley.

"Did you heal me?"

Caiduc shook his head.

Then, what did?

Blood pooled around me and wet my shirt and the sides of my pants. I wasn't even woozy. I shook my head. "I was stupid. That demon shouldn't have gotten the better of me."

"You wanted to lose."

"No, I didn't." But did I? Did I want it all to end?

"You look tired."

Tired. That didn't begin to describe how I felt. Tired, lied to, confused, and abandoned. Abandoned a long time ago.

"I need to ask my mother about my abilities. She knows what she did to me."

"You want to see her."

"No, I need to. I need to use everything in my arsenal to defend myself."

Something glowed down the alleyway.

I stood.

"Where are we? Are we near the bar?"

Caiduc nodded. "You want a drink?"

I ran to the glow and stopped. A portal glowed in the opposite alleyway behind a chain-link fence. A tall man walked through. He had a gold watch upon his wrist. I didn't see his face, but it was Bob.

"Help me over this fence." The portal wouldn't stay open for long.

Caiduc stood next to me, scratching his wrist. "Oh, no. You shouldn't go."

"I have to know what he's up to. I don't trust him." I grabbed the chain-link fence and climbed. I jumped down on the other side.

Without time to consider my choices, I raced through the glowing portal.

Twenty Three

Y stomach lurched as I stepped on the other side of the portal. Bob stood on the edge of a cliff. A woman stood beside him.

I ducked and crawled behind a rock.

The woman had honey-colored skin and long, blonde hair, but when I looked down, I realized she wasn't a woman. Her legs would look more natural on a horse or a mule. They were long, hairy, and ended in hooves.

"Onoseklis. My gem on Earth." Bob hugged the woman. Her naked arms wrapped around his obsidian black suit.

The sky was dark and crowded with clouds. A full moon glowed white with dark, wispy tendrils of smoke curling over its face.

"More are coming," Bob said.

The woman looked over the cliff toward the moon.

"I'm moving as quickly as I can," Bob said. "I want to get you back where you belong."

The woman looked at Bob with urgency in her eyes. She grabbed his hands. "I belong to the caves, and the wind, and to you."

Her knuckles were white as she clasped him. Her hold was like a badger's jaws around the neck of a wolverine. If she let go, he would devour her.

Bob gulped. "I'll be back soon. I will send them tomorrow. Find a place for them, Ono."

She frowned.

"I know the Jikininki were difficult to control. I won't send any more of them. This time they will be Furies. I'm sure you can deal with a few winged goblins."

Ono looked to the moon.

Bob cocked his head to side. "I will see you again." He kissed her hand, but she didn't look at him.

Bob spread his fingers and opened a portal. He stepped through. The portal glowed next to Ono.

It's too close. I can't go through without her seeing me.

Ono stared longingly at the portal, and then, it zipped out of existence.

"What are you doing?"

My heart leapt to my throat. Caiduc knelt behind the rock beside me.

Perfect timing.

I grabbed his hand. "Get me out of here."

I burst through the water into the alley. My blood was still spilled on the concrete. I was drenched in it. It wet the side of my pants and shirt as if someone dipped me in a large bucket of red paint.

When I got back to the house, it was ten minutes to midnight. I had walked around the block a few times. Part of me was afraid to confront Nash or Tom about the angels. I think I was afraid they wouldn't have a good enough explanation, and I would have to live with the fact that I made innocent angels fall.

I searched for Nash in the living room, kitchen, and library. I walked out onto the library balcony and looked over the training field.

There were plenty more rooms Nash could be in, but I was so tired. I decided to end my search. I figured it would be better to ask him in the morning with a clear head after a good night's rest.

Hopefully my guilt would be assuaged tomorrow.

Lucifer might be lying. Nash would probably tell me that all the angels we had targeted were pointed out by her. Then, we could at least have a real discussion about what Lucifer was really up to and what we were going to do about it.

I stepped around the corner. My skin leapt. A gray t-shirt came into view.

Tom stood in front of me, a large book in his hands. "What happened to you?" He looked down at my bloody clothes.

"I got into a knife fight," I said.

"You're joking."

"Nope. Listen. Bob's up to something."

"Yeah. You said that."

"No. You don't understand. I followed him through the portal. He talked to this demon. He's the Redeemer, and I think he wants Nash dead."

Tom had his mouth open like he was trying to catch flies.

"Are you going to say anything?"

"I don't know what to say."

"Say, you'll talk to Nash. He'll hate that I followed Bob, but I had to. I had to know what he was up to."

"Okay," Tom said.

"There was something else I wanted to…" I touched my temple. My head throbbed. "Never mind."

"I'll talk to him."

"Good," I said. "As soon as you see him?"

Tom nodded. "Yeah. Let me handle it. You look like hell."

"Why? Is my skin gray?"

"Your hair is matted in blood." I pulled the ends of my hair in front of my face. The dyed ends were crusted in a darker shade of red.

I ducked Tom and pulled myself upstairs. I threw my bloodied clothes in the hamper in the bathroom and let the water warm in the shower. The blood came off my body in swirls of water down the drain.

Bob was the Redeemer. He did this to me. He convinced my mother to perform the spell on me. But why? I was part of his plan that included demons, fallen angels, and Nash's murder.

The side where the demon twisted the knife was smooth and unmarred. I ran my hand over the skin. No pain. But I was in pain. *What or who had healed me?*

I wrapped myself in a bathrobe and didn't bother changing into my pajamas. I slipped under the covers and drifted into a fitful, nightmare-fueled slumber.

THE floor was warm beneath my feet. The room was white without lines or shadows and seemed to go on into infinity whether I looked up, down, or on either side.

I looked over my shoulder.

"Hello, young heretic."

In front of me stood Michael, the Archangel. I reached for my sword, but it wasn't at my side. Instead, I wore a white dress that trailed to the floor and not the bathrobe I fell asleep in.

"This is a dream," I said.

"No. I've come to visit you in *here*." Michael tapped the side of his head.

"That's not possible."

"It is once you've tasted angel blood."

I narrowed my eyes at him. I drank angel blood like witches drink demon blood. The spell turned me into a monster, but it also gave me powers I didn't understand. "That's why you want to kill me."

"You need to go where you belong. I didn't ask for anyone to do this to you. But what you are, what you do is a sin. It's vile."

"And you have to stop me or you'll fall."

Michael nodded his head slowly.

"Is that what God told you to do?"

Laughter came from behind me.

I turned around. The blue eyes of my parents' murderer disarmed me. I screamed and rushed him, beating my hands against his chest, touching his bare, exposed arms, but he wouldn't fall.

I clenched my teeth and continued to beat him until he grabbed my wrists and threw me off him.

My body hit the floor, but it didn't hurt. I stood. "You monster."

"What are you doing here?" Michael asked.

"Dispelling your lies, Michael," Raphael said.

Michael's mouth was a hard line.

"Like the one you tell—"

"Something's wrong with you," Michael said. "Something's been wrong with you since the Fall."

"That's what you'd have the others believe, isn't it? Tell her what really happened to her parents," Raphael shouted. "Tell her where they are now."

What did he mean? He killed my parents. I saw it with my own eyes.

Uriel, Raguel, and Phanuel joined Michael. They appeared from mist and became solid.

Standing with Raphael were Sariel and Gabriel.

The Seven Archangels of Heaven. I recognized them from the books in Nash's library. Each carried their weapon.

Uriel held a flaming, blue broadsword. Raguel gripped chains attached to large, silver plates that balanced a collection of silver spiked orbs. Phanuel carried a long, glowing staff with a silver cross at the top. Sariel had a silver shield as tall as she was. Gabriel held his silver trumpet.

Uriel flew at Raphael, but Sariel stepped in front of him, blocking Uriel's blow with her shield. Sariel's armor shone. The blade sparked off her shield.

Phanuel and Raguel rushed forward. Phanuel ran at Raphael, and their silver staffs met. Raguel swung his silver plates attached to long chains.

Sariel ducked as one of the plates flew for her head. Michael drew his broadsword.

Four against three.

They struggled.

Michael bore his blade down on Raphael. Sariel deflected Uriel and Phanuel's blows with her shield, turning in time to stop Raguel's attack. The plates glanced off the shield and flew across the white room.

I ducked as the plates came at me.

"If I break you in here," Michael said. "You'll never be the same."

"Break my mind," Raphael said, "then meet me on the battlefield, and I'll break your body."

Michael shoved, and Raphael stumbled back.

Raphael let out a curse.

Angels could curse like sailors.

He attacked Michael, dealing a barrage of blows. He fought like a madman with no proper form. Michael leapt back. It was like playing chess with someone who didn't know the game. You think its going to be easy, but it's the unknowing player that you can't read.

Raphael shouted, beating Michael's chest plate with his staff. Phanuel launched forward, but Raphael swung his staff, causing Phanuel to block his attack.

Raphael plowed into Phanuel, knocking him to the ground. He turned and met Michael's broadsword.

Michael twisted and spun, his sword coming down on Raphael's staff. They both ducked as Raguel's plate flew over their heads.

Gabriel pressed his lips to his horn and blew. We knelt to the ground and covered our ears, the sound didn't seem to effect Gabriel. But the pain was in our heads. He couldn't hurt us in a dream just like I couldn't make Raphael fall. The pain felt so real. Could it hurt our *minds*?

I stood. The angels settled back to their sides. Sariel and Gabriel with Raphael. Uriel, Raguel, and Phanuel with Michael.

Raphael glared at Michael.

"Tell her!" Raphael's mouth twisted in a grimace.

"You are broken," Michael said. "You should have fallen a long time ago."

"I'm not your puppet, Michael," Raphael said.

"And I'm not yours." I stepped up to him. "I can't make you fall here. That means you can't hurt me either. If you come after me, I'll light your feathers up so fast, it'll make your head spin. I'm tired of the lies. I'm a threat to each one of you, and I want answers. I want answers right now!"

The pain exploded from me. The force blasted the angels back, lost in the endless, white room.

My head was against the pillow as I stared up at my bedroom ceiling. I was standing only a moment ago. I touched Raphael. I had my parents' murderer in my grasp.

The world is a bugle, and its music screams.

"Damn it." I sat up in bed and threw my pillow across the room.

Twenty four

I yawned and stretched in bed then glanced over at the clock. It was eleven in the morning. I hadn't planned to sleep in, but I tossed for hours before I could sleep without being awakened by a bad dream.

I pulled on a fresh shirt and slipped on my shoes. I had to find Nash. I couldn't wait any longer to ask him about the angels.

As I walked down the hall, voices echoed from downstairs.

At the foot of the stairs Nash talked with Adriel. Kiran leaned against one of the columns in the foyer next to Adrianna. Tom faced Adriel and Nash with his back to me. Chandra stood in the corner with her arms folded.

"I'm not going," Adriel said. "It's a barbaric ritual, and I won't be a part of it."

"You have to," Nash said. "Everyone in the Outer Region must go."

"What's happening?" I asked.

Nash and Adriel stopped talking and looked up at me.

"We're getting a new Chancellor," Adrianna said.

I climbed down the stairs to join them. "What happened to the old one?"

"He was tossed into the Pit." Tom turned his head to look at me.

"What did he do?" I asked.

Tom shrugged and turned away again.

I sighed. Now wasn't the best time to bring up our angel hunting strategy. Whatever they were talking about sounded like a big deal, but I wanted to get this out on the table.

"Nash, I need to talk to you," I said.

"Not now, Lia. We do this first. We can talk as soon as we get back." His voice was dismissive. He was probably still angry about yesterday when I unceremoniously broke it off with him. Maybe *I* should be giving *him* space.

I folded my arms. "So, we're all going where?" I asked.

"You don't have to go," Nash said. "You are human. You don't belong to Lucifer."

"Certainly feels that way sometimes," I said.

"We'll be back after noon," Nash said.

I needed to hear that we hadn't attacked innocent angels on purpose. But I also wanted to know what was going on. What were we going to see that had Adriel so upset?

"Wait," I said. "I'll go."

"You are not going to want to do that," Kiran said.

"Why not?" I asked.

"It can get gruesome," Adrianna said.

I glanced over at Adriel. "I've seen the Angel District. I can't imagine it's much worse than that."

I had been to the Circles too, but I wasn't prepared to tell them that yet.

"Get ready to eat those words," Tom said.

My hand gripped the handle of the passenger side door when I noticed Adriel, Chandra, Adrianna, and Kiran getting into another car. Kiran got into the driver's seat.

Had I known we were taking another car, I would have chosen to ride with Kiran, but my hand was on Nash's door handle. It would look awkward if I switched cars. Instead, I opened the door to the back seat and slipped in as Tom sat down across from me.

He eyed me quizzically.

Nash slammed his door shut and started the engine.

I was thankful he didn't look back at me, but I saw his eyes narrow in the mirror as he backed the car out of the driveway.

That would have been the perfect time to ask them about what Lucifer said, but awkwardness lingered in the air and made it difficult for me to speak. We rode in silence.

Nash stopped the car abruptly, and the seatbelt cut into my chest as the car jolted to a halt.

We were at the Pit.

"They're doing it here?" I asked. Demons don't want to be anywhere near the Pit.

"It has to be done here," Nash said.

A large crowd of people, well, demons, gathered several yards away from the Pit. They talked amongst themselves. Nash weaved through the crowd, and Tom and I followed him until we met up with the others.

Four men, carrying a podium, emerged from the leafless trees. Lucifer walked behind them. She wore her blood red judge's robe with red stiletto heels.

The men set the podium down before the crowd, and Lucifer stood behind it. The crowd had quieted as they waited for Lucifer to take her place.

I recalled the trial and the heckling and laughter that issued from the crowd. There was none of that here.

They turned their heads toward the trees.

A figure walked from among them. Her skin was pallid, her featherless wings hung from her back, and she wore nothing but an iron collar.

The first angel I made fall—Andromeda.

"Are you ready?" Lucifer asked.

Andromeda looked up at her. "I am, Morning Star."

"What is she doing?" I glanced over at Nash. "She's an angel. She hates Lucifer."

Nash was silent.

"She's a fallen angel," Kiran said. "She wishes for her soul to be demonized."

I shook my head. There was no way Andromeda had agreed to this. Just a day ago, she screamed at Adriel for being a traitor. So much hate smoldered in her eyes, I thought it would reach out and smother me. Now, she wanted her soul to be demonized?

Two men stood on either side of Andromeda. The men held hacksaws, made of what I was certain was Arcadian Steel. Each man grabbed a hold of one of Andromeda's featherless wings and pulled. The wings fanned out. In unison, they placed their hacksaws where the wings grew from the shoulder blades. They began to cut.

Dark blood dripped down Andromeda's body as the men sawed. Her chest pounded as if the air was forced out of her lungs. A loud scream escaped her lips, and tears squeezed from her eyes. Andromeda knelt to the ground. The men bent with her and continued to saw as she wailed.

I felt rustling behind me. I turned. Adriel weaved his way through the crowd and away from the horrid scene.

Another scream assaulted my ears. I wanted to go with him, but I hesitated too long to catch up with him. Nash would surely follow me if I left, and I didn't want him to get into any trouble for leaving.

Instead, I closed my eyes until the screams stopped.

When I opened them, Andromeda knelt in her own blood. The bones of her wings lay like rotting branches beside her.

Demons rushed in from the crowd and smeared her face, chest, and arms with her own blood until she was covered.

"Do you accept this?" Lucifer asked.

Andromeda lifted her head. "Yes," she said.

Andromeda gathered up her wings and stood. She turned around, and the crowd parted to allow her passage. She approached the Pit.

I covered my mouth with my hands. At first, I was afraid she might jump, but Andromeda stopped at the edge. She held her detached wings over the abyss.

She stood for a long moment. *Is that regret in her eyes? No, it's determination.* She let them drop. The bones fell from her arms, and she turned back to the crowd.

She started to walk, but struggled as she tried, as if the bones of her body were breaking. Something moved under the skin, crunching and crackling.

Andromeda's body began to change. Her breasts flattened against her chest until it looked like a man's, her face elongated and began to grow thick hair, something ropey grew from her tailbone, and her feet transformed into scaled bird-like talons.

The iron collar snapped as Andromeda's neck grew to accommodate the large mule-like head. She stopped in front of Lucifer and knelt.

The air was dead.

Lucifer looked down at Andromeda. "You're the new Chancellor now," she said. "What is your name, demon?"

Andromeda's once light, high-pitched voice came out in a deep echo. "Adramelech."

Twenty five

LUCIFER left with her servants, carrying the large podium after her. Adramelech followed behind her. Her long tail lashed out like a whip cutting through the air.

I stared after her. "Why would she do that?"

Adrianna put her hand on my shoulder. "Maybe she thought it would be better than being in the Angel District."

"They turned her into a monster," I said.

I clenched my teeth and turned to Nash. "She wasn't one of them."

"Let's get out of here." Tom took my arm and walked with me over to Kiran's car.

I kept my head down as we drove back to the house.

The car door slammed. Nash made his way toward the house.

I rushed out of Kiran's car.

"Who does he think he is?" Nash asked. "He could have gotten us all tossed into the Pit."

Nash yanked open the front door.

I followed behind him.

Adriel sat on the steps inside. Nash approached him.

"Stand up!" Nash said.

Adriel stood, standing chest to chest with Nash.

"You might not like it," Nash said, "but you're one of us now. You're not special. You're not an angel. When we have to look, you have to look."

"I will never be one of you," Adriel said. "You've let go of hope. You're a maggot. Down here with all the other maggots, watching displays of cruelty and enjoying it."

Nash balled his hand into a fist and punched Adriel square in the jaw.

Adriel struggled back, catching himself on one of the marble steps. He stood with all the grace of a tightrope walker and swung back at Nash.

In a series of blows and dodges, Adriel found himself against the wall, his fists raised and knuckles bruised.

Adriel moved his head to the side, and Nash missed him by mere inches. A crack ran through the plaster where Nash's fist hit the wall. Nash's knuckles were bloodied.

Adriel pushed him into the center of the room and rushed at him with another punch to the face.

"Stop it!" I yelled. I stepped in between them.

They were forced apart, their backs hitting opposite walls. Larger cracks patterned the plaster.

Nash and Adriel, on their hands and knees, struggled for breath after the wind had been knocked out of them.

Nash was the first to get to his feet. He looked over at Adriel and then at me. His gaze lingered on me for a long moment. Then, he turned and stormed out the front door.

I knelt beside Adriel and offered him my hand. We stood up together. "I'm sorry," I said. "You were being idiots."

"The only idiot I see is him." Chandra leaned against one of the columns with her arms folded, watching Adriel. "Lucifer could have thrown you in the Pit, you know that? You really think she missed a six-foot fallen angel leaving her new chancellor's coronation?"

Adriel hung his head. "It was disgusting. I couldn't look at it."

"You should have seen her after she tossed her wings into the Pit," Adrianna said. "I don't think I could live with a face like that."

Adriel turned away from me and marched down the hall. The backdoor slammed, and I shot a look of disappointment toward Adrianna.

"Sorry," she said.

I looked around the room. "Where'd Tom go?"

Chandra pointed down the hall.

I left them in the foyer and opened the door to the library. Tom read at the desk, disappearing into another book.

I stood across from him and slammed my hands on the desk. "I need answers."

Tom closed the book and sighed. "I thought I'd come here until things calmed down."

"How did Nash know which angels were in Raphael's army?" I asked.

Tom hesitated. His nostrils flared. "It wasn't a clean process."

"How did he know?"

"We determined it based on a series of intel," Tom said.

"What intel?"

"We used . . . Jinni."

I narrowed my eyes. Jinni? Nash was distrustful of Jinni. Why would he use them to help him find out which angels to hunt?

"Why are you asking me this?" Tom stood. His fingertips pressed into the desk.

"Because you got it wrong. Andromeda wasn't working for Raphael. And now, she's turned into that thing. How could you be so reckless?"

"It was the best way," he said. "The only way we had. Angels weren't just going to point Raphael's followers out to us. They wouldn't talk to us. Most of them wouldn't know anyway, and if they found out about you, they would have tried to kill you just like Michael is trying to do."

I folded my arms. "What's going on between Nash and Adriel?"

He paused.

"Tom!"

"They were . . . *born* at the same time."

"So, they're brothers?"

"Yes, they are from the same order of angels," he said.

So, Nash was Seraphim.

"How did Nash get down here?" I asked.

Tom pressed his lips together.

"Tom?" I urged.

"He was part of the original Fall."

The original Fall. That was when the angels battled in Heaven. The first time they rebelled against God.

"He fell with Lucifer?"

"Yes."

"Where is Nash now?" I asked.

Tom looked at me. "He's with her."

My hands left the table as if it was a hot stove. I marched out the library and to the front door. I didn't notice if anyone was at the landing. I walked outside and ran toward Lucifer's tower.

Adrenaline coursed through my veins.

I rushed through the sliding doors and passed the secretary.

Her eyes went wide. "You need an appoint…"

I marched straight to the elevator, reached into my pocket, and jabbed the silver key into the hole. The elevator lurched up, and my stomach went with it. My teeth clenched.

The door to Lucifer's office was partly ajar. I was ready to march in and demand to know what was going on when I saw something through the crack in the door that made me stop in my tracks.

Nash sat in the chair opposite Lucifer. He got up and walked over to her. She stood. He whispered something in her ear.

Then, he kissed her!

She crawled backward onto the desk. Nash kept his lips locked on hers as he remained glued to her body.

I turned away and flattened my back against the wall. I bit down on my knuckle as I heard paper rustle in the air, and glass hit the floor. I tore myself away from the wall and hurried down the hallway. I jabbed at the button by the elevator door.

I rocked from side to side. The doors couldn't open quickly enough. I wanted nothing more than to be in my bedroom and screaming into a pillow.

A chime sounded, and the doors opened. I stepped inside.

My breath came in short gasps. I couldn't get enough air into my lungs. I pressed the button to the first floor, and the door closed.

My hands found the back railing of the elevator and encircled it as I descended. Tears dripped off my chin and into my mouth as I continued to gasp for air.

That wasn't the kiss of a new relationship. That was the kiss of two people who had been together for a long time.

AS I left the elevator and walked to the sliding doors, I could hear the secretary saying something, but the meaning of her words was lost in my jumbled brain.

The stale, still air did not help me to breathe more deeply. I stopped in the middle of the parking lot and told myself to breathe until finally, with a sharp intake of breath, the panic was over.

I put my hands over my face and wiped at the tears.

I couldn't go back to Nash's house.

He had lied to me. He *was lying* to me.

I turned the corner and walked down the alleyway. I pressed my back against the brick wall and slumped to the ground.

I didn't care about anything. I didn't care if Sam and Delilah found me again or some other demon hell-bent on hijacking my body. Let them come. I'll run them through with my dagger.

The back of my head hit the brick wall. I wanted blood on my hands, a lot of it.

What was I going to do? Lucifer wanted Heaven and Hell for herself. That's why she was having me attack the angels. This had nothing to do with Raphael's plan. They were probably on the same side.

Adriel and Nash were brothers.

Nash was in bed with the enemy.

I didn't know who to trust anymore.

I was suffocating in this place. If I wanted the truth, I needed to find it on my own. I needed to discover more about the strange powers I had, and if my father was alive. I wasn't going to find him in Sheol. Maybe he knew something about all this. Maybe he could help me.

"You're crying." Caiduc knelt across from me. He looked at me with his head cocked to the side.

"Yes." A short burst of laughter followed my voice like an unwelcomed guest.

"Why?" he asked. This time, he didn't sound like he was studying me. His voice was soft, concerned.

"Because I can't trust anyone." I swallowed and tasted salt at the back of my throat.

Caiduc's branch-like arm reached out to me, and he touched my shoulder.

I was being comforted by a Jinn, one that I thought had come to ruin me. But I was wrong about everything.

I looked down at my hands. There was power there, and there was power inside me, power I didn't know how to harness, but power that could save me. The only person I could trust now was myself.

"Caiduc."

"Yes," he said.

"Can you take me somewhere?" I asked.

"Anywhere you wish."

seven princes

OB swung the brass knocker.

The door opened.

"Bub." Her voice was honey.

"Ashmedai." Bob smiled.

Ash's eyes smiled back at Bob. They were deep-set, rich brown like chocolate. Black curls framed her face. He was drawn to her lush, red lips and the ample bosom that was practically spilling out of her dress.

"Come in, you old dog." Her voice was smooth like aged wine.

Bob stepped into the house. The walls were trimmed in gold. Crystal chandeliers hung from the ceiling. Velvet, red curtains warmed the windows.

One could never have enough gold, crystal, and velvet. Bob grinned like a child ready to ride the Ferris Wheel.

"You like it." Ash was the only woman in Sheol who could look into his eyes without gazing up. She could change that if she wanted to, but she knew *he* didn't want her to.

"I've saved a bottle for you." Ash reached into the wine cabinet and pulled out a bottle of Cabernet Sauvignon. "I've waited to taste this for three hundred years."

"I don't know how you had the patience." Bob sat at the table covered with a silk cloth. The chair was plush and framed in twists of gold. On the table, two wine glasses waited to be filled.

Ash poured the wine.

Bob swished the wine in his glass and brought it up to his nose. "Mmm." The wine had notes of vanilla, black pepper, and cherry.

As Ash moved to sit in the chair opposite him, Bob watched her pale leg slip from the slit in her long, red dress.

Ash caught his eyes. "What do I have to do to keep your eyes on my face?" she asked.

"I want my eyes everywhere." A devilish smile crept across Bob's face.

"You glutton." Ash rested her face on her hands. "How about this?" Her eyes changed from chocolate brown to sea green with gold creeping around the pupils.

"So, pretty, but you know I didn't just come here for the company," Bob said, "engaging as it may be."

"Of course." A smile snaked across Ash's lips. "Our army is safe," Ash said. "Your fallen friend couldn't dispense with them all."

"You talked to Belphegor?"

"Bell's harder to talk to than a wall. He won't even look at me. Can you imagine?"

"I cannot."

Ash took a sip of her wine.

"We have to make sure he's on our side," Bob said.

"I don't even know what he likes. I worked all my charms." Her bosom swelled beneath her dress.

Ash really did love herself. So much so, she even tried to seduce the splinters of herself. Bob was one of those fragments, made into an individual by Lucifer's fractured soul.

"And the others?"

"I met with Leviathan. They won't be a problem. They want what everyone else has. They helped us get the Balban."

"But not Mammon."

"I can't talk to Mammon, Bub. Mammon hoards pretty things. He would want to keep me forever, and how could I refuse such a willing participant."

Only one name did not cross Lust's lips. *Satan*. Wrath. Lucifer had him locked up tight in the Ninth Circle. But all would be in place soon. Bob needed to be patient, something he didn't like being.

Lucifer would find out shortly. Nothing was worse to Lucifer than treachery. Worse still was the snake that ate itself.

Ash grabbed Bob's tie and pulled him until he leaned over the table, his face close to hers. "We are the same in our desires. We both can't get enough." Her voice was fire on air, trails of smoke intoxicating him.

"Oh, dear, you lust for one thing and one thing only. I want *everything*." He said the last word through his teeth and crushed his lips against hers.

excerpt

If you enjoyed
THE SEVEN ARCHANGELS OF HEAVEN,
look out for

THE SEVEN PRINCES OF HELL

Book Three of the Arcadian Steel Sequence

By L. M. Peralta

the seven
princes of hell

THE ARCADIAN STEEL SEQUENCE

BOOK THREE

L. M. PERALTA

prologue

1 UCIFER lifted the curtain and gazed out the window above the clouds. Light emitted from the tear in the sky, a tear the angels made. Angels in Hell. Her kingdom. Raphael had no right. The angels would return, but this time Lucifer and her army would have a weapon that not even Michael could resist.

Lucifer had a prisoner, a prisoner Michael had searched out for centuries. She had kept him for a long time down in the bowels of Hell.

She found him scribbling notes in a cave, hiding because he could not Veil himself. Poor creature. Such an abomination.

She smiled. Michael would be pacing Heaven's pearly gates right now, wondering what she wanted with the one-winged angel, the one he so despised.

She let the curtain fall. Darkness encased the room, but a lamp pushed the darkness away, making the shadows fade in its glow.

She intended to win this war, and if it costs Heaven a few angels, that was no skin off her back.

Michael issued the decree, banishing her to Hell, a place that didn't yet exist. He was all too happy to carry out the *order*. All the angels loved Lucifer. She had been beautiful and strong, the strongest light in Heaven.

But she made Hell work. Pride would never let her lose. Her tongue was as silver as her armor when she fell, and she used it to embolden the angels who fell beside her.

She separated her soul into seven distinct personalities: Pride, Gluttony, Greed, Lust, Sloth, Envy, and Wrath. *The Seven Princes of Hell.*

She brought fire and ice to the hellish Circles. Sheol was a barren wasteland until she molded it from the darkness. She knew ways of tormenting human souls and manipulating desires.

She dared Michael to come. She would be ready.

Lucifer's heels clicked along the floor as she paced the room. The blackened bones, which had once displayed beautiful, white feathers, were tucked against her back. She stopped and observed the man sitting in the chair before her.

His back was turned. Stacks of books rose in front him. A single white feathered wing graced one side of his back. On the other side was a stump.

The walls were covered in drawings of the Staff, the only weapon that could kill angels. Scribbled notes surrounded the drawings. Gibberish.

Lucifer approached the table.

The angel's back muscles tensed as her voice tickled his ear. "Is it finished?"

His hand gripped protectively around the Staff. Etched into the weapon was a story from long ago when angels mated with humans. "What will you do with it?" he asked.

"I will use it for its purpose."

"To kill him?"

"Perhaps."

"He'll hunt me down, you know," the one-winged angel said. "Especially after he hears I helped you." His voice trembled like a dried leaf, threatened by the wind to lose its place on the tree.

Lucifer placed her hands on his shoulders and pressed them down into a more relaxed position. "If he wants you, my skilled friend, he'll have to go through me."

"You don't mean that. You will cast me out now that I am no use to you." The one-winged angel lowered his head.

Why did he sound so frightened? She hadn't meant to scare him. Maybe it was the way her voice sometimes overlapped itself with a deeper one.

That was the consequence of splitting yourself into seven. Fragments were left inside her like tiny pieces of glass that the broom missed.

"Why would I lie to you?" Lucifer tried to keep the deeper voice back.

"Because you lie to everyone. I don't think you mean to anymore. You just do."

Lucifer raked her long fingernails along his shoulders. "That bastard tossed me out of my own home. You can guarantee I want that Staff deep in his heart. He's the greatest liar of us all."

One

THE demon lunged at me.

I wrenched a cushion from the sofa. The blade sank into the fabric and the fluffy bowels.

Caiduc cowered behind a folding screen.

The Jinn was good for nothing in a fight. He was afraid. Something I didn't understand since his true form was impervious, right? So, why was he frightened of everything that moved?

I tossed the pillow aside and reached for my dagger. The room looked ransacked.

Fragments of glass from the vase I threw at the demon littered floor. The television screen was cracked when I was thrown against it. Tufts of pillow guts snowed down.

Who had broken the lamp?

This was *not* where I asked Caiduc to bring me.

The demon grinned at me with his pointed, yellow teeth. He had blotches of flaky, burnt skin. The rest of him looked human.

He rushed me.

Damn it.

He had a kitchen knife. I had a dagger of Arcadian Steel.

Our blades met. His cracked in two.

The blade clattered to the floor. The handle was still in the demon's grasp. His face fell.

I rammed my dagger into his shoulder. Dark blood oozed over my hand. The blood was hot and thicker than a human's.

It covered my hand like gummy tar. *Gross.*

"Witch." He ground his teeth.

"Cockroach." I twisted the dagger.

Pain rode up my side. The demon brought his fist into me again. I winced.

I yanked my dagger out of his shoulder, ready to give him a mortal wound, but he punched me again. I doubled over.

This was *not* going well.

I looked up.

A clawed hand swiped across my cheek. The side of my face burned. Drops of red blood spattered the floor.

Shit!

How would I explain this one to Nash and Adriel?

The demon dove at me again.

I wouldn't have to do any explaining if I were dead. No, I still might. Nash would march into the Circles and pull me out just to tell me how stupid I was.

I threw myself to the floor, and the demon narrowly missed me. Holding my side, I sank my dagger into his foot. Blood sprayed my face.

The demon howled.

Wasn't expecting that one, huh, buddy?

I rolled onto my back and stood, trying to straighten myself despite the pain in my side. Was his hand made of brick?

I could see more of him now. His eyes were solid red. His head was covered in burnt skin that couldn't keep the blood in.

What had he been doing in this house? Did he *live* here?

But now was no time for a demon census report.

The demon picked up a golden Buddha and swung it at me. I stepped back, and the back of my leg hit the coffee table. I fell onto the glass surface.

Before I knew what was happening, the demon was on top of me. The Buddha clenched in his hand.

My dagger had fallen under the glass table, out of my reach.

The demon raised the Buddha like he was playing Whac-A-Mole.

Shit! Shit! Shit!

A crack ran through the glass table. My mind burned. I slammed my fist onto the surface.

The glass shattered.

I hit the floor. It felt like I had pebbles under my back. The demon fell with me, but I barely noticed his weight.

My hand gripped the dagger. He swung the Buddha toward my head, but I was faster. I plunged my blade into his neck.

"Go back to Hell!" I screamed.

His mouth morphed into a circle. The Buddha fell from his hand.

I withdrew my dagger. Blood spurted from his wound. He was falling on top of me, but he disappeared to dust before the descent.

I laid on the floor, my arms stretched out. A burst of laughter erupted from my lungs. It hurt my side to laugh.

I hoped all my ribs were intact. I sat up, which wasn't easy to do.

Caiduc stood before me, scratching his wrist.

"Well, you weren't any help," I said.

"You told me not to," he said.

"I told you not to transport me. Didn't mean I couldn't use your help. Are you feeling okay?"

"Yes." Caiduc's eyes darted.

My lips pursed into a frown.

Caiduc touched the string of wooden beads dangling from his ear.

"Let's go," I said. "I have no idea where you've brought us."

I tried to stand, but pain flared up my side. "Some help."

Caiduc approached me with his hands held to his chest. He gingerly offered one to me.

I took his branchy hand in mine and used his weight as leverage to hoist myself up. I brushed the crumbles of glass from my back.

"You fought well," Caiduc said. "You are getting better."

Did he want me to get better? Was that why he hadn't stepped in with his mysterious Jinni magic? Or was it because he didn't want me to see what he could do? Maybe that would be against Jinni code or something.

"At least I didn't get myself stabbed this time." When that demon stabbed me back in Sheol, I would have died if someone hadn't come and healed me.

I stepped over the cushions, the pillows, and the broken glass. Tearing open the front door, I walked out into the street. Rain misted the cobblestone road.

I missed the rain.

The white face of the tower peeked from the trees blanketing the hill. *Fengdu Ghost City*.

"Huh, this is the right place. You were close, Caiduc."

I followed the road. Despite the misty rain, people explored the city. Tour guides spoke over loud speakers. Tourists carried umbrellas and backpacks.

Trying to make myself inconspicuous, I joined a group of tourists as I moved through the city. We climbed the steps lined with devil sculptures. Splotches of green stained the statues.

After we went over the bridge, I separated myself from the crowd. The green hills overlapped each other in the distance. Water met the rocky base of the island.

Past the river was a tiered tower with red columns and eaves that curled up at their points.

This place was beautiful.

Without Adriel to guide me, I became lost in the twists and turns of the streets. Night fell before I found a familiar street and followed it. Caiduc trailed behind me.

"Why did you attack that demon?" Caiduc asked.

"Because he's a demon."

"But your friends are demons."

"That's different," I said. "My friends don't possess people. They don't make people do bad things."

"They did though. They all had contracts with Lucifer. That's why they are demons."

"Look, I don't want to talk to you about morality."

"Is that because it confuses you?" he asked.

"No, it's because I'm not Tom. I don't like talking for the sake of it."

The small shop sat among the clusters of buildings at the base of the green hill. Its timber beams were straight and narrow. The corners of the roof curved up to the sky. The sign above the door read: *Miss Jiao's Tea House.*

"This is it," I said.

Mist curled through the dark streets. The cobblestone walkway was damp from the rain. Clouds covered the moon and stars, and streetlamps let off a cold, blue glow.

Caiduc stood beside me with his hands clasped. "Do I have to go in?" His fingers trembled.

"Not if you don't want to."

"I won't then." Caiduc disappeared.

Demons were one thing, but I wondered what would make a Jinn so afraid of a small woman like Jiao. She was no taller than four eleven, and her slim frame was far from imposing.

I opened the door to the tea house. The bell chimed above the door. "Hello?"

Low tables surrounded by sitting mats were evenly spaced on the tiled floor. Wooden columns trimmed in gold held up the recessed ceiling. Lanterns with red tassels hung from every fourth ceiling tile.

A cherry blossom grew in the center of the room. It wasn't there the first time I visited. The tree was in full bloom. Pink flowers littered the floor around it.

I walked up to the tree and cradled a delicate, pink flower.

"Don't touch that!"

I jumped.

An old woman stepped from behind the folding wall. She carried a tea kettle. She wore a black robe with a thick, red band around her waist. She looked frail. Her brown skin was thin and wrinkled. Her hair was as white as snow and wispy like the feathers of a bird.

"I'm sorry. I'm looking for Jiao."

She glanced up at me. "You're the girl who came with Adriel."

"That's right." *How did she know that?* She wasn't here when I came with Adriel. Maybe she watched us from that folding screen in the back.

"What happened to you?"

I touched my cheek. The blood had dried. "It's nothing. Is Jiao here?"

The old woman smirked. She set the tea kettle down on one of the low tables. "Sit," she said.

I looked around before approaching the table. Maybe this was Jiao's grandmother or maybe her great-grandmother. I sat at the table with her as she poured the tea.

"Thank you." I reached for the cup.

She slapped my hand away. "Do you want to be a babe in arms again?"

I raised my eyebrows. "I'm sorry I thought..."

"You assumed," the old woman said. She lifted the tea cup and took a long sip from it.

My eyes widened.

The wrinkles on her face disappeared like someone pulled her skin tight. Her gray hair darkened to a rich, glossy black. Her eyes brightened, and her frail body grew less bony. Her back straightened. Her lips became plumper.

"Jiao?" I asked.

"You think I would let some old woman take over my tea house?"

"But you're..."

"If you call me old, I just might force some of this tea down your throat. You'll be a third trimester fetus on the floor before you can blink." The bite in her tone told me not to ask any questions. It also told me something stressed her out more than my sudden appearance.

"I need your help," I said.

Jiao raised an eyebrow before narrowing her eyes. "Adriel has you thinking I do favors?"

"I need to find my father. Well, both my fathers actually..."

Jiao raised an eyebrow.

"...and my mom, my adoptive mom."

"And I'm assuming your *other* father adopted you."

I nodded. "Can you find them for me?"

"Well, that's an awful lot of people that went missing on you."

"My mom and dad died."

Jiao shook her head. "Can't find dead people," she said. "Unless you want to find out where they're buried."

"You can't find out where they . . . went?"

"Hell no," Jiao said. "What kind of teas do you think I'm brewing? You don't mess with the afterlife. *I* don't mess with the afterlife." She folded her arms. I didn't know if she was trying to convince me or herself.

"But my dad, my bio-dad I mean, he's not dead. He's alive somewhere. I just don't know where he is."

"I can't find people without something they have touched."

"But I don't have anything. I never knew him."

"Well, you're out of luck," Jiao said. "It's not like Google. You're going to need more than a name. Speaking of, have you tried Google yet?"

I doubted an internet search would be of much help. All I *had* was a name. It wouldn't be as easy as Jiao was making it out to be. Besides after what my bio-mom said about him wanting to get away from her, maybe he changed his name.

"You should probably start there before you start messing with magic," Jiao said.

Magic. Witchcraft. What if Adrianna was right?

"I need to ask you something."

Jiao sipped her tea, and the circles under her eyes diminished. She had lost fifty maybe sixty years in a matter of minutes. She looked like the twenty-something college girl I thought she was when I'd first met her.

"I have this power," I said. "I can move people with my mind."

"What do you mean?"

"I can toss them against walls, throw them backward. When I was sixteen, I threw myself from a burning car. I don't know how I'm doing it. I think I might be a witch."

Jiao paused and put her cup down. "Witches need incantations and herbs. What you are doing isn't witchcraft."

"Then what is it?"

Jiao shook her head. "Witchcraft is something that is taught. Did anyone ever teach you?"

"No."

"Did you ever drink demon blood?"

"No." I drank angel blood. Should I tell her that?

"Then, what you are doing is something else entirely. Give me your hands."

"What are you going to do?"

"I'm going to bite your fingers off." Jaio chomped her teeth. My skin jumped.

She rolled her eyes. "I'm just going to take a look."

I placed my hands across the table. Jiao clasped them in hers and closed her eyes. She had a bored look like she was leafing through a magazine in the waiting room of a doctor's office. But something changed. A pained expression flashed across her face. She released my hands.

"What? What did you see?"

"What are you?" she hissed. "You stole an angel's grace?"

I shook my head. "I don't know what you're talking about."

"Get out!" she screamed. "Get out now!"

I stood up, and she pushed me out the door.

Two

RAIN fell outside Miss Jiao's Tea House. It felt good on my skin even though I had been tossed out into it. The answers I needed weren't here. I would never find my father, and if my powers didn't come from witchcraft, where did they come from?

You drank angel blood. That had to be the origin of my powers. But something seemed so wrong about it. That's why I hesitated to tell Jiao. And now that she knew, she was afraid of me or angry at me or both.

I had done worse things than drink angel blood. I made angels fall, angels that weren't working for Raphael.

Mom and Dad. Where were they? Had they gone to Heaven? How could I know for sure? Wherever they were, that's where I wanted to be, even if it meant an eternity in Sheol. I would make it work.

I couldn't imagine them being assigned to any of the Circles. They were good people.

I shook my head. I changed my contract. I didn't have a choice on where I would be going.

Caiduc looked up at me. "Where to?"

"Huh?"

"Where do you want to go?"

Home. "Bring me back to Sheol," I said. "I should have never come here."

Caiduc's branchy fingers touched my arm.

The flash was blinding. Water crashed around me.

I blinked until my vision came back into focus. I was in my room at Nash's place with its cold, unwelcoming hospital-white walls and the chill that wouldn't leave the air.

Glancing around the room, I discovered Caiduc gone. Maybe he could sense I needed a moment alone with my thoughts. But no matter what I needed, I didn't want to be alone.

So many questions were left unanswered. How could I know I was doing the right thing if I didn't know enough?

I pulled a sweater on. I reached for the door.

Wait.

That nasty cut on my cheek.

I couldn't walk downstairs like this. Nash would see the cut, and I wouldn't hear the end of it.

Maybe I could cover it up.

I leaned over the sink and peered into the bathroom mirror. I pressed down on my cheek. Dried blood flaked from the cut. The skin pulled apart.

Too deep to cover up.

Damn it!

I wet a towel and dabbed the cut. It looked better without the dried blood, but it still looked nasty.

I sighed and dropped the towel to the ground.

I'm going to have to be honest with Nash. At least one of us wouldn't be lying.

Wait. What was that?

The area around the cut seemed to shimmer. I peered closer. The skin sealed up like Playdough pressed together.

My mouth hung open as I touched the skin where the cut had been. The skin was smooth. What in the world? Had *I* done that?

My side no longer hurt either. Somehow, I had healed that too. No one helped me as I bled in that alley. I had helped myself.

Whoa. It would be great if I knew how to control it.

I rinsed my face and wandered down the hall to the stairs. As I reached the bottom of the stairs, the front door opened, and Nash walked in.

I kept my head down and tried to pass him, but he grabbed my arm.

"Lia…" My name left his lips in a breath.

I clenched my teeth. How dare he? I worried about a kiss while he had done much more with the Queen of Hell.

I tried to shrug him off, but he maintained his grip.

"I can't let you go," he whispered.

Liar. He let me go the moment he slipped into Lucifer's arms.

Why should I be surprised? They were one in the same, both fallen angels. I was human, temporary, and damned to the Circles. I shook my head. That might be the way it worked when you're immortal, but it wasn't the way it worked with me.

His words echoed in my head: *I can't let you go.*

"You have to, eventually," I said. "Bob made it very clear to me. Lucifer needs to fill my bio-mom's place when she leaves. So, once I've defeated Raphael, my mom will be released to Heaven. Then, it's off to the Seventh Circle of Hell for me." A man signed a contract to take Lydia's place, but that was a band-aid. After what he had done to that girl in the basement, he was destined for Hell. He had his place to fill, and I had mine.

"I won't let that happen," Nash said. His voice was like gravel.

He sounded so sincere, like always, but I couldn't trust him.

"How are you going to stop the Devil?" I spat. I pulled my arm away from him and walked out the door.

I felt his gaze on my back, but I didn't turn to look at him. I didn't know where I was going, but I couldn't bear to be in the same room with Nash for another second.

Chandra was right. Nash moved fast. But something told me that he was seeing Lucifer long before we broke up. That kiss they shared was passionate, but it was also too comfortable, too familiar. Their bodies molded together like the missing pieces of a puzzle.

I walked a couple blocks before I unclenched my fists, and the tension left my shoulders.

"Lia?"

I turned around.

"I saw you leave," Adriel said.

"When?" I asked.

"I was on the stairs."

"You saw me and Nash." My lip quivered.

Adriel put his arms around me. He didn't judge. He didn't press. He held me as I cried against him.

I was warm and safe in his arms. I never wanted to leave.

CHANDRA and I crossed staffs.

She pushed me back. I swayed and caught myself before I stumbled to the ground. She lunged forward, her staff above me.

I held my staff in two hands and blocked her blow. She tried hitting me with the end of the staff, but I managed to block that one too.

Chandra ground her teeth.

She rocked back. I imitated her, and our weapons met in the middle.

Chandra jabbed her staff at me. I pivoted to defend, knocking her weapon off course. She approached me, twirling her staff as I retreated. She swung at me. I blocked.

Chandra forced my staff to the ground with hers. Her staff swung up. *She's trying to take my head off!* I ducked, and her staff whooshed above me.

She buffeted my legs.

I winced, but maintained my balance. I blocked a second blow to my face.

Chandra twisted her staff. It was behind my legs, but before I could defend, the ground rushed up to meet me.

Chandra smirked.

I thought I was getting better, but I'd never be able to beat Chandra.

She went to the weapons table and grabbed her water bottle. I stood, rubbing my back. Good thing we trained on the grass.

Adriel fought with Nash farther down the field. Nash gave Adriel a room in his house although Adriel didn't have any belongings to keep there, and like Nash, he never slept. They were getting along, but they were far from friends.

They were brothers. Both Seraphim. Now both fallen angels.

"Hello, sweetheart."

I spun.

Bob stood with his hands in his pockets. He wore his customary black suit, black shirt, and red tie. His height was impressive. It wasn't practical to be so tall.

"What do you want?" I asked.

"My key." Bob held out his hand.

"I don't have it," I said.

He narrowed his eyes.

"After I took it from you, I lost it. Might have left it in the elevator. Don't know."

Bob smiled.

What did it take to wipe that grin off his face? Did I have to hit him again? I did have a staff in my hands.

"That's too bad. You're going to get me into a lot of trouble."

I don't care. Bob was the Redeemer, and he was trying to get Nash killed, but why?

Maybe he didn't like how Lucifer favored Nash. Although I couldn't imagine Bob and Lucifer together.

"What are you doing here?" Nash stepped up beside me. He folded his arms.

"I'm always a welcomed guest here." Bob grinned. "Why don't you invite me for dinner? My trunk is full of food."

"I don't cook meat."

"And I don't eat meat." Bob winked. "Well, not tonight anyway. I'll be a vegetarian just for you, just for tonight."

The last thing I wanted was to have dinner with Bob. It would be like a mouse dining with a cat. The mouse could never be sure when the cat might ignore the food and take a bite of mousy flesh instead.

After seeing Bob alone with a table full of food, I kept having dreams about him gorging himself sick. All that food had to go somewhere. If it wasn't ending up on Bob's lanky frame, it must be ending up on the floor.

"I can't host tonight," Nash said. "We're hunting."

This was the first I was hearing of it. Why didn't he tell me?

"Well, some other time." Bob turned on his heels and left the training field.

"What did he want?" Nash asked.

"I stole his key," I said.

Nash raised an eyebrow.

"His elevator key." I moved my staff from one hand to the other.

"Where is it?"

What was that on his face? Nerves, anxiety, why?

"I lost it," I said. I didn't feel so bad about lying to him. He was lying to me.

"You shouldn't be taking things from one of the Princes of Hell," Nash said.

I cocked my head. "Why aren't you a Prince of Hell? Lucifer seems to like you enough."

Nash looked to side. "You don't understand what the Princes of Hell are."

"Lucifer's seven personalities. She split herself up into pieces. Bob is one of those pieces."

"I'm not one of Lucifer's personalities," Nash said. "We're not that close."

"But you are close." I tossed him the staff. "I have to get ready. I didn't know we were demon hunting tonight. Or were you lying about that?"

I turned and marched toward the house. When I got to my bedroom, I tied my hair in a tight bun and grabbed my sword and dagger. I stopped at the window in the hallway outside my room.

Tom and Kiran trained on the field. They met blades a few times. Tom stopped and dropped his sword. He said something to Kiran. Tom's brow furrowed, and he frowned. Kiran stepped forward and pressed a finger to his lips.

What are they up to? Whatever it was, Kiran wanted to keep it quiet. *They're hiding something too. Why not?* Everyone else has something to hide.

*   *   *

MY head hit the brick wall, and my world spun. I tried to pick myself up, but in my dizziness, I stumbled. Water dripped from the ceiling of the dark basement.

Drip. Drip.

I opened my eyes. It felt like I was underwater. My vision blurred. Sounds dulled. *The world is a fiddle, and its music screams.*

I held my head between my hands, trying to stop the world from spinning and blurring like paints mixing on a palette.

The Surgat stood under the swinging light bulb as it blinked on and off. The demon held a massive sword shaped like a giant old-style key, its edges ridged and ending in a sharp, straight horizontal tip. The blade met Nash's with a clang.

Adrianna knelt in one corner of the room as she put pressure on a wound on Kiran's leg. Adriel approached and reached out his hand to touch the wound, but pulled back. *He can't heal anymore.*

But I can? Can I heal others? I wasn't sure how I healed myself.

Adriel looked toward me. He was coming to see if I was okay. *No, you have to help Nash.*

Chandra came up behind the demon while he and Nash fought. The silver keys around the Surgat's neck clinked together as he ducked to avoid Chandra's brass knuckles meeting his skull.

Chandra attempted to hit the demon again, but one long arm swung back and grabbed her wrist. The Surgat twisted. *Crack!*

Chandra screamed. Her hand hung limp, folding down against her arm. *Clink!* The brass knuckles slipped from her fingers.

Nash ground his teeth. His sword was caught on one of the ridges in the Surgat's blade. The Surgat swung his sword, and Nash's blade clattered to the ground.

The Surgat's long, thin leg kicked Nash in the chest, sending him backward onto the concrete floor. He turned his gray, skinny body to Chandra. His black eyes leaked smoke.

Gripping Chandra around the neck, he lifted her from the floor. He turned her and bent her body forward.

Adriel gripped his sword and rushed the demon, but he was too late.

The demon took his large key blade and plunged it into Chandra's back and turned it.

Chandra's mouth leaked blood and spit. She lifted her head. Her head was so close to her spine that her neck sloped like a snake's. Her eyes were solid black.

The Surgat released her.

Chandra's skin hardened to a thick, black shell. Her hands became pinchers. She grew a long black tail with a stinger. Her hair turned red and grew in turfs down her back. She gazed at me.

Oh shit!

Chandra's pinchers snapped at me.

I pinned myself to the wall and narrowly avoided being sliced in half.

"Chandra, it's me!" Like that would help. Chandra *did* want to kill me, but what did that demon do her.

Nash's sword met the Surgat's blade. "He controls her now."

Adriel's longsword blocked Chandra's pincher from attacking me again. The blade glanced off the shell, but Chandra couldn't move it anymore.

She turned on Adriel, her stinger whipping around behind her. The stinger lunged forward. Adriel dodged it, and Chandra buried the stinger into the floor.

She pulled the stinger out, causing concrete pebbles and dust to pop into the air. Adriel blocked another pincher as Chandra reached for him.

Clang!

Nash's blade met the Surgat's sword.

The sword. That's what set Chandra against us. I needed to get that key blade to turn her back.

What could I do?

I ran to the demon and leapt onto his back. I grabbed the necklace. It had a hundred keys strung around it, making it heavy. I yanked it, cutting into the demon's neck.

The Surgat tried to reach behind himself to grab me, but I held tight. Chandra pinned Adriel to the ground.

He buffeted her in the head with his sword, but the shell acted like armor. Perhaps it could only be penetrated by pure Arcadian Steel and not the lesser alloy of the blade Adriel wielded.

But we weren't trying to kill Chandra.

With his sword and my distraction, Nash forced the key blade from the demon's grasp. He slashed the Surgat's chest. The demon howled.

I leapt from his back and grabbed the blade. It was so heavy I had to drag it to where Chandra had Adriel pinned.

With every ounce of strength I possessed, I lifted the blade and sank it into Chandra's back. I turned the key.

Chandra's body went limp like a doll's. *Did I kill her?*

The shell turned back to smooth skin. The tail disappeared.

Adriel rolled from under her.

Chandra fell to her knees. "What happened?" She grabbed her broken wrist.

"You lost control of yourself and your Veil," Adrianna said. "You tried to kill Adriel and Lia."

Keys rattled.

I turned.

Nash and Adriel ran the Surgat through with their swords, Nash from the front, Adriel from behind.

The demon turned to smoke, and his necklace of keys dropped to the floor.

Nash knelt and inspected the keys, taking one and turning it in his hands. "These keys can open any lock in the world."

"There are more than a hundred locks in the world," I said.

"They work like skeleton keys," Nash said. "Large groups of locks can be opened with one key. You just have to know which one."

I shrugged. "Maybe we can gift one to Bob since I lost his."

Nash gave me a look that said he wasn't in the mood for my jokes. When *was* he in the mood for jokes? I wished he would stop looking at me like a snake that had crawled into his boot.

He lifted the string of keys from the ground. "Let's get out of here." He opened the portal.

Adrianna helped Kiran to his feet and walked with him through the opening. Chandra following, scooping up her brass knuckles.

"What are you going to use those keys for?" I asked.

"I don't know," Nash said. "But they might come in handy."

"They are dangerous," Adriel said. "They open doors you should not enter."

I doubted Nash would heed his warning.

MUSIC blared through my earbuds. I folded my arms against the railing of the balcony as I gazed upon the training field.

My head and neck still ached from the battle with the Surgat. I wished I knew how to control my special healing ability or any of my abilities for that matter. How many more did I possess and didn't know about?

The one that made angels fall was easy to understand. I touch them, and puff—flames. It was the getting to them that was the hard part, but at least that ability never failed.

But who could I turn to to teach me about my powers? I was force-fed angel blood. Was there anyone else like me?

Adriel leaned his arms against the railing.

I pulled the wires of my earbuds, and they popped out of my ears.

"You have a key that you're not supposed to have," Adriel said.

"Yeah," I said. "But I'm not returning it. Bob's the Redeemer, and he's trying to have Nash killed. I'm going to find out why."

"You're not going to talk to Nash about it."

I looked at my hands. "I don't want to talk to Nash at all." I sighed. "Last time we discussed it…"

He kissed me. Then he tried to take it back, but you can't take back a kiss any more than you can take back the feelings it awakens.

"…he didn't seem to take it very seriously. I didn't know it was Bob, but I knew someone was after him."

"He wants to stop him *and you*," Adriel said.

"But why? That's what I keep wondering. Bob has as much of an interest as Lucifer in stopping Raphael or Michael or any angel. Why does Bob want Nash dead if he's the head of the team that kills angels?"

Adriel shook his head.

"I'm going to find out," I said. "No one is going to keep any more secrets from me."

Three

OONLIGHT flooded through the open window. A steady summer breeze rolled in. My mouth was dry so I got out of bed to get a glass of water.

Something crinkled under my bare feet. Stooping, I picked it up. It was a picture drawn by a young child.

A flat two-dimensional house was drawn in the background. In the foreground were three stick figures with the traditional round circles for heads. Two of the figures had triangles drawn midway up their torsos to depict dresses. The two taller figures were a mother and a father, and the little girl in the center was me.

I smiled at the childish attempt, so like the drawings I used to draw in school when I was little. My finger traced the drawing of my father. Where was he, and why didn't he try to find me?

I placed the drawing on the desk beside the door and wandered down the hallway. The walls were bare, and the tiled floor was cold against my feet.

I stopped outside the door to my mother's bedroom. Her back was to me. She placed something inside the drawer at her bedside.

"What's that mommy?" The words tumbled out of my mouth expectantly like I was in a living memory where all the lines were pre-written.

My mom paused with the object still in her hand and the drawer still open. She turned to me.

She held a book. She approached and knelt to look at me. "This?" she asked. "This was your father's. It's called *A Tale of Two Cities.*"

I touched the book gingerly as if it was something sacred.

"It's the only thing he left us. So, it's special," she said. "You must never take it out without asking."

"Can you read it to me?" I asked.

"For a little while." She put the book on the dresser and helped me onto the bed. She curled up beside me and opened the book to the first page: *It was the best of times, it was the worst of times, it was the age of wisdom, it was the age of foolishness, it was the epoch of belief, it was the epoch of incredulity, it was the season of Light, it was the season of Darkness...*"

I sat up abruptly. Sweat painted my brow. That was it. Something my father had touched.

"Caiduc?" I whispered into the darkness.

Caiduc's dark form appeared on the edge of my bed. If I had seen him in the night, I might have jumped out of my skin. But I was used to him now. Even if his nightly visits were creepy.

He turned his head to me.

"Can you take me somewhere?" I asked.

Caiduc nodded. "Where do you want to go?"

"I know where I can find something of my father's to bring back to Jiao. I need to go back to my childhood home. Can you bring me?"

Caiduc nodded.

Jinn powers were confusing. How could he know where my childhood home was? To know that, he must be omniscient.

Getting up from bed, I grabbed my dagger and belt and wrapped it around my waist. I wore my pajamas: a t-shirt and a pair of shorts. I didn't bother getting dressed.

I pulled on my boots and tied back my hair. "I'm ready."

Caiduc gripped my arm, and *splash!*

I gasped in the air.

Caiduc and I stood in the bare living room that used to belong to my mother. It had never been hers, but she and I had occupied it. The house smelled musty. No one lived there for years.

I wondered if it was a happy home like Mom and Dad's was. I still remembered the wooden, creaky stairs, the worn bannister, the old floorboards, and Dad's studio that was connected to the house. I frowned. Did they let it go to shambles like this?

I guess I own it now. Although I wasn't sure how all that was going to work out since I was a runaway, and all my paperwork was with family services.

I'd figure all that out later. The house wasn't what mattered to me. The memories did, and I carried those with me.

I bumped into what I thought might be a couch and a coffee table, but I found the hallway.

"What are you looking for?" Caiduc asked. "Maybe I could help."

"It's a book." I felt my way along the wall. "Hopefully it's still in my mother's bedside drawer where she left it."

I stopped abruptly. My bio-mom's room was bare except for a large silver cage and silver blood that had dried upon the floor.

Silver shoeprints blanketed the ground. The police who found me all those years ago couldn't see the blood that pooled there.

A memory flashed before my eyes of me crying in the corner of the room. My face was stained with the blood of the angel that my mother had killed. A stranger approached me in a police uniform, holding out his hands like I was a wild animal.

Not there. Not there. Not there.

"It's not in here," I said. "She moved all the furniture."

I glanced at the door to the adjoining room, a small study that we had rarely ever used. I opened the door.

My mother's bed and mattress were piled inside along with her room's other furnishings, clothes, and long mirror. I climbed over the bed to the small bedside drawer and opened it.

The old paperback book nestled inside. I pulled it from the drawer and met Caiduc back out in the hallway.

"Is that what you were looking for?" he asked.

"It is," I said. "Hopefully, it's good enough for Jiao to help me find my father."

I looked down at the book. *A Tale of Two Cities*. The memory played in my head again like a movie, like I wasn't really there.

"What will you say to him when you find him?" Caiduc asked.

I hesitated a moment, not because I didn't know what I planned to say but because it was difficult for me to say it. I'd better get used to it if I had to say it to my dad soon. "Why didn't you try to find me?"

I turned the paperback book over in my hands. To me, that old book was more valuable than any of the books in Nash's library. I read over the first chapter three times.

Every time I heard my mother's voice reading it back to me. It felt strange to remember her. I was two people with two families: Lia Hebert, daughter of Micha and Alexandria Hebert, and Rachel Palermo, daughter of Robert and Lydia Palermo.

Rachel. I didn't *feel* like a Rachel. *My name is Lia.*

I opened my bedside drawer and placed the book inside.

On my way to the training field, I stopped outside the library. Adriel sat on the couch with a book in his hands.

"What are you reading?" I sat beside him.

He looked up, eyes wide. "Ah, nothing." He closed the book.

I read the title. "*Jikininki: The Corpse-Eating Specters.* I didn't know you were interested in demons. I've seen a Jikininki. I could tell you about it, if you want."

"I…" He put the book on the table beside the couch. "That's okay," he said. "I was just . . . browsing."

"I found a book today," I said. "*A Tale of Two Cities.* I started reading it. It was a favorite of my dad's. My real dad, not the one who adopted me. He was a painter. Didn't read much. But he was brilliant. Just the most beautiful paintings."

"I've seen your father's paintings."

"You have?"

Adriel nodded. "They are *moving.*"

"Thank you." An ache rose in my throat. Tears wet my eyes. I tried to blink them away. "I'm so afraid that they're not up there. They deserve to be, but…"

Adriel took my hands. "They're in Heaven."

"How do you know?"

"Because of you. Only good people could have made you what you are."

"But good people end up here," I said.

Adriel shook his head.

"But they do, and spend an eternity suffering. How is that fair?"

"People who have done wrong have sin in their hearts. They are capable of a countless number of wrongs. So, though the punishment is eternal, it is appropriate."

"But can't you change your mind?" I asked. "People change all the time. Sometimes they don't know what they're doing is wrong. Given time, like say an eternity in Hell, they might *find God*."

I clamped my mouth shut. I was starting to sound like Tom.

"Brava!"

Speak of the Devil.

Tom sat in the chair across from us. "Whoa, Lia. I didn't think you had it in you." He looked at Adriel. "She's right. If God's so merciful, where is his mercy when someone down here repents? I've never seen someone ripped out of the Circles with a one-way ticket to Arcadia."

Adriel frowned. "Hell is not infinity. It is an unchangeable present."

Tom narrowed his eyes. "Did you just throw Sisyphus at me? Tell me, Seraph, what *is* the difference between infinity and an unchanging present?"

Adriel glared at him.

Tom's voice raised in pitch. "Because once I have your answer, I'll truck over to the Circles to tell old Sisyphus, 'It's okay. You're not rolling a boulder up a hill forever. You're rolling a boulder up a hill today. It just so happens that every day is today.'"

Happy Groundhog Day! I thought.

Adriel stood. "I will not stay here while you make a mockery of God's justice." He left the room.

"Why do you do that?" I asked.

"Because it's so much fun," Tom said. "Finally, someone who can hold his own in a debate. Too bad he's gets so heated. I was just getting to the good stuff."

"It's not good for him. Every time you mention it, he's has to think about Heaven." *A place to which he can't return. Because of me.*

"I guess I could argue with you instead," Tom said. "You showed some brilliance just now. Too bad we're on the same side of the debate." He winked.

"Hope I'm not interrupting." Bob stepped into the library. "So many books." He looked around the room. "I've always been impressed by Nash's collection."

"Ah, look at that." Tom picked up the book Adriel had been reading. "I found the book I want." He flashed a tight-lipped smile and ducked out of the room.

"The boss wants to see you, sweetheart," Bob said.

What did Lucifer want with me now? "Fine," I said.

I walked with Bob to his car and sat in the passenger seat. Bob folded in after me, turning the ignition.

Redeemer. I'm on to you.

"Is this about the key?" I asked.

He turned to me and grinned. "No."

I settled back in my seat with my arms folded and braced myself for the ride.

Bob drove like someone was going to drown his cat if he didn't make it to his destination in under ten minutes. The cat drowned. We made it in thirteen.

"What is this about?" I asked as we got into the elevator.

"I can't tell you that, sweetheart." Bob pushed a button, and the doors closed.

I folded my arms.

Bob pulled a key out of his pocket and turned it in the keyhole in the elevator panel. *So, he got a new one.*

The elevator jolted as it took us up.

"Why does everything have to be a secret around here?" I asked.

"You'll find out soon." Bob put his hands in his pockets.

"I don't like surprises." It wasn't surprises I didn't like but bad news. Every time I saw Bob, it was bad news. I wanted to brace myself for it, like you would as you neared the peak before the rollercoaster drops you, but I needed an inkling of what I was preparing myself for.

"This shouldn't come as a surprise."

Maybe Lucifer didn't like that we hadn't gone out to burn down angels in over a year. But she wouldn't be calling me in for that. She would have spoken with Nash.

Or maybe this was about Adriel. I had made him fall, but I did that to save him from the Pit. Shortly after that, I asked that he be released from the Angel District. Did Lucifer think I might be playing both sides?

Perhaps Bob *did* tell her about the key, and I would be lectured on how I couldn't go around beating up on Lucifer's right-hand demon.

Show me your true face, Beelzebub. It'll make it easier to kick you in the teeth.

The elevator chimed, and the doors opened. I followed Bob down the hall. A clone secretary passed us with a silver platter of food.

The scent of roasted asparagus wafted down the hall. I peered over my shoulder as she placed the platter down inside one of the rooms. She closed the door and locked it with a key from her skirt pocket.

You don't deliver food to empty rooms. Lucifer was keeping someone locked up. My mother?

Bob opened the door to Lucifer's office. "After you, sweetheart."

I walked past him into the room. Lucifer lounged on the sofa across from the two black, leather chairs. But she wasn't the only one in the room.

Nash stood at the window, sipping from a mug.

Of course, he was here already.

He didn't look at me when I walked in.

Lucifer stood from the sofa and sat behind her mahogany desk. "Sit." She gestured to the chair across from the desk.

I frowned, but sat.

Nash hadn't moved. What was so damn interesting at the window?

Lucifer's fingers twined together. Bob was behind me. I felt like I was trapped between a snake and a scorpion.

Lucifer smiled. Her lips were a different shade of red every day. Today they reminded me of a traffic light.

If Nash was here, why did she need me? Nash could deliver her message. Then I wouldn't have to sit across from her like a zebra trying to stare down a tiger.

"Why am I here?"

Nash shot me a look. I wasn't surprised the first look of the day was a jab.

Lucifer continued to smile like she was made of stone and I was made of glass. I could shout and complain all I want, but in the end, she could shatter me.

But I wasn't going to let her frighten me.

"I've spoken with Nash," Lucifer said. "But I wanted to make sure you heard this from me."

Was her trust in Nash breaking?

"There's an angel out in the desert. I've asked Nash to find him. Now, that I have you, I have the leverage I need to bring him down here."

I folded my arms. "What do you want with this angel?"

Lucifer's glare pinned me. Good thing she separated herself from Wrath or she might have reached over the table and scratched my eyes out. "His name is Azazel. And he is very important to me. Thousands of years ago, Michael ordered Raphael to bind and blindfold him and leave him in the desert to suffer."

"Didn't really answer my question."

Nash stabbed me with his eyes.

"I don't have to answer your questions. I want Azazel taken with his Grace intact. That's why you are not to touch him. You will be there as a threat but not a weapon. Do you understand?"

"Yeah. It'll bring me joy to set a guy free that Michael and Raphael hate for some reason. Thank you for the opportunity. Is that it? Or are you going to tell me, you need twenty more angels from me?"

Lucifer's lips curled into a smile. She's thinking of all the ways she will have me tortured once I'm down here permanently. "That's it," she said.

four

NASH sighed. As he gripped the wheel, his knuckles turned white.

"What are *you* sighing about?"

He looked at me like I asked him if Earth was round. "Lucifer is the Queen of Hell."

I narrowed my eyes at him. "Don't talk to me like I'm stupid."

Nash shook his head. "Well, you didn't seem to know that back there. Are you trying to get me thrown into the Pit?"

I folded my arms. "Lucifer won't throw *you* into the Pit."

"Lucifer uses people," Nash said. "I'm a tool to her. Like you."

Does Lucifer passionately kiss her tools?

"Are you afraid she'll replace you with Azazel? Who is he anyway?"

"He was one of the Watchers, a group of fallen angels who mated with human women. He spearheaded the whole thing. That's why God ordered Raphael to tie him up in a desert. He didn't want the other angels to be corrupted."

"I thought Lucifer said Michael asked Raphael to do that."

"God speaks through Michael."

"Well, isn't that convenient for Michael? But why does Lucifer think Azazel isn't fallen?"

"Because he would only be fallen if he thought what he had done was wrong."

"But God didn't want him to do it, so…"

"Just because God didn't endorse it, doesn't make it wrong."

"Wait. Isn't God the moral compass on everything?"

Nash shook his head. "This is too much for you."

"Stop doing that, and tell me the truth."

"Azazel thought by mixing angels and humans that he could make humans better. But instead he made more imperfect beings. Michael had them hunted down."

"Except one," I said.

Nash nodded. "Metatron. He ran. But when Michael finds him, he'll kill him."

"No one knows where he is?"

Nash looked out the window. "No."

"So, Azazel, what use is he to Lucifer?"

"She's angry with Michael. Eternity is a long time to reflect on sins of the past. Sometimes you repent, other times you decide what you'd done wasn't quite a sin after all."

"But you can't go back," I said. "Hell is forever."

"It's messed up." Nash turned the key in the ignition.

I knocked on the door. Jiao's tea shop was probably closed, but even if it was broad daylight I doubted Jiao would appreciate me walking right on in. She yelled at the top of her lungs for me to leave last time.

Still, I wasn't sure if she was in the tea room. Both times I had gone to see her, she was in the back.

I knocked harder this time.

A curse and the shuffle of feet came from behind the door. I braced myself for a hard push back into the street. The lock clicked, and the door opened.

Jiao stood in a robe, her hand clasping it to her small body. Standing this close to her, I realized how short she was. I'm no giant, but Jiao was easily a foot shorter than me.

"You again," she spat. "I told you to get lost."

"Yeah, you suspected me of stealing an angel's Grace," I said. "I didn't steal anything. Something was forced on me. I—"

"I'm going to stop you right there and pretend that I didn't hear that," Jiao said.

"Why?" I asked.

"Never mind. Just leave now."

She was scared. She would deny it, but that look in her eyes screamed everything. My mother had done something terrible, probably irreversible, and it frightened the hell out of Jiao.

"Please," I said. "I still need your help, and I'll keep knocking at your door all night to get it."

Jiao's eyes darted left and right.

"If I help you," she hissed, "you'll leave me alone for good?"

I nodded.

"Come in before I change my mind." Jiao opened the door wider.

I stepped inside.

"You still want to find your father?" she asked.

"Yeah, that's why I'm here."

"And you remember what that would require?"

"I have it here." I pulled the book for the inside of my coat. "It was my dad's."

"Come with me." Jiao led me past the partition to the back of the tea shop.

The hallway was lit with paper lanterns. She turned the corner into a room with shelves full of jars lining the wall. The jars contained powders and pastes of various colors.

"Sit," Jiao said.

I took a seat on one of the cushions next to a low table. On the table was a large, silver dish. I clenched my father's book to my chest.

Jiao grabbed a pot, a jar, and scroll from the shelf and sat down across from me. "Give it to me." She gestured toward the book.

My hand shook as I passed the book to her. I wanted it back as soon as it left my hands. It was the only thing I had left of my bio-dad.

I reached up and gripped the cross and locket that hung around my neck. I could always find comfort there.

Jiao placed my dad's book in the silver tray and took out a long, wooden stick. She blew on the end of the stick, and a tiny flame sparked.

She lit the corner of the book and set it ablaze.

My heart dropped into my stomach. "No!" I reached out.

Jiao put a hand up to stop me. "Do you want to find your father or not?"

I set my jaw, but I settled back. I clenched my fists as the book's pages came under assault by the flames. The fire burned it unnaturally quick and completely until what was once the only thing of my father's that I owned, turned to dust.

Jiao scooped up the remnants of the book in her hands and poured it into the small pot. The dust dissolved into the hot water. Jiao opened the jar, reached in with two fingers, and scooped out a small amount of powder.

She sprinkled the powder into the pot. She unrolled the scroll. It was a map. She crumpled it in both hands until it was nothing more than a tight ball.

She placed the crumpled paper deep into the pot and covered it with the lid.

"Now, we wait," she said.

"How long?" I asked.

"Tell me about Sheol," Jiao said. It came out like a demand.

I hesitated. "Why do you think I would know anything about that?" I asked.

"You're walking around with a Jinn," Jiao said. "They make appearances on Earth but very rarely. They like to hang out in Sheol."

"How did you know about that?"

"The Jinn?"

I nodded. Caiduc stayed far away from the tea house. Something frightened him.

"Let's just say I have a long history with Jinni. I can smell them. Now, tell me about Hell."

"Hell is . . . different than you'd expect." I wondered if telling Jiao would be against some code and would get me into trouble or something. But then again, what did I care? I already had a place in the Seventh Circle.

"Different how?"

"Can I ask why you want to know?"

"You can ask, but I won't answer," she said.

"What do you want to know about it?"

"Well, everything you know."

"I spend most of my time in the Outer Region. It's a place for demons who complete their contracts. It's . . . okay, I guess. Better than the Seventh Circle. That's all fire, boiling blood, and harpies. And then, there's the Pit."

"The Pit?" The word was a whisper on her tongue.

"Yeah, the name says it all. It's big and endless. If I had to guess, I'd say it's probably bigger than this whole city."

Jiao glanced down. "It's ready." She lifted the top off the pot and gently pulled the map out with a pair of silver tongs. She placed the map on the table.

I marveled at it. The brew that it had bathed in was dark, so dark that it should have turned the page amber, but the map was mostly clean and white except for one spot.

"He's in Hattiesburg, Mississippi."

Hattiesburg. The only spot on the map that had been darkened by the tea. *He's was so close. Maybe two or three hours away all my life.* If I haven't landed in Hell, I could have thumbed a ride to Hattiesburg.

I had never been to Hattiesburg, but I imagined it would be very difficult to find him without a more precise location.

"Hattiesburg is a big place. Any way you could be more specific?" I asked. *A street address maybe?*

Jiao narrowed her eyes. "You know his name?" she asked.

I nodded. "Robert Palermo."

"Then, I'm sure the rest could be done on the Internet. Don't rely on magic to hand you everything on a silver platter."

Her words were biting.

"Thank you." I got up from my seat. At least, I wouldn't have to search the entire United States and knock on the door of each Robert Palermo in the White Pages.

"Remember our deal." Jiao looked up at me. "You don't bother me again."

"Agreed," I said.

I met Caiduc across the street from the tea shop. He scratched his wrists.

"Did the witch find him?" Caiduc asked.

"He's in Hattiesburg," I said. "I don't know his exact address, but at least we only have one city to search rather than the whole world. I need to get to a public library. One in Hattiesburg would do if you can manage."

*   *   *

CLEAR water splashed upon my face, but I came out dry on the other side. I stood between two towering shelves. Gray carpet trailed under my feet, and the musty smell of old books filled my nose.

How funny. The sterile smell of Nash's house could overcome the antique scent of books. But this place was consumed by it, although I'm sure the books were far less ancient.

Was this a university library? Without meaning to, I remembered Carson. I remembered feeling normal.

And then a demon showed up in his apartment, and I had to tell him at the risk of sounding crazy. I did sound crazy and scared him away.

What had that demon done to him?

I couldn't think about it. Nothing to do now. I imagined the demon, sinking its claws into Carson's shoulder, whispering for him to do terrible things, things that would land him a spot in Hell.

Things that made middle-aged men lock up girls in basements and drain their blood.

I shook my head.

Not there. Not there. Not there.

"Can I help you?"

I jumped.

A woman wearing glasses and a cardigan narrowed her eyes at me. *The librarian?*

"Umm. No. I was looking for the computers."

She eyed me up and down. "You can't sleep here, you know."

I furrowed my brow. "Of course not. I just need to Google something."

What made her think I planned on sleeping here? I wasn't homeless.

I glanced down at what I was wearing. My shirt was a bit wrinkled. But I showered this morning so I'm sure I smelled fine.

Whatever.

I walked to the computer terminals in the center of the library and logged in under guest. I searched Robert Palermo. The first link that came up was a university site. I clicked on it.

There he was. My father's picture came up on the screen along with a short bio. He was a Professor of Literature at the University of Southern Mississippi. He graduated from Loyola University. Recommended reading: A Tale of Two Cities.

The page had no home address, but at least I knew for sure that he was in the city. I clicked back to the search results and scanned the page. A White Pages listing popped up so I clicked the link.

Two Robert Palermos lived in Hattiesburg. One of them had to be him. I jotted the addresses down on a piece of paper and shoved it into my pocket.

Behind the library, I showed Caiduc the first address. "I have two," I said. "Can you take me to this one?"

Caiduc nodded. His earring swung. His rough hand gripped my arm.

I got dizzy from all the in-a-flash traveling, but at least Jinni transportation wasn't as nauseating as portal travel. I held onto Caiduc's shoulder for a second.

"Are you alright?"

"I'm feeling a little sick that's all." I left Caiduc and walked up to the house.

I knocked on the door, and a blond man answered. I remembered my father's face and this wasn't him.

"Sorry," I said. "I must have gotten the wrong house."

The man gave me a tight-lipped smile and shut the door on me.

One down, one to go.

Clenching Caiduc's hand behind the fence, he transported us to the second address. I climbed out of the bushes and brushed the leaves off my clothes.

White picket fences and manicured lawns accented each house along the clear, evening covered street. Trees grew on the median, and all the houses were at least two stories.

I spotted the address. The house was three stories with white flowers in the yard and bushes lining the red brick foundation. Stairs led up to a covered porch. The house must have had twenty windows.

I walked up the driveway. On one side of the house was a massive bay window. Inside a family was having dinner.

A mother, father, and two girls. They were laughing. At the head of the table was a man I recognized—my father. His dark hair was streaked with gray. He helped his youngest daughter cut up her food before leaning back to enjoy his meal.

I swallowed. I could taste the salt of my tears in the back of my throat. He had forgotten me. If I came back into his life now, I would ruin his perfect family. They were his future. I wasn't even a memory.

"You're crying," Caiduc said.

I wiped the tears from my cheeks. "I don't know what I expected," I said.

"Do you want to go in?" he asked.

But I wasn't crying because I felt abandoned by him. I might have wanted a future with him, but he didn't raise me. He wasn't my dad.

I expected him to fill that role for me, but that wouldn't erase the pain.

Mom and Dad were gone. Raphael took them from me. Only one place existed where I could fight him.

I shook my head. "I want to go back where I belong."

five

I opened my eyes. Caiduc clasped my hands. We knelt together in my room. His dark eyes were sad. Mine were crying. Caiduc placed his branchy fingers against my cheek.

Nothing was said, but nothing was more comforting than the silence that drifted between us. I let the stillness of the room wrap around me, and I wasn't vulnerable anymore.

Safe. For now.

But not for long. Lucifer, Nash, Raphael, Michael, Bob. All of them were up to something. As much as I wanted to take advantage of Caiduc's abilities to mend my abandonment wounds, I needed him for something much more serious.

My first target would be Lucifer. I had to find out what she was up to. People with reputations for lying don't usually tell the truth. I also wanted to get a hold of my contract. Maybe it contained some loophole that could get me out of the whole thing.

The second part should be easy. I was sure Bob would happily get me a copy of my contract. It was signed in *my* blood after all. I was entitled to it.

I hoped I didn't have to oust him as the Redeemer to get what I wanted. Not yet.

But spying on Lucifer, that's where I would need Caiduc's help.

The Jinn seemed pretty content with helping me though I had no idea why. That had been on my list of concerns for some time, but Nash had assured me that finding the answer to that question would be harder than solving a Rubik's Cube.

Maybe Jinn just get bored. Maybe I was Caiduc's entertainment.

It was nice to see that, although he might be terrifying to look at, Caiduc had a heart. Jinn seemed a lot closer to humans than angels or demons.

A car engine turned over.

Caiduc smiled with his eyes before disappearing before mine. The coldness of the room felt heavy.

I walked to the window and peered outside. Nash pulled away from the house. I imagined he was going to see Lucifer so that he could paw her all over her desk.

I marched into the bathroom and rinsed my face with cold water. Strands of my hair were wet from falling into the sink. I rubbed my face with a towel.

I hated myself for thinking about him. He was doing what Chandra said he would. *He doesn't like you,* I thought. *Move on.* He certainly had.

Wrapping myself in the covers, I lay in bed, hoping that sleep would veil me in darkness. I drifted as I listened to the music on my MP3 player.

One moment I was in my room at Nash's house, and then my world shattered like pieces of glass on a broken mirror. I was downstairs in the living room.

Adriel sat on the couch, drinking a cup of coffee. I didn't like how he reminded me of Nash. They were so different, but they looked so much alike now. I wondered why I hadn't seen it before.

He continued to sip his coffee without looking my way.

"Adriel?" I said.

I expected him to turn toward me, but his eyes remained on the white wall. What was he thinking about?

"Adriel? I shouted.

He looked around. His eyes froze on me but saw through me. He turned back to his coffee.

As I approached him, my eyes blinked open. I was in bed. The covers were tight around me.

What in the Hell was that? Maybe it was one of those psychic dream conversations like the one with my mother and the other with the Seven Archangels of Heaven.

But Adriel couldn't hear me. Why was that?

The air outside the covers was cold on my face. My stomach grumbled. The warm sanctuary of the covers beckoned me to stay, but my stomach growled like a hungry animal.

My feet met the cold, marble floor, and I padded across the room to the door and into the hallway. I hesitated at the top of the stairs. Light came from the living room.

Nash? But didn't he leave? How long ago was that?

I tiptoed down the stairs and peered into the living room. Adriel nursed a cup of coffee. Just like in the dream. Or psychic vision.

I needed to learn how to control that. And my other powers too.

"Adriel?"

He turned and looked my way.

"Hi," he said. "Hope I didn't scare you. Nash asked me to watch over you while he was away."

"Did he now?" I failed to keep the ire out of my voice.

"Are you okay?" Adriel asked. "It's the middle of the night. You normally sleep through it. Lately that has changed."

How did he know I slept through the night? Oh, that's right. He's been watching me for years.

"I'm fine," I said. "I just skipped dinner, and now I'm so hungry I could eat an entire buffet."

Adriel frowned and cocked an eyebrow. Did he have to take everything so literal?

I blushed. "Well, maybe only half a buffet. Depends on the size of the restaurant."

"I'll help you make something," Adriel said. "I don't know my way around the kitchen, but I'll do whatever I can."

I laughed.

"What's so funny?"

"I just imagined you in an apron cutting vegetables."

"Why's that so funny?"

"You're a warrior, and you're cutting up veggies."

"Nash is a warrior."

"True. I guess I've just never imagined him in the same way."

"Well, anything so I could take a break from this coffee. The stuff's disgusting." He put the mug down on the table.

"You're telling me."

We made spaghetti. I took out onions, mushrooms, green peppers, garlic, tomatoes, and pasta. That sounded right.

"Can you cut up the rest of the vegetables while I sauté the onions?"

"Sure, can you demonstrate?"

He really didn't know his way around a kitchen if I had to show him how to cut mushrooms, but I gladly demonstrated how to cut each vegetable. I was no Emeril Lagasse, but I had helped Mom in the kitchen a few times.

Working together, we had the kitchen smelling pretty good. I had drained and rinsed the pasta. We hung out on the couch while the sauce finished cooking.

Adriel didn't lounge on the couch like Nash did. Instead, he perched on the edge of it with his feet firmly planted on the floor. If he sat back, he'd crush his featherless wings. They hung on either side of him.

"I saw my father," I said, "my bio-dad I mean."

"When?" he asked.

"Yesterday."

"But how?"

"I don't want to tell you that."

Adriel narrowed his eyes. "Lia…"

"But I want to tell you this: I went to meet him. I know it might not change anything. I mean, I'm eighteen now. I missed so much time with him, and I wouldn't take it back because I loved my Mom and Dad. I'm so glad they were the ones who raised me. But he's my dad too."

"He must have been happy to see you after all this time."

I shook my head. "I chickened out."

"Why didn't you meet him?"

"I couldn't do that to him. He left me for a reason. I'm pretty sure he wouldn't want me turning up at his doorstep."

"What if that's exactly what he wants?"

My eyes held Adriel's.

The timer on the stove went off.

"Sauce is ready. I'd better go make sure it doesn't burn."

I took a serving bowl from the cabinet and loaded in the pasta, smothering it with sauce. As I reached for the bowl, Adriel said, "Let me get that."

He lifted the bowl from the counter and headed for the dining room.

"Wait," I said.

Adriel turned.

I didn't like the idea of that big dining room table causing a gulf between me and Adriel. "Let's eat on the sofa. Nash will never know."

Adriel walked to living room while I grabbed the plates and forks. I put some of the pasta on my plate and rubbed my hands together. "Here goes." I put a forkful in my mouth. "Umm."

I nodded my head as I chewed. I had taken four or five mouthfuls by the time I noticed Adriel hadn't served himself any.

"Try it," I said. "It's good."

He forked some of the pasta onto his plate. "Sorry," he said. "I'm not used to eating."

"Angels never eat?" I asked between bites.

"No," he said. "I've never felt hunger like I do now. It's strange." Dubiously he loaded the spaghetti onto his fork. More than half of it slid off his fork before it made it to his mouth.

I stifled a giggle.

Adriel looked over at me.

"Sorry," I said.

He smiled. "It's okay. I watched humans eat before. It's harder than it looks."

"Not once you get the hang of it," I said.

"Thank you," Adriel said.

I grinned. "Everyone gets the hang of it eventually."

"No." His eyes held mine. "After Sydriel went missing, I was in a very bad place. She and I were close. My heart was dark and cold when I thought something must have happened to her."

He looked down for a moment before meeting my eyes again. "It wasn't the best time in my life. I wondered if I would ever return to Heaven."

He gently took my hand in his. "But watching you, being your guardian angel, it changed me. I wanted to protect what Sydriel vowed to protect."

I looked down at our joined hands. "You're not my guardian angel anymore," I said. "I don't want you jumping in front of Raphael to protect me."

"You don't understand, Lia." His thumb stroked the palm of my hand, and I felt my pulse quicken. "It doesn't matter if I no longer have my wings. I made a vow, and I must keep it."

KIRAN swung his sword. He widened his stance, his knees bent. He glanced at me as I approached, but continued practicing.

I copied his stance and followed his movements. Even without a sword, my actions were clumsy.

"Drop your shoulders," Kiran said. "You're too stiff."

I sighed. "No amount of instruction can help me beat Chandra."

"You're not trying to beat Chandra."

"Yes, I am."

Kiran shook his head. "Because you know that beating Chandra will mean you will spar against me next. You don't want to spar against me." He didn't say it with smugness in his voice the way Tom might have said it. It was a fact.

"I'll fight you. I'm just not ready. It would be like a snail racing a cheetah."

"You have no reason to lie to me," Kiran said, "and yet you do."

"I'm not lying to you."

"Then you are lying to yourself."

I stopped mid-stance and folded my arms.

"You're afraid that if you beat me, you'll be ready. That you'll have to face the angel that murdered your parents."

I narrowed my eyes. "I want to kill Raphael. You could put him in front of me today, and I would set him on fire."

"But you are still afraid of death."

"Everyone's afraid of death." I stopped. "Well, everyone who is alive is afraid of death."

"You are afraid of something."

Was I? Raphael was ready for me. He was hunting me.

I looked down. "Failure."

"You cannot be afraid of failure," Kiran said, "or you will be frozen forever."

"I don't freeze. I don't hesitate. I act. Despite my fears."

Then why haven't you asked Caiduc to take you to Raphael?

"I'm not the one who's lying," I said.

I grabbed the copy of *A Tale of Two Cities* from Nash's shelf. The book didn't hold the same value to me as my dad's copy, but at least I would get to read it.

Curling up in a chair, I read as I sipped my hot chocolate. Christmas was tomorrow, and I would be celebrating in Sheol. Of course, they didn't celebrate Christmas in Hell.

This would be the third Christmas I missed with my family: Uncle Jonah. I couldn't even send him a Christmas card.

I looked up from my book.

Tom stood at one of the shelves with a book open in his hands.

"Oh, hey. I didn't see you there," I said.

He was unmoving.

"Tom?"

I stood. "Hey." I approached him. "What did I do to deserve the silent treatment?" I reached out to touch his arm.

He disappeared.

What the...?

"You should have a book in your hand if you're going to be in here." Tom walked into the library with a book under his arm.

"Where did you go?" I asked.

"I just got here," Tom said.

"No, you were standing right there." I indicated the spot where Tom stood only moments ago.

Tom cocked his head. "Are you feeling okay?"

I put my hand to my head. "Yeah, I just . . . need to sit down."

"Maybe you should."

Was I doing the dream psychic thing or was that something else? I'd seen Tom standing in Nash's library a thousand times. Could it have been a memory? A memory playing out in real time?

I walked back to the couch and slumped down.

"Where were you this morning?" Tom asked.

"I was training with Kiran."

Tom stiffened. "You train with him a lot without Nash's supervision?"

"No, just this morning. I'm not going to make a habit of it though. Kiran thinks I'm holding back."

"Are you?"

I folded my arms. "Any luck with Lucifer's latest project?"

"You mean finding Azazel? I have a stack of books taller than me upstairs. Tons of references to Dudael, but no indication of where Dudael is. I'm not going to go running around the desert in a headcloth in search of a place that might not exist. In fact…"

I needed to learn how to control my powers. I wasn't a witch. Witches drank demon blood. So, I was the opposite of one, whatever that was called.

Jiao seemed to know something she didn't want to talk about. Maybe she could help me. But she didn't want me anywhere near her.

"You're not listening to me," Tom said.

"Yes, I am," I said. "You were talking about hiking in the desert in a headcloth. I think that's good idea."

Maybe if I got her something she wanted. What had Adriel given to her last time? Tea! But I'm sure she wouldn't be interested in Chamomile.

She was very interested in Hell.

"Tom, are there any special teas in Sheol?"

He raised an eyebrow. "Nash has some Da Hong Pao. It's the most expensive tea in the world."

"That's not what I'm talking about."

"Tea leaves grow on trees in the Third Circle. They're useless to demons."

"Why? What does the tea do?"

"It makes the drinker immortal, ageless."

"So, it's Eterna-Tea."

"Very clever." He smirked. "It's called Void Mortem."

Useless to demons, but very useful to anyone with a finite lifespan.